One step and I hit the heavy mix of odors like an invisible wall that stopped me in my tracks. Reacting to the smell, my stomach gave a pitching roll like a dinghy in a hurricane, but it was the sight that caused me to involuntarily contract my hands—and thus my trigger finger. The shot sounded like the big bang that unleashed the universe. It resounded against the walls and sent wild echoes flying down the canyon.

Yet my eyes were so locked onto the sight before me that I didn't flinch at the noise. The barn had been roofed in used tin, and sunlight poured through the hundreds of old nail holes so that the body strung upside down from the rafter seemed suspended in golden rain.

★

"...an engrossing read..."

—Mystery News

"Martin displays a rich knowledge of the Texas-Mexico frontier..."

—Publishers Weekly

ALLANA MARTIN

DEATH OF AN EVANGELISTA

WORLDWIDE.

TORONTO • NEW YORK • LONDON
AMSTERDAM • PARIS • SYDNEY • HAMBURG
STOCKHOLM • ATHENS • TOKYO • MILAN
MADRID • WARSAW • BUDAPEST • AUCKLAND

To Mareea Lunetta Martin

DEATH OF AN EVANGELISTA

A Worldwide Mystery/January 2000

First published by St. Martin's Press, Incorporated.

ISBN 0-373-26335-X

Printed in U.S.A.

The first Catholic priests arrived in Mexico less than two years after the Spanish Conquest of the Aztec empire. Anti-Catholic legislation first appeared in the 1830s, two decades after the first organized rebellion broke out against Spanish rule. After the constitution of 1857 codified La Ley de las Iglesias, the Law of the Churches, a three-year civil war broke out. An article of the 1917 constitution declared the Church an enemy of the State. In 1926, the Church's opposition to the 1917 constitution led to the Cristero rebellion, a Church-versus-State civil war that lasted until 1929. Fighting between warlords and competing generals extended the civil war and expanded the death toll, by some estimates to over a million.

Evangelista is the term used in Mexico for any Protestant as well as for those who proselytize.

"It is not a shame to kill,
   but to kill and get caught is a shame."

—A well-known saying *(dicho)* in Mexico

ONE

THE ONLY TIME I saw the German he was already dead, a cerise ice pop melting down his shirtfront in a rivulet that split in two around the hilt of the knife jutting from beneath his breastbone, the deep cranberry color getting lost in the blood that seeped from the wound.

I had left the second-floor dentist's office and stepped onto the sidewalk facing the *zócalo*, the main plaza with an ancient church at one end and the Presidencia at the other. The sun shone and a dry wind brought the scent of sugar and cinnamon from the *panadería* across the street where pastries and bread were baked in the huge wood-fired brick ovens of a building that had once housed Pancho Villa's headquarters in Ojinaga.

All the parking spaces next to the plaza were reserved for taxis. I looked around for Chuy Garza, the taxi driver who had picked me up in Presidio. I had left my pickup parked behind the customs inspection station on the U.S. side of the border. Since the peso crisis, vehicle thefts had jumped twenty percent on both sides of the river, and four-wheel drive, *doble tracción* as it was called in Mexico, constituted a thieves' delight.

Chuy had driven across the international bridge, picked me up where I waited by my pickup, and dropped me at the dentist's, promising to wait for me. I knew that didn't mean he wouldn't work local fares for the better part of the ninety minutes my root canal would take. He had a family to support, and it was only ten days until December 25. I live in *la frontera*, the borderland of Texas where it fronts

Mexico along the Rio Grande. For *fronterizos,* the Christmas season begins on December 12, the feast day of the Virgin of Guadalupe. This year, my buoyant holiday spirit had been deflated by the abscessed tooth.

I rubbed my jaw. Beneath the novocaine's deadening, I detected a slight throbbing. I considered going into the *farmacia* at the corner, where pills can be purchased one at a time without a prescription, and requesting a painkiller, but I didn't feel like waiting. I thought I had some pills in an old bottle in my medicine chest, and I felt confident the pain wouldn't be too bad in the hour it would take me to get home. My mistake.

I toe-tapped for five minutes. No Chuy. I'd take another taxi, knowing he'd understand. Appointments and schedules are casual on border time, geared to the improvisation of the moment. I crossed the street. No attendant manned the bright green taxi kiosk on the near side of the plaza, itself quiet on a Monday morning. Only three vendors, selling shoeshines, cotton candy, and *pan dulce,* roamed the corners trying to persuade drivers to buy as they slowed before turning. In front of the palace a half dozen bench sitters dozed, protected by the building from the wind.

On the far side of the plaza a pale green Pontiac Le Mans, vintage 1978, hugged the curb, its dust-coated surface giving the impression it had been parked there for decades. Hire taxis in Ojinaga are generally American cars of old and mixed vintage, held together with baling wire, kept running by ingenuity. Fares are negotiated, not metered. The Pontiac had its driver's-side window rolled down, and no one sat behind the wheel.

Where there's a taxi, there's a driver lurking close by. I crossed the street optimistically, opened the back door, and got halfway in before I saw the passenger.

"Sorry," I said to the man on the far side of the seat,

his face tilted toward the window glass. "I didn't know the cab was taken."

Even as I backed out, I saw the hands palms up and slack in the lap, the bunched-up jacket, the melting *paleta* caught on the shirt collar.

"Are you ill? Do you need help?"

I sat on the edge of the seat, leaned across and touched his shoulder. And saw the hilt of the knife where it lay almost flat against his diaphragm. Driven in low and upward.

I swung around to get out and came nose to nose with a potbellied, bowlegged man in his forties wearing a tight short-sleeved shirt, brown pants, and a baseball cap. He was bent over, staring in the taxi door, effectively blocking my escape.

"This is my taxi," he said proudly. "I will convey you and the señor wherever you wish to go." He moved to close the door. I shoved it back with my hand.

"He's dead," I said thickly, the local anesthetic from the dental surgery still operative enough to make me mumble my words. "Move, and let me out."

The taxi driver leaned farther in to peer over my shoulder at the passenger.

"The señor is ill?"

"Dead."

"No, no. Not to worry. The señor is perhaps faint. A little tequila and lime juice and he will be fine."

"There's a knife in his chest. Let me get out."

He understood that well enough to give me a panicked glance before stretching across so that I had to flatten myself against the back of the seat while he inspected his passenger. "Madre Dios!" he cried. Then he moved. Almost leaping backward, he placed himself protectively behind the door from me, holding on to it as if his legs might fold up.

"You should not have done this thing in my taxi," he hissed. "I am a poor man trying to make a living. Why have you killed this man in my taxi?" His voice rose, wailing. "Why do you cause this terrible trouble—"

"Be quiet! Or we'll both be in trouble. I didn't kill him. I don't even know him."

"Listen to you. You can hardly talk. You're drunk."

I shook my head, got out, and glared down into his round, frightened eyes. "I came out of the dentist's office. I needed a taxi. I got into the car. He was sitting there. Dead."

"Chale!"

His exclamation indicated extreme disbelief.

We both noticed the sound of the diesel engine at the same time. The Humvee, automatic weapons bristling from the back, rolled down the side street and came to a stop only a few feet from us.

I glanced around. The plaza had emptied of vendors and bench sitters. Had I not been caught by the taxi driver, I'd have cleared out already, too. One does not, in Mexico, voluntarily become a witness to any crime.

Two helmeted soldiers, one armed with an automatic weapon, stepped out of the Humvee.

Ojinaga had recently granted the military fifty-five acres for a base to house six hundred soldiers, ostensibly to conduct roadblocks and sweeps for drugs. In reality, the base was to deter guerrillas operating in the Sierra Madre Occidental from moving into Chihuahua State, according to some members of the Mexican press. Rebels were known to be crossing from the neighboring state of Sinaloa.

"What's the problem here?" the weapon-toting soldier demanded.

"No problem. No problem," the cabbie said, waving his hands in denial. They ignored him.

The second soldier had walked around to the far side of the taxi. He peered, gave one startled look at the backseat passenger, and yelled to his companion.

I glanced back at the cabbie. His eyes rolled in all directions looking for a place to run. Like me, fear of being shot in pursuit under *la ley de fuga,* the law of escape, kept his feet welded to the pavement. I was afraid to breathe loudly, let alone move. All I could do was keep my numbed lips closed.

The first soldier opened the door. The body slipped sideways. The soldier grabbed the dead man's jacket, yanked the body back into a sitting position, and went through the pockets, coming up with a wallet.

He opened it, smiled, and extracted a considerable amount of cash before flipping casually through the plastic frames. One item gave him pause. He held out the open wallet to the other soldier, who looked, frowned, and said something too low for me to hear. I watched dumbfounded as the soldier put back all the money save one bill and replaced the wallet in the dead man's pocket.

The soldier caught me looking, winked, waved the single bill in the air before slipping it into his breast pocket and saying, "Feliz Navidad." He slammed the dead man's door.

The soldiers came back around the taxi and stood one to each side of the cabbie and me.

"Keys," demanded the unarmed soldier to the cabbie.

Trembling, the little man handed over the keys to his taxi. The soldier walked to the driver's side, opened the door, climbed behind the wheel, and started the motor.

"Get in," the other soldier said, nudging the cabbie and me toward the Humvee with the barrel of his weapon. I climbed in, but the cabbie made one last effort to plead his innocence. "I've done nothing. I have six children, a grandson, and my old mother is very sick—"

"Tell your troubles to someone who cares," the soldier told him. He grabbed the cabbie by the arm and hoisted him in.

The soldier maneuvered the Humvee into a tighter turn than I would have thought possible, and we moved off in the direction the vehicle had come from, the taxi with the second soldier behind the wheel following, its dead passenger lolling in the seat. We wove through the streets, our driver impatiently honking at slow traffic. Pedestrians on the sidewalks gawked at the cabbie and me with mingled expressions of curiosity and pity in their faces.

TWO

THE SOLDIERS drove us past the statue of Los Niños Heroes to the headquarters of the army garrison, a series of concrete-block buildings less than a quarter mile past the Ojinaga customs kiosk.

The cabbie kept muttering, "I am abandoned by God." I understood how he felt. Knowing that every day the garrison personnel saw the statue memorializing the martyrs to a war that ended with Mexico surrendering half of its territory to the United States did not comfort me. To prevent myself from feeling equally lost to hope, I concentrated on what I knew about Mexican law. The military could hold a prisoner for twenty-four hours. After that they had to turn the poor unfortunate over to the *federales,* who could hold a prisoner as long as it took to get the desired result. No doubt about it. Cabbie and I were in severe trouble.

The Humvee moved along a road marked off by white-painted stones past a watchtower and manned, sandbagged bunkers, and stopped in front of a low building with two soldiers in full battle regalia posted out front.

"Out," our driver told us. I climbed out, but the cabbie seemed unable to move, frozen by his fear. The soldier came around and hauled him out. "Muévete, pendejo," he said. Move, asshole. He shoved the little man forward and his fellow soldier joined him, prodding us along with their weapons.

And these two were just the ranks.

They kept us between them as we passed into an anteroom where four more uniformed men watched a bullfight on a wall-mounted television. Our escorts channeled us down a hallway and into the bowels of the building. We stopped in front of one of a series of doors. The soldier by my side threw it open and gestured for me to enter.

I stepped in and turned to see the cabbie looking back at me as the other soldier hauled him farther along the corridor. He had a slack-faced look of dread, and his eyes said plainly, *See what you have done to me.*

"You have identification?" my soldier said.

I dug out my billfold and handed it over. If I hadn't, I'd have been frisked as gently as he'd gone over the corpse.

He left, slamming the door shut. I heard the lock click.

The room was small, square, windowless, and dingy. It held one table and one chair. I leaned against the wall. An old man from an *ejido* who'd been detained by the military had told me once, "Don't make any jokes with the army. They have no sense of humor."

And no sense of time. By my watch I had been waiting for an hour before strong footsteps approached the door and stopped. I squared my shoulders and tried not to look as sick, scared, or intimidated as I felt. At least the dentist's medication had worn off and I'd be able to speak plainly.

The door swung inward, opened by the soldier who had taken my billfold. He moved aside to make room for a second person.

The man who entered the room wore an immaculate uniform, the creased pants tucked into glossy leather, knee-high boots. Both hands sported gold rings. One diamond-encrusted number wrapped his ring finger, and on the other hand a sparkling horseshoe hid his pinkie finger. A jewel-inlaid Rolex encircled a thick, hairy wrist.

Now I knew he would take a bribe. The question was, how big a bite would he expect?

I took in other inauspicious details. On one side of his hand-tooled belt hung a large scabbard, and the butt of an automatic protruded from the waistband of his pants.

The Humvee driver stepped in behind his superior officer, rolled out the chair from the table, positioned it behind his boss, and steadied it. The man in charge sat down, waved a finger, and the soldier jumped to shut the door, then positioned himself in front of it.

The bejeweled dazzler said, "I am Comandante Zurita. You are Texana Jones."

Who was I to disagree? I nodded.

"This is your correct name?" Strong inflection on this question.

Another nod. I couldn't seem to find my voice.

"Americana?"

Again I nodded. My hair is dark brown and my complexion the golden brown of the Mediterranean, both characteristics reflecting the dominant genes of my father's Italian ancestry. I am often taken for a light-skinned Mexican.

"This Polvo place you live is where?"

"Fifty miles upriver from Presidio."

"You speak Spanish like a native." A pause. He drummed his fingers on the table, and the rings flashed. "We have a small problem."

His choice of words chilled me. In Spanish, understatement is the norm. If someone tells you he owns a *casita,* a little house, expect a mansion. If a problem is described as small, it isn't.

The *comandante* said, "The taxi driver claims to know nothing. He says the dead man must have killed himself."

I silently thanked the poor cabbie for not accusing me to the *comandante.*

"What do you have to say about this crime?" As he spoke, he lifted the biggest knife since Jim Bowie's out of the scabbard at his belt and held it, the index finger of his left hand poised on the tip. "A souvenir from Chiapas," he said.

Visions of dead *indios* danced in my head. The Mexican military had recently killed large numbers of Indians in Chiapas State. My palms were sweaty. My jaw ached. Nerves had left me cotton-mouthed. I cleared my throat. My recitation of the facts took three sentences.

He tapped the knifepoint with the tip of his finger. "You just *happened* to come out of the dentist's office and get into a taxi with the murdered man, a bolillo."

A slang expression, the term refers to a foreign person. I took this to mean the dead man was not an American, since we're usually called *americanos* or, more commonly but less politely, *gringos*. So, a tourist from some other country then.

The death of any foreign national makes headlines. Headlines mean blame *must* be fixed on someone, guilty or not. Who better than another foreigner?

That would be me.

Time, I decided, to try the *mordida,* the bite, the bribe, the take, the tip, the gratuity, the consideration. Call it what you like. It is the oil of the society from bottom to top. The taxi driver bribed the kiosk operator for his space on the plaza. Traffic cops earned most of their income from violators who held a couple of dollars out the window as they ran the stop sign at the corner. The postal worker needed a tip to remember a customer's mail. Journalists accepted gratuities from politicians. Politicians received "a little consideration" from the drug lords. And so on, and so on. The more power you had, the bigger the bite you expected. Murder took a big bite, maybe bigger than I could afford.

I cleared my throat and spoke the traditional phrase for

introducing the subject of the *mordida*. "Is there no other way of arranging this matter?"

Normally, there would be an equally polite response followed by an exchange of cash. Since after paying the dentist ninety dollars in cash, I had only ten dollars in ones and ten five-hundred-peso notes in my billfold, and since the *comandante* would have been informed of the dismal state of my cash flow by the soldier who took it, we would agree on an amount to be conveyed before my release. I could only hope that my husband would think I was worth it, and bring the cash across. I'd heard of the military taking checks, but I doubted they'd accept mine.

The *comandante*, however, wasn't playing. In what I took to be an unmistakably negative response, he said nothing, but rose to his feet and replaced the knife in its scabbard. Giving me a quizzical look, he turned to go. The soldier opened the door and followed his boss out. The turn of the lock sounded final.

I sat down and put my head in my hands. This case seemed to have *federales* written all over it.

Another hour.

Footsteps, the door opened, and a soldier I had never seen came in and instructed me to stand up and follow him. We quick-marched down a long hall to a cell. He unlocked and swung the cell door open. I could be here forever. No one would know where I was. My brain clicked into high gear as I scrambled to think of a way out. That's when it registered. The *comandante's* watch. The Rolex. It reminded me... My fogged brain made a connection. A name popped into my head just as the soldier's hand found the small of my back to shove me into the cell.

"Please ask the *comandante* to speak with me again. I have something that it's in his interest to hear."

The soldier hardly gave me a glance as he shut the cell

door. His cold expression told me nothing, least of all whether or not he'd deliver the message.

Another hour passed. I had almost given up. The soldier returned, unlocked the cell, and with a jerk of his head motioned me out. We followed our trail back to what I thought of as the interrogation room.

Fifteen more minutes. I jumped up when I heard the footsteps. The *comandante* entered, two soldiers in tow. This time he did not sit down. His arms crossed tightly over his thick chest, his eyes slits of suspicion, he stood with legs planted like stout support posts at a fence corner.

I lifted my chin and looked directly into his cold eyes, trying to sound confident but keeping my voice free of any hint of personal criticism or blame. Please God, let the name alone be enough.

"I wish to spare you any difficulty or embarrassment you might suffer because your men detained me. I ask that you telephone Señor Gordon Suarez. He will vouch for me. I assure you, if you call now there will be no trouble for you over this incident."

He stared, expressionless.

"Don Ghee will vouch for me." *Don* is a title of respect, an honorific used with someone known personally. I tossed in the nickname Ghee to emphasize the personal aspect.

Over the *comandante's* head the two soldiers eyed each other and moved out of the way as their commanding officer grabbed the chair, rolled it around to me, and said, "Please, señora, be seated."

One for me. He'd used the courtesy of *señora* for the first time. I lowered myself into the chair in what I hoped was a regal manner.

"So you know Señor Suarez." A weak statement more than a question.

"He's a friend," I said.

The *comandante's* eyes turned speculative. He wanted to ask how close a friend but he dared not. Gordon Mateo Suarez was one of the most influential, wealthy men in Mexico, an arms dealer, among his other enterprises, who supplied the *comandante's* army—and probably the rebels they fought, as well. A man whose money bought political influence in more capitals than just Mexico City, it was said.

The *comandante* babbled, "You had only to mention this earlier, señora." Greatly respectful now, he switched his Spanish to the florid *usted* form. "It is most regrettable that you have been delayed. Can I get anything for you? A Coke, some food, perhaps…"

"I'd like a glass of water."

"Please, come with me." As I stood up, he took my elbow gently. We glided together down the hall and into what I assumed, judging by the comfortable furnishings, was his office. He paused to cut off the *telenovela,* the soap opera, blaring from the console against the wall opposite the wide desk, then asked me to be seated on the couch, opened a small refrigerator next to the credenza with the Chivas Regal, and took out a bottle of Perrier, which he opened and handed to me. He helped himself to a strong shot of whiskey.

While I gulped Perrier, the *comandante* explained that he himself would drive me back into town, or home.

I asked to be dropped at the plaza.

"Whatever the señora wishes." He opened a drawer of his desk, took out my billfold, and brought it to me.

"You have my apology for those fools of soldiers detaining you. I hope you will forget that this morning's unpleasantness happened."

I told him it was *poquita cosa.* A trifling thing.

"About the taxi driver," I said tentatively.

The *comandante* waved his hand at me, forestalling further comment. "A friend of Señor Suarez should not waste time or effort on one of no consequence."

Translated: The taxi man goes down for the murder so that you don't have to. I knew when to quit.

He added, "Please, the next time you see Señor Suarez, you will convey to him my good wishes."

I assured him I would.

He smiled, and we walked together to his vehicle, a conversion van with a cloth cover over the spare tire mounted on the rear that read: Happy Trails/The Stouts of Idaho.

The *comandante* handed me into the captain's seat and took the wheel.

"How do you like it," he said, making a sweeping gesture toward the back of the van. I looked around. The vehicle had been equipped with carpet, a sofa bed, a television, and a minibar.

"Very nice," I said.

"It is, isn't it," the *comandante* agreed cheerfully.

He had personalized his confiscated vehicle. A tiny metallic skeleton dangled from the rearview mirror. On the dash lay a copy of *Proceso,* Mexico's best-known news magazine. The cover photo showed a masked man dressed in military gear and brandishing an AK-47. The headline read: Rebels Attack Huatulco Resort. The subhead quoted the guerrilla leader as saying, "We can bring Mexico to its knees."

The *comandante,* noticing where my attention lay, said, "With our new tanks, helicopters, machine guns, and rocket launchers, we will muzzle those dogs."

He drove like a *troquero,* a Mexican trucker, bold to the point of being reckless, flying up the road.

Turning to face me, and swerving off the road, the *com-*

andante said, "I have a saying. It's not where you've been that matters, it's where you're going."

And whether or not you get there, I thought, cinching my seat belt tighter. As we hit traffic, he sped up, skimming fenders, ignoring the brakes, and hitting the horn until we squealed to a halt at the plaza.

He wished me "Que la vaya bien," and pulled away.

I stood very still until a hand touched my shoulder and I jumped a foot.

"The shoeshine man told me you and the cabbie was grabbed by the army," Chuy said. "You okay? I hear that comandante is a real mordelón."

A big biter, much given to the take.

I told Chuy, "I'm okay. I just want to go home."

"You got it." He brought around his cab.

I was so wrung out, I barely managed a thank-you.

He drove with tempered speed through Ojinaga's streets. He had to. His vehicle was so refitted with scavenged parts that nothing quite functioned as it should, including the truck gearshift fitted into a hole cut in the floorboard.

Toward the bridge traffic dwindled. We skirted around an old man leading a burro painted to look like a zebra and loaded down with pots and pans for sale, a pack of cur dogs, and a handful of kids walking in their plastic shoes and carrying string bags of groceries. We passed the hospital on the right, with its chain-link fence, the ambulance inside, behind the padlocked gate. After that, there was an open zone, and then the bridge over the Rio Grande.

Chuy paid the toll leaving Mexico, and with a nod passed to the front of a short line approaching the U.S. Customs booth. The inspectors waved him through as they do most of the regular taxi drivers, and he pulled into the parking area where I'd left my pickup. The space is small, with head-in parking for only eight vehicles. Mine was not

among them. My white Ford supercab with its *doble tracción,* winch, and mud tires was gone. "Mala suerte!" Chuy
said. Bad luck.

Me and the Stouts of Idaho. I turned and stared glumly
back into Mexico, the destination of nearly all the vehicles
stolen along the border. "Damn," I said, and then repeated
it twice more. Thrice cursed.

Chuy said, "Come on. I'll drive you home."

I nodded and got back into the taxi, sinking down into
the threadbare seat that Chuy had covered with a tucked-
in piece of brown fabric. Considering the questionable re-
liability of his vehicle's transmission, Chuy made good
time through Presidio. From there it was slow going because of the washboard effect of the road, which allowed
for natural drainage of our infrequent rains into the wide
river valley. I watched the passing landscape of creosote
bushes and the gray-green of salt cedars marking the river,
the electric line running on wooden poles, and the bullet-
pocked sign warning of free-range cattle. The sound wave
hit us as we crossed the cattle guard at the twenty-nine-
mile point. I squeezed my hands tight over my ears and
ducked involuntarily as the brain-piercing roar enveloped
us. I felt the car swerve, then stop abruptly as the British
Tornado passed directly overhead only a hundred feet from
the ground.

Ears ringing, I sat up barely in time to see the jet fighter
as a rapidly diminishing dot against the clear sky. Cussing
the pilot in two languages, Chuy got out to inspect the
damage. The car had veered off the road, and the right front
tire had blown out. I hadn't even heard the tire go because
of the jet noise. Chuy loosened the lugs, jacked up the front
end, tossed the ruptured tire into the trunk, and put on a
threadbare spare. We spent the rest of the trip making in-
dignant comments about the jets flying out of Holloman

Air Force Base in New Mexico. The river run seemed to be a favorite for pilot training, and the whole region was their playground. A public hearing had been held with staid and defensive representatives of the Departments of State, Justice, Interior, and Defense. The Border Patrol had complained that the low-level jet flights endangered their helicopters. Irate ranchers had told of injuries to stampeding cattle and panicked horses crashing into barbed-wire fences. As county vet, my husband Clay had assessed the cost to stockmen for dead and injured livestock. Dozens of people had furiously asserted that moving vehicles seemed to be favored for buzzing. The government drones had promised more hearings to look into the situation.

When we reached the trading post, my home as well as my business, I got out my billfold to pay Chuy the ten dollars he charged for the trip and discovered that the *comandante* had returned everything but my cash.

THREE

I KNEW SOMETHING was wrong when I saw the ladder, the paint bucket and brushes, and the unfinished sign propped against the side of the building.

Against the signboard's yellow background all the lettering had been neatly penciled in, but only the first four lines had been painted:

El Polvo

Population	125
Dogs	52
Elevation	2,594

Cadillac Charlie, free spirit and on-and-off employee of nearly everyone in *la frontera,* had agreed not only to mind the trading post for me while I was away, but Monday being a slow business day, he'd guaranteed to have the sign finished by the time I got home, and that should have been hours ago.

Bad things happen in threes. I invited Chuy to come in and have a soft drink on the house while I got his money from the register and found out what was going on with the normally reliable Charlie.

The bell on the double doors jangled as we walked in, and the big, red-bearded man perched on the stool behind the long wooden counter looked up from the book lying open before him and greeted us in a cheerful baritone.

"Morning, Padre," Chuy responded. "What's that you're reading?"

"A biography." Father Jack Raff closed the book to stare at the cover. "An early Christmas gift from a friend in Cincinnati. I was hoping for the latest Tom Clancy. I love all that techno stuff."

In his orange crewneck sweater, patched jeans, and tennis shoes, Father Jack looked anything but priestly. An ex-boxer, he had piercing blue eyes, a slab face beneath the curly beard, a much-battered nose, and wide hands with thick fingers callused by the manual labor he performed around the border communities to help his flock, and that included anyone who needed him, Catholic or not.

"Did Charlie run out on me because I was so late?" I said as I stepped around the counter and opened the register, extracting the cash for Chuy. "I had a spot of trouble."

"Charlie was faithful. Unfortunately, also injudicious."

"What happened?" What now?

"He challenged Pete Rosales to a raw chile eating contest. They started with jalapeños, moved to serranos, and finished off with a handful of those tiny, fiery red ones... what are they called?"

"Chiles piquín," I said.

Chuy said, "Who won?"

"It was a tie," Father Jack said, "but about an hour after they'd congratulated one another on their invincible stomachs and Pete had left for home, Charlie's lower digestive track proved vincible after all. I found him sitting on the ground beside your sign, moaning about his insides being on fire and swilling ice water like it was free beer. Clay came in about that time, and we considered what to do. I suggested emetic action, but your husband, as the closest thing to a medical man, thought that digestion was too far along for that to be entirely effective and recommended calling the emergency service to airlift Charlie out by helicopter."

My husband, Clay, maintains his veterinary office in a converted trailer behind the trading post when he's not out on call to the big ranches that make up most of our region.

Father Jack said, "I've talked to the doctor. He cleaned Charlie out coming and going, so to speak, poured a quart of industrial-strength antacid down him, let him rest for an hour, and then released him. Clay's gone to pick him up."

"When did he leave?" I asked, checking my watch.

"A little after two."

Nearly five now. The hospital is in Alpine, in the adjacent county. Clay would have gone the short route, eighty-seven miles one way, over half on the bladed road through Pinto Canyon. He'd take the smoother ride the long way through Presidio to bring Charlie home. Everything in the Trans-Pecos is miles from anything else. We're always buying new tires, and the term "impulse shopper" is not in our vocabulary. Most spread out of all is our sparse population, which means we don't bother with the speed limit too much on the nearly empty roads. Knowing how Clay drove, I calculated that they'd be home within the hour.

I thanked Father Jack for keeping an eye on things in Charlie's place. Mostly, when I have to run an errand, I put up the CLOSED sign and find my customers waiting for me when I get back. In an emergency, Lucy at the Polvo post office has a key.

"Glad to help," Father Jack said.

I liked the priest. Like most newcomers to our mixed

culture of the borderland, he'd started out with some good intentions and a lot of misconceptions, but he'd come a long way since his arrival four years earlier along our stretch of the river. A member of a religious order that provided priests for mission churches, Father Jack had started big, intending to end what he called our cultural and economic deprivation. His earliest effort had been a goat cheese cooperative. Everyone had politely smiled, agreed with him that it would be a good thing, and helped to clean out the dilapidated warehouse that an obliging soul, happy to be relieved of the tax burden, had donated to the project. When the time came for the start-up, no one seemed to be able to corral the needed goats for milk production. Maybe mañana, maybe next week, maybe next month, the locals told Father Jack, the border way of saying no. Thus he had learned about both our spirit of cooperation and our self-sufficiency and independence from schedule and constraints. These days he channeled his missionary's zeal into the more important things, like helping someone from a rancho or *ejido* across the river make a long-distance telephone call for the first time, or building a chicken coop for a river widow, the local term for a woman on the other side whose husband spends most of the year working in the U.S. Father Jack had even learned river Spanish, a mix of Spanish and English used up and down the border, so that a cheeseburger becomes "hamburger *con queso*."

"I didn't have any customers," Father Jack added, "except for a couple of gasoline fill-ups. I was careful counting out change, so I don't think I messed up your bookkeeping."

"You couldn't hurt it much. My bookkeeping is mostly maintaining overdue credit accounts. And with the Customs Service closing down our border crossing, business isn't likely to pick up. Half my customers come from the other side.''

Five miles above El Polvo there is a narrow spot on the river that the locals from both sides have used for generations to visit friends and relatives living opposite, the border version of crossing the street. Decades ago, before the irrigation in New Mexico and below El Paso sucked the river nearly dry, people had to cross by boat or on horseback. Now you could drive and barely wet the tires, or sling your shoes over your shoulder and wade. The ease of crossing tempted the dishonest as well as the desperate. A few weeks ago the Mexican authorities had captured six men smuggling in military equipment left over from the Gulf War, including camouflage uniforms and gas masks. The resulting diplomatic jockeying had culminated in an announcement from the El Paso office of the Customs Service that all unofficial river crossings would be closed.

It's a long way from the Rio Grande to the Potomac. The border is a boundary only on the map. The physical space it defines is as fluid as the river that marks it. Nothing, least of all the border, is static. Along its entire length, the effects of the Conquest continue into the present, reshaping the future by creating new faces, new ways of life, new worlds. Even the words change: *mojado,* illegal alien, undocumented, or yanqui, gringo, *norteamericano.* And more and more, *narcotraficante.*

Father Jack said, ''The customs pronouncement didn't stop Pete from coming over, I notice.''

I smiled. ''Official dictates don't mean much to anybody around here, especially Pete Rosales. To him Texas is just occupied Mexico. Washington doesn't have a clue.''

Father Jack had slipped into his windbreaker, a bright blue with an emblem of Our Lady of Guadalupe in red, gold, and blue on the back. Everybody in El Polvo had chipped in for it, a presentation gift on the third anniversary of his arrival. As he started around the counter, a big paw shot out from underneath and hooked his ankle.

"Phobe, we've played enough," he said, reaching down to disengage the claws from his jeans. The response was a disgruntled meow, rather Siamese in tone, as the bobcat came prancing out from her favorite hiding place on the lower shelf beneath the register.

Father Jack started down the aisle between the grocery and hardware displays, and I stroked Phobe's ears to give him time to get away. Then I felt a twinge of guilt. The priest had given half a day to minding the store for me. I owed him. "Stay for supper," I said. "You too, Chuy."

"Thanks, but I got to get home," Chuy said.

Father Jack also declined. "You look as if it's been a hectic day," he said as I handed Chuy his money.

"Sure sorry about your trouble, Señora Jones," Chuy said, folding the ones into his breast pocket. "Bad enough getting hauled away by the army without having a fine vehicle like that pickup stolen."

"What!" Father Jack said.

"From right behind the customs stop," I said, throwing up my arms and letting my frustration show. Chuy had his hand on the door, and I called to him, "Do you know the other taxi driver's name?"

He turned. "The one they arrested with you? Sure, Oscar Jurado. Been driving that Pontiac for ten years." He waved good-bye and left. We heard a chugging and clanging as he drove off.

Father Jack said speculatively, "So—you got away from the army. You must have friends at city hall. But then, everything in Mexico is negotiable, except the virginity of the Virgin of Guadalupe."

That's what I like about Father Jack. He can joke about the things he takes seriously.

Father Jack said speculatively, "So—you got away from the army. You must have friends at city hall." His expression begged for further details. We *fronterizos* thrive on isolation, but as a by-product we are insatiably curious about the events of one another's lives.

And we love talking. I was no exception. I promised him the whole story as soon as I took something for my tooth.

Both Father Jack and the bobcat waited for me while I went to the back. I couldn't find the prescription pain pills, so I downed three ibuprofen tablets and rejoined the priest. As I told him about my conversation with the *comandante,* Phobe jumped up onto the counter and sat right in front of me, her golden unblinking eyes looking into mine with such intensity and affinity that she seemed to be listening to the climax of my tale.

"So I thought to mention the name of a Mexican rancher we met. Clay culled his herd during the drought. He's the most influential person we know, although—"

"We know somebody influential?" my husband said from behind me. Just hearing his voice eased my tension more than any tranquilizer. Clay is six foot one, slim, and gray-haired. His face reflects both his sense of humor and the sense of decency that dominate his personality. The only person he's ever impatient with is himself. We laugh a lot together.

"Ghee," I said, answering his question.

He gave me a wide-eyed look. "If you had to invoke that big a gun you must have been in trouble."

"I was." I peered around him and through the door. "Where's Charlie? I thought you were bringing him back."

"I left him at your dad's bunkhouse. He'll have more

room and more privacy there. Don't worry, I called first. Your dad said he'd look after him. And I promised him we'd look after his car. It's parked around back.''

Charlie drives and mostly lives out of a pristine 1955 white Fleetwood Cadillac that he calls "White Bess." It's fully equipped in more ways than any automobile I know, including camping gear, Charlie's wardrobe, and a modest library.

Clay said, "Charlie is one sick puppy. It'll be a long time before he eats chile peppers again. The doctor told him to stick to a baked-potato-and-water diet for three or four days—''

''As if Charlie will,'' I said.

''He may. Did you know he had an ulcer?''

''Charlie?'' I said. ''He seems so laid-back.''

Clay said, ''Suffered with it for years after Nam.''

''When he gets home, I must pay him a visit and try to persuade him to be kind to his stomach,'' Father Jack said. Then, like a backyard gossip who can't wait to tell the news, he added, ''Your wife's been involved in a skirmish with the Mexican military.''

''I told her to give up smuggling,'' Clay said.

''Don't be facetious. Father Jack might not know you're kidding.''

''If this is going to be a long story, let's get comfortable,'' Clay said.

I know my husband. Comfortable meant sitting in a rocking chair with his feet up and a glass of whiskey in his hands.

Clay said, ''Come on, Padre.''

We moved into the living area of our private quarters, one of a series of long, informal rooms that stretch the length of the back of the trading post.

Father Jack settled in by the fireplace, Clay lit the kindling, and I kicked off my shoes, relaxed against the fat cushions at one end of the couch, and put my feet up. Phobe climbed up behind me and settled at my neck, from time to time nibbling at my hair. I didn't worry about her claws marking the sofa's fabric. Our furniture was already well worn before we adopted the bobcat. Clay poured the drinks and took the other chair by the fire.

Sipping appreciatively, Father Jack pronounced in a hushed voice, "My, my. Crown Royal."

Clay smiled and lifted his glass. "My father-in-law gives me a bottle on my birthday and at Christmas."

"Grand stuff," Father Jack said. "I'll have to visit you more often."

Clay held up the bottle and gave it a hard look. "Nearly empty. Good thing the season is upon us."

For a few moments we enjoyed the mellow result of the brewer's art and listened to the crackling of the dry wood as it burned.

"So," Clay said, breaking our meditative stillness, "how come you had to invoke Ghee's name?"

During my lengthy explanation Clay's face grew more and more somber. "I knew you should have gone to the dentist in Alpine," he said when I finished.

"The man in Ojinaga is a good dentist."

"He's a cheap dentist."

"I know, I know. Don't say it. You get what you pay for. The problem is, sometimes you have to pay for what you can afford. Anyway, the dentist didn't have anything to do with what happened."

"If you'd gone to Alpine, there wouldn't have been any trouble."

I smiled, knowing that only retroactive worry made him scold.

He said, "At least the insurance company can't claim you parked the pickup in an unsafe place."

"That reminds me, I'd better call our agent."

"Wait until tomorrow," Clay told me. "Relax. Enjoy your drink."

"The dead man looked like a tourist, you said. Anything special you remember about the way he looked?" Father Jack asked.

"No. I don't know. His face was…well, it was hard to tell." I thought about it. I had a sharp image of his hands. They had looked strong, with well-kept nails. His hair had been gray and thinning, and cut very short.

"What about his clothes?" Clay said. "Tourist tacky?"

I shook my head. "Expensive. He carried dollars. The bill the soldier took from the wallet and waved at me looked like a twenty. The comandante called him a bolillo."

Clay said, "Then we'll be reading about it in the paper. Funny the soldiers didn't just hand you over to the federales after their show of force. I can't imagine when they saw you and the cabbie arguing that they stopped for any reason except a show of unnecessary force. They certainly didn't expect to find a dead man."

"Not unless they killed him," Father Jack said jokingly.

I got to my feet. "Time for some food."

Father Jack half rose as if to go; I motioned him down, and Clay added a little more incentive to the priest's glass. I held mine out for an equal refill, grateful now I hadn't taken a prescription pain pill so I could indulge a bit. I took my glass with me to the counter, opened the refrigerator, and got out the makings for sandwiches. Phobe followed, and reminded me that she too was hungry by nipping me on the ankle. I went back to the refrigerator, took out her food log, a prepared combination of horse meat, vitamins, and minerals. Everything the domesticated bobcat needs for good health. I sliced off a substantial hunk and chopped it into chunks in her pan. She gnawed happily while I prepared the human meal.

Behind me the conversation turned local as Father Jack talked about a phenomenon he had dubbed the *Fairistas*.

"More visitors come to Rhea Fair's grave every day. Adelaida bought a sterling silver milagro to leave there."

Adelaida was Father Jack's housekeeper, and so twisted from arthritis that her employment was a charitable act on the part of the priest. Rhea Fair had been a local *curandera* or healing woman. In the three years since her death she had become a folk saint. People from both sides of the river journeyed to her grave and prayed to her for a cure for their ailments or to bring them good fortune. They left paper flowers, river stones, and the small gifts of food that are called *promesas,* a promise that if a cure is granted, they'll grace the saint's tomb or image with *milagros,* miracles, little trinkets in the shape of the body parts. One can buy arms, legs, heads, eyes of brass outside any church. In some churches, the saints' images are festooned with so many *milagros* tied on with string that the priests must cut them off daily to make room for more. *Milagros* lay piled atop Rhea Fair's grave.

"How do you feel about it?" Clay asked the priest.

"I keep a watchful eye on developments and try to persuade people like Adelaida to venerate the saint if she wishes, but to save the money for medicine."

"You think there's something to Rhea's sainthood?" Clay asked him.

"The idea of sainthood is older than the Church, if you count as a saint anyone who has died and gone to heaven. Look at Moses and Elijah. They appeared with Christ at the Transfiguration. The Greek Orthodox Church accepts popular acclaim in recognizing saints. We used to. Saints come when they're needed. Rhea might not have been of the right faith, but I'm sure her life was right. I don't mind that people pray to the curandera for intercession. The faithful dead are part of the community of saints. Though in matters like this, the Church has to proceed with caution.''

I set the table and called the two over. Father Jack asked about Clay's practice. I'm used to conversation over the dinner table about such things as abscesses, cancer eyes, afterbirth, castration, heat cycles, and artificial insemination, but I try to stifle my husband's enthusiasm for the fine details of his work when we have company. Father Jack chewed rhythmically, showing no sign of loss of appetite from Clay's graphic description of a particular procedure. I relaxed. The food eased my physical fatigue as the whiskey had soothed my nerves. Throughout the meal Phobe lay under the table, batting my foot with her paws. A good moment in a terrible day.

When we finished eating, Phobe and I returned to the couch. Clay and Father Jack cleared up and washed the dishes. Afterward we sat in the glow of the dwindling firelight and drank the café au lait Clay had made with real half-and-half, just the way I like it. Almost, but not quite, I forgot my stolen truck.

''I think you should put the Closed sign on the door and take tomorrow off,'' Clay said.

I rubbed the back of my neck. ''The Closed sign will be up, but so will I. I promised to make a delivery to La Noria.'' I looked at Clay. ''I'll have to use your pickup.'' He nodded.

''I've heard that name ever since I moved out here,'' Father Jack said.

''One of the best watered ranches in the whole of the Trans-Pecos,'' Clay said.

"And they spend money locally, bless them," I added.

"I've been meaning to get up that way for some time," Father Jack said thoughtfully. "Not to the Haro place, but to visit Electra Reaves."

Clay said, "Checking out the competition?"

The priest gave a wry smile.

"Is Electra really competition?" I asked. "I thought most people just listened politely to her proselytizing and went right on going to Mass."

"She's not as successful as the Jehovah's Witnesses, Mormons, Seventh-Day Adventists, and Baptists have been in converting in Mexico. At least in the larger towns on the other side. Ms. Reaves's strength is at the ranchos and ejidos," Father Jack said. "Seems they're abandoning incense, relics, and saints in favor of Bible study and witnessing."

Clay shook his head. "She's either a very brave or a very foolish lady. Some folks on the other side equate Protestants preaching conversion to the devil stealing souls."

"Some people on this side aren't crazy about it," I said. "I've seen signs in a few windows saying 'This is a Catholic home. Evangelistas not welcome.'"

"That disturbs me," Father Jack said. "I discourage it where I can. Hate is a dangerous sin. I heard that two Mormons disappeared a few weeks ago from their house in...one of the more remote villages. Can't recall the name."

"Santiago de Gracia," Clay said. "The bodies won't turn up. If it had been a Mexican, now..."

"They'd have done what?"

"Beaten him badly and publicly. And if he continued to preach his gospel, kill him. Not quickly or pleasantly, either. There was one case where a Protestant convert had been so successful that he started to organize the workers into a union. The town council, so to speak, came into his house one night and dragged him out. The next morning they found him tied to a tree with—"

"Stop!" I said. "Don't tell the rest. The details are too awful."

"I take it he died a martyr's death," Father Jack said. "A pity religion and politics have to get mixed. The Church has a bit of history in that regard."

"Your power for understatement is admirable," I told him.

He laughed heartily. "You're right about that." Then he paused, and added, "I think perhaps it's time I met Electra Reaves."

"I'd like to see her place myself. I've been there once, when the Nells Ranch used it for a guest cabin. That must have been ten years ago, long before they sold it to the couple from Santa Fe. Why don't you come with me to La Noria tomorrow? You'll enjoy meeting Federico Haro. He's a grand old man. On the way back we'll stop at Electra's, and I'll introduce you. She buys supplies from me. I don't think she'll mind if we stop by."

"Great."

"I warn you, I make an early start."

"What time?"

"Daylight."

"I'll see you at sunup," Father Jack said, rising to his feet and getting out his keys.

Clay and I stood on the porch and waved good-bye as the priest took off in his truck, red taillights glowing against the dark like animal eyes caught in a hunter's spotlight.

I closed the doors behind us, giving the lock the extra turn it needed to close properly. I flipped the switch on the exterior Christmas lights, and the trading post, outlined in gold, shone into the night. While I emptied the register,

Clay went to feed the two dogs he was tending in the kennels.

After my shower I tumbled into bed. Phobe joined me, settling on Clay's pillow so that he had to get another from the closet when he came to bed.

"If I'd known we'd end up with a twenty-five pound bobcat for a pet, I'd have bought a king-size bed," he said, pulling Phobe on her pillow to the middle. She thought he was playing, and pawed his arms, trying to entice him to roughhouse. Since he thinks this is unwise with any wild animal, he rubbed her belly instead, and she purred loudly, kneading her claws into the foam pillow. We'd had feather ones until she attacked and shredded them the first summer we had her.

"What do you suppose is behind this interest of Father Jack in the Reaves woman?" Clay said.

"Does there have to be something behind it?"

"He's not going all that way to convert her." He leaned on his elbow and looked at me. "You blue?"

"Postprandial depression."

"You're mourning for your pickup. We'll go next week and buy you another."

"We can't afford it until we get the insurance check."

"We'll manage. Cheer up." He kissed my cheek and settled under the covers.

"Maybe Father Jack thinks Electra is stealing souls and has to be stopped."

I'd meant it as a feeble joke. Instead of laughing, Clay said, "I've noticed religion gets real serious in sectarian matters."

He pounded his pillow into shape and, as always, fell asleep almost instantly, while I lay still and worried over the events of the day.

FOUR

I WOKE TO the smell of coffee and the sound of Phobe's rubber squeaky-mouse. I stretched, sat up, cut on the bedside lamp, and eyeballed the clock. Five-thirty a.m. My jaw had ached all night, but exhaustion had won out over discomfort. I'd stayed in bed rather than trudge to the bathroom for a pill.

I stayed flat on my back, dreading getting up, then shoved the covers back, letting the cold air hit me. That got my feet to the carpet. I grabbed my robe and headed for the bath, where I knew Clay would have lit the propane heater. And found cold. Meaning Clay had gone out sometime during the night on a call, and I had slept through the telephone's ringing.

I lit the heater and stood under the hot shower to loosen my stiff muscles. I emerged, face scrubbed bright but spirit sluggish, brushed my teeth, and crawled back into bed. I slept deeply until Clay came in with a tray loaded with coffee, buttery toast, and a bowl heaped with apricot preserves.

"Rise and shine and greet the glory of a new day," he intoned with brisk cheer, setting the tray down on the table. I love everything about the man but his crack-of-dawn exuberance.

"When did you get home?"

"About twenty minutes ago. I washed my hands and wiped my feet before I fixed the coffee."

"Where have you been?"

"Delivering the pups at Lucy's. Six of them."

Lucy, the postmistress, had for years owned a mellow old dog that Clay had put to sleep last summer before its cancer became painful. The new dog, a lovable female named Mandy, had arrived on the doorstep two weeks ago, pregnant and without benefit of pedigree or marriage, as far as we knew.

I yawned and propped myself against the pillows in anticipation. "Six? A lot of dogs to find homes for."

Clay placed the tray across my lap, saying, "Lucy's grandchildren have dibs on all of them." He poured my coffee, the half-and-half already pooled and waiting in the bottom of the mug. I am a slow starter to the day, and I rely on coffee, strong coffee, to get me going. Phooey on those who decry caffeine. I'll take theirs, mine, and everyone's. Three deep swallows and I felt better. Clay reached for a piece of toast, and I noticed how tired he looked.

"Take a shower and get into bed," I suggested.

"Can't. Jerry Ayrs called five minutes ago. He's got a horse down."

Ayrs leased Red Mountain Ranch. He was a hardworking cowboy and a good man. I was sorry he had trouble.

I finished two cups of coffee while Clay did a quick shave, brushed his teeth, and left. I heard his van pull out as I dressed. He'd only recently bought the specially fitted mobile clinic. A convenient investment, though an expensive one, since his practice covers two sides of the river, roughly four thousand square miles, and both large and small animals.

I took the tray back to the kitchen, washed up, and fed Phobe. I was in the front of the trading post packing up the supplies for La Noria when Father Jack arrived. With him acting as helper, we loaded the pickup in time for him to enjoy a cup of coffee. We waited on daylight to start our journey.

La Noria Ranch sits on the far side of a deep canyon at the end of twenty-one dirt miles of bone-jarring trail known as Muerto del Burro, Death of the Donkey road, for the hundreds of beasts that wore out their lives hauling supplies along the route. Intent upon negotiating the rutted track, I made no conversation. Father Jack focused on the severe landscape, speaking only once to point out three mule deer scrambling up an invisible path in the rock. Late-summer rain had helped the deer population survive the dire effects of what had been a prolonged drought, saving the hunting season, a godsend for ranchers whose income had already dwindled from loss of livestock through forced sale at low prices to an overloaded market.

We traveled the canyon in shadow. The sun had yet to reach the narrow floor but had colored the tips of the volcanic uplift of the mountains a molten gold. We passed between vast walls of layered rock striated with the dim history of geologic time, moving through a landscape of white brush, lechugilla, Spanish dagger, and greasewood that changed into juniper-studded mountainsides rising several thousand feet to empty into a grama grass savanna domed by the sky.

The entrance of La Noria, functional and practical, proclaimed its owner's personality. A modest metal sign displaying the ranch name hung on one wing of the gate.

"What do you know about Federico Haro?" I asked Father Jack as we passed over the cattle guard and rolled onto a graded road curving away across the golden brown grass spiked with yucca.

"I know he's a man of means. The Church always knows who's who in the neighborhood."

"He came to this country in the early thirties, running tequila from Mexico into Texas. He ended up working for a rancher in Uvalde—"

"What's that?" Father Jack said, his attention distracted by a red dot moving on the horizon.

"Somebody coming."

Ahead the land rose gently toward the north.

Father Jack kept his eyes on the red dot speeding toward us, but returned to our conversation.

"I take it the Haro being touted as an up-and-coming power in Texas politics is a relative?"

I nodded. "Henry is a grandson. They say he'll be the first Hispanic governor of Texas someday."

"He's somebody's protégé..."

"Bascom Davis, the land commissioner. Davis has announced he'll run for lieutenant governor in the next election. Henry was his aide for a couple of years, and Davis backed his successful run for the Texas House." The mention of Davis reminded me of Clay and the call he'd had that morning. Bascom Davis owned the thirty thousand acres Jerry Ayrs leased in return for maintaining the roads, fences, and water wells, plus handling hunting parties for guests.

"What's Davis's angle in grooming the Haro grandson for higher political office?" A pause and Father Jack answered his own question. "I guess having helped Henry Haro's political career would get the Hispanics behind Davis in South Texas, where he's the weakest on votes."

"And some people think the clergy are naive."

Father Jack said, "I remember reading somewhere that Davis wants to have the biggest political landslide in the history of Texas politics."

"Not like Landslide Lyndon, I hope."

"I doubt there'll be any dead men voting in this election."

The red dot had grown to identifiable size. A Jeep Cherokee sped down the slope.

"Going like pharaoh's chariot," Father Jack said as the vehicle hurled past us.

In my rearview mirror I followed the Jeep's bouncing progress. "That was Carlos Haro."

"The expression on his face would chill oatmeal. Which Haro is he?"

"Henry's uncle. Federico's youngest son."

"How many children does the old man have?"

"Four. One daughter, three sons."

"Do they live around here?"

"Carlos does. He trained as a silversmith in Taxco. His workshop is in Marfa. You might chat him up sometime to make something for the Church. Don Federico's only daughter lives in California, but her daughter moved in at the ranch about a year ago. Alberto, Henry's father, lives in San Antonio. He runs a business development service for American and European investors in Mexico."

"Taking advantage of NAFTA."

"Trying to. The peso devaluation, the recent political shift of power, and the fear of what the rebels might stir up doesn't exactly encourage investors."

"That leaves one more son. There's usually one ne'er-do-well in every large family."

"Not in this family. They have golden lives. Eduardo owns an irrigated farm below Presidio. He specializes in organically grown onions and peppers. Ships the stuff by special order all over the United States."

"Not Salubre Produce, by any chance?"

"That's it. Have you tried any of it?"

"Don't mock a fat old priest. On my stipend I do well to afford the pesticide-laced stuff."

We had come into first sight of the Haro ranch house, all five thousand square feet of it. Built in the forties, from rock gathered from the foothills of the ranch, it was shaped almost like a castle, with a flat roof and rounded towers united by a two-story central great room. Other buildings were visible beyond the house. The treeless compound was turfed in clumps of native grass.

I followed the drive around back and parked. Near the open-fronted stable a dark-haired young woman dressed in a red shirt, khaki pants, and boots held the reins of a paint horse, stroking its velvet nose while watching us get out.

Two stocky, barrel-chested men, one in his forties, the other in his twenties, but otherwise weather-hardened clones of each other, hurried out of a nearby shop building to unload the boxes of groceries, sacks of feed, and other supplies from the back of the pickup.

"The cases of motor oil you ordered are underneath the roll of barbed wire, Lalo," I said to the young man as he smiled at me. He nodded, greeted Father Jack with a cheerful "Buenos días," and bent his back to the task. His father, Eliseo Silva, deaf since a childhood illness, acknowledged us with a deep nod and picked up two boxes, one under each arm.

While the men unloaded the pickup, Alicia Lagos unsaddled the horse and led him back to his stall, shut the alley gate behind her, and joined us. Up close the Haro granddaughter showed her age as nearer thirty than twenty. While not pretty, she had a pleasant face, with the wide Haro forehead, a deeply pointed chin, and brown eyes under straight brows. I introduced Father Jack. She gave him an acute look, as if she wanted to ask or say something, but thought better of it. Instead, as Lalo came back for another box, she told him, "When you unpack the horse supplies, leave the Shine-Brite out for me on the shelf in the tack room."

"Grooming one of the horses for a show?" I asked.

She laughed lightly. "It's for me. That horse shampoo

is better than any salon formula, especially if you have dry hair like mine.''

"If that is Carlos," a firm voice spoke from somewhere above our heads, "I have nothing more to say to him. Tell him to go back to his studio."

We looked up. From an open casement window on the second floor of the house we could see the white-shirted upper torso of an elderly man.

"It isn't Carlos, Grandfather. We have guests," Alicia called up to him.

A hand fluttered a welcome. "Come up. Come up."

Alicia seconded the invitation, and we followed her into a wide corridor that opened onto a stone-paved solarium. In the center of the area was a wide well rimmed in stone.

"That's the ojo de agua," Alicia explained to Father Jack.

"Eye of water?"

"That's the literal translation," she said. "It's a spring. That's what the ranch is named for. La Noria means the well. When the original owners first dug for water, they hit a sweet-flowing spring. We pump water from the well to a holding tank in the fourth tower. From there it's piped by blackline to stock troughs in most of the pastures."

In front of us a staircase and several doors led from the solarium. Alicia opened one and said in rapid Spanish, "Two more for coffee, Tina."

On either side of the staircase stood a stuffed mountain lion mounted on an ebony base. The wild animals had been fixed in a snarling stance, posed eternally as if facing the dogs that had cornered them for the mounted hunters. Rather than appearing fiercely alive, as intended, their dulled fur and glass eyes emphasized dusty death. We mounted the stairs and entered Federico Haro's private aerie.

An undivided space of a thousand square feet open to the roof rafters made a fitting backdrop for the white-haired man in corduroy slacks, long-sleeved shirt, and Italian shoes. At eighty-eight Federico Haro looked thirty years younger. Of average height, he gave the impression of being taller because he carried himself erectly. He had the understated strength of the physically active man he was, still riding out each day to oversee the activities of his ranch. Alert black eyes, a strong nose, and sculpted lips punctuated the handsome face. Only the fine wrinkles of the skin betrayed the generosity of time that marked his life span.

He stood in the center of a collection of blue-green couches and chairs that composed a seating area demarcated by a large woven rug in fine wool. Along one wall, a heavy brass bed gleamed in the light beneath wide windows flanked by carved tables covered with books. A series of folding doors in another wall concealed a private bath, a kitchenette, and a well-stocked bar. The sharp masculine atmosphere of the loftlike space was softened by the presence of a well-dressed middle-aged Mexican woman whose soft brown bulk rested easily in one of the armchairs.

"Texana knows everyone, of course," Alicia said, introducing Father Jack.

As he always did, Haro said, "Your servant," giving us both the soft, formal handshake of Old Mexico.

Alicia turned to the seated woman. "This is Señora Severa Salinas."

The woman acknowledged us with a smile and a serene look. Rumor had it that she had been Haro's mistress since the death of his wife.

"Be seated. Be seated, both of you," Haro said.

The couches were comfortable, deep enough for my long legs, firm enough to support the back. As I did each time

I visited La Noria, I thought how perfect everything here seemed to be. With the near world enclosed by these walls and the far world encompassed by the rimrock, it seemed impossible to be disturbed by anything beyond.

Haro, sitting in a straight-backed chair that might have been made especially for him, nodded his head slightly and said, "Here is everything a man needs. A priest, two lovely friends, and a loving relative. But I warn you, Padre, if you've come to save my soul, an old man like me has a litany of sins behind him."

"What's the old rhyme about salvation?" Father Jack said. "Between the horse and the ground, salvation he found."

Haro said. "I can't think of a better way to die than riding across my land."

"Grandfather is going to live to be a hundred," Alicia said, smiling.

Easy footsteps crossed the wood floor toward us. Tina, the cook and housekeeper, carrying the coffee and a plate of sweet rolls, served us, handing her employer a glass of watery-looking milk, and departed.

"Goat's milk," Haro explained.

"Grandfather's had a touch of indigestion lately," Alicia said, with all the imagined need for explaining the foibles or illnesses of the old that the young seem to feel is necessary. "Too much spicy food."

Father Jack patted his ample stomach. "I know the feeling."

Haro said, "Why should food I've eaten all my life bother me now? Too much family. That's my trouble."

Alicia's hands tightened in her lap as she stared down at the floor.

Haro looked past us to the view beyond the window. He sighed deeply. "Forgive my irritability. My son Carlos is

turning into a grumpy old man, and he's making me one.''
He lifted his glass to his lips, finished the milk, and blotted
his mouth with the linen napkin. "Goat's milk," he said
again, his tone dreamy. "In Guadalupita I drank it every
day as a boy. In the bad years, goats provided all our food.''

Picking up the cue, Father Jack moved in smoothly. "Is
that where you were born?"

Haro, looking at the priest, said reflectively, "It was a
tiny village in southern Jalisco."

Father Jack knew an entrance line when he heard it. He
set his coffee aside and prepared to listen. Alicia smiled
indulgently, knowing her grandfather was now on a safe
subject. I, too, had heard Don Federico's history more than
once, but I didn't mind. He was a natural storyteller, and
his tale had all the poignancy and drama of a life lived, as
the ancient Chinese curse goes, in interesting times.

FIVE

In my time Guadalupita was not to be found on any map. When I was a boy, the two hundred and thirty-four of us seemed a great number. I hear that three thousand people live there today.

"During the sixteenth century, the village had converted from the old gods and the old ways to the Catholicism of Spain, and had built a church. The Dominican friars recorded the first infant baptism in the church in 1564.

"In my childhood, the only educated person among us was the priest, a pious, silver-tongued old man named Juan Baptiste, who tended bees. He was a hero to all the village because he had fought alongside us against bandits. He founded a school in Guadalapita, and brought two Daughters of Mary to teach catechism and sewing to the girls. In the months between harvest and the next planting he taught the boys to cipher and to read and write. A few parents sent their sons to him for extra lessons in Latin, mathematics, and philosophy. My brother Bernardo attended those classes.

"The padre tried to improve our lives, to expose us to ideas beyond the experience of the village. Thanks to his teaching and influence, the village boasted eighteen young men attending the seminary in Zamora, my brother among them.

"As you can imagine, this was a source of great pride to all of us in Guadalupita. We were devout. Every child in the village knew the Pater Noster, the Ave Maria, Countless prayers flowed to heaven from our lips.

"Madrinas and padrinos taught their godchildren the cautionary tale of the devil on the snorting black horse. He yanked a bad man onto the saddle in front of him and carried him high into the sky. The poor sinner twisted and struggled, but he couldn't escape the devil's clutches, until he pulled his rosary from his pocket. Seeing that, the devil shrieked and dropped the sinner, who landed on the ground unhurt. Thus were we taught to pray our beads as a means of redemption.

"The source of our faith and much of our sanctity rested in the relic of a saint, a boy murdered by a gachupín, a spur wearer, as our ancestors called the Spanish. The saint's legend told that, in the fourth generation after the Conquest, a Spaniard, drunk on pulque, rode down an old woman as she crossed the street. A goat herder named José Zuño went to help the woman to her feet just as the gachupín turned his horse to ride over her again. The goat herder pushed the woman out of the way. The infuriated Spaniard rode down the boy. The goat herder crumpled into the dust of the street.

"After the Spaniard galloped off, the old woman crept out from her hiding place and went to the boy. The gapuchín's spurs had slashed his eyes, blinding him. The woman led him to her hut, bound up his wounds, and watched over him all night. At daybreak she left him to go for food.

"When she returned, he was gone. She alerted the villagers. They found him on the wild thorny slopes with his goats. His eyes were healed, his face unmarked. He told them nothing, but the villagers persuaded the priest to speak to him. Later, he told them that José Zuño had had a vision of Our Lady, who miraculously healed him.

"The tale of the boy's recovery infuriated the Spaniard when he heard it. A few weeks later, some villagers found José facedown on the hillside, dead, his left hand cut off.

Under cover of night, they brought the body back and buried it. The priest placed the severed hand in a carved box and put it in the sepulchre of the altar, and people came there to pray to José.

"Over the following decades in Guadalupita there occurred no major epidemics. No one was killed by a wild animal. No one died a violent death. Many prayers were answered through the intercession of the goat herder saint, and the village prospered in its quiet way.

"In the year of my birth, President Díaz announced that political parties were forming and there would be a democratic vote for the next election. In the bigger towns all over Mexico, people were taking sides, dividing into political camps. We did not know it, but the unrest had begun. Mexico would have democracy, all right. The bloodiest kind of democracy. Not even the saint's hand could save us from ourselves. My childhood memories are of gunfire, women crying, and my family and the other villagers running and hiding in the hills. I was a young man before I saw women dressed in colors instead of the black of mourning.

"All the time, the political unrest to the north was growing and spreading. Overnight, it seemed, things fell apart. The villagers had heard of promises of the new democracy. What they got was roving bands of revolutionaries making the roads unsafe for travel, robbing the ranches, and killing and raping, looting the poor of the little they had, in the name of the revolutionary leader of the moment. Blood and money was the motto of the villains who claimed to be freeing us into greater prosperity by drunkenness, slaughter, and rape.

"Sometimes, if there were few raiders, the village fought them off like the bandits they were. If there were many, we took to the hills until they had gone, taking every last

chicken with them. The chavistas looted the church, taking
even the sacred communion chalices, and set fire to it, but
a rain put out the fire before the building could be damaged.

"A few years went by, and the violence of the revolution
died down so that we returned to nearly our normal routine
of seasonal planting. Our beloved Padre Juan died in the
terrible flu epidemic that swept the world, and my brother
Bernardo returned to Guadalupita from the seminary, where
he had been teaching, to replace him.

"When I was fourteen, General Plutarco Elías Calles's
first act as the new president of the Republic was to suspend
all Church ceremonies. In Guadalupita my brother followed
the Calles law in things visible. He did not wear the cassock
in public. The bells did not ring to call the faithful to Mass.
As to things spiritual, he said his Daily Office in private.
He administered the sacrament to us in our homes. Outside the village, in the large towns, seminaries and church
schools closed, and the clergy lived in fear. Those who
agreed with the Calles law derided church supporters as
'mochos.' Guadalupita was one hundred percent mochos.

"My brother saw such national division as dangerous.
He feared that faith was shallow-seated in most of Mexico
and the anticlerical, socialist movement would win and take
Guadalupita with it. He decided to fight against those who
would destroy what he believed in. Already other areas of
Mexico had rebelled. The cristero movement grew rapidly.
My brother decided to join them, and he preached to the
village to come with him. Forty men, ranging in age from
eighteen to forty, most of the able-bodied men of the village, agreed with him.

"I was not one of them. I had seen all the fighting I
needed in the years my brother had been tucked away at
the seminary.

"Others from neighboring villages joined in support, and

they set the first day of June as the date of their insurrection. As one who opposed Bernardo, I was scorned. After the men rode out to the cheers of almost all the village, and I went with the women and children to the church to pray, I left Guadalupita on foot to take my chance in Mexico City or Guadalajara.

"The following morning, while the roosters still crowed in the plaza, a party of government soldiers rode in and attacked.

"From the hills I turned back for one last look at my home and saw the dark cloud of smoke rising into the sky like the devil's black horse. I ran all the way home.

"The ashes were still hot when I got there. The soldiers had broken up every cooking pot and piece of household furniture, piled the rubble in the plaza, drenched it with kerosene and set it on fire, then torched the houses. The village was silent. The dead were everywhere, the earth itself defiled with blood. I found the bodies of my mother and three of my sisters huddled together. The others I found with their children. A few old men had died with pistols in their hands, trying to defend the village. The cattle and pigs and sheep had been driven into the countryside. Even the dogs had run away. The church had been looted and desecrated. The roof had burned, but the walls still stood. I searched the sepulchre of the smashed altar. The relic was gone. It took me four days to bury the bodies.

"Once more, I set out on my journey. I made my way from village to village, sometimes living off the land, sometimes working for food, sometimes begging. From time to time I heard news of my brother and his band of cristeros. They were fighting in the east. Five hundred men had joined their ranks. In hand-to-hand fighting, they had taken seven villages, killed many of the opposition, with only a small loss of life to their numbers. People were saying that Padre Bernardo's band could not be stopped.

"Two months later, at a ranchería in northwestern Michoacán, I met Bernardo. He had taken to wearing a military uniform and carrying a pistol, a rifle, and a machete. He was jubilant about the cristero victories, eager to move on to greater battles. I told him what had happened to Guadalupita. I cursed that our saint's relic that had protected us had been stolen by the revolutionaries. Bernardo took me aside, and from his saddlebag withdrew the carved box.

"'We had greater need of it. The village can be rebuilt. We fight for the soul of Mexico.' Those were his words.

"My brother, who had preached meekness and the virtuous life, had summoned men to fight and kill and die. Worse, he had betrayed his family, his faith, his village."

Federico Haro looked directly at Father Jack as he said this. It was the finale of his story, and he sat with statue stillness and waited for the priest's reaction.

Father Jack leaned forward, rested his arms on his knees. "What happened to your brother?"

Haro narrowed his eyes slightly, as if focusing his thoughts inward. "I never saw him again," he said. The tone conveyed finality of mind as well as circumstance, the familial wound still raw.

Alicia, who had risen to collect our cups and plates, said, "I want to videotape Grandfather recounting his life's story, but he won't let me. I tell him he's an important part of Hispanic history."

"That word again," Haro said.

"Grandfather disapproves of the term 'Hispanic.'"

"It's inaccurate," Haro said. "It lumps Mexicans together with all the other Spanish speakers we have nothing in common with, such as Argentina or Peru. We Mexicans are Spaniards by way of Tenochtitlán and Chichén-Itzá. We should be proud of that history. Not watering our heritage down with vague terms like Hispanic.''

Alicia gave her grandfather a look of momentary disdain mingled with pity.

"Good point," Father Jack said. "Like calling me an Anglo just because I speak English and despite the fact that I'm not Protestant." He gestured toward me. "Or in Texana's case, she comes from Mediterranean rather than Anglo-Saxon heritage."

Haro nodded. "It's refreshing to be understood. Sometimes, with my grandchildren, I think I'm speaking to the wind."

Severa stopped any further rancorous comments by mentioning Henry's political success.

Haro smiled broadly, and said, "He will make the Haro name mean something to this state and, I hope, this country. Our good friend Bascom Davis has been of remarkable help to Henry both politically and personally. They are partners in the horse business."

"Grandfather always says if you find yourself on the opposite side of an argument with Mr. Davis, you've picked the wrong side."

"I'll tell it, I'll tell it," Haro told his granddaughter. "Bascom loves his whiskey, his poker, and good conversation, but he's all politician at heart. He knows when to take a stand and when to cut a deal. He's the old Texas at its best, a good combination for the new Texas my grandson will represent."

He recounted several tales of Henry's achievements. When he started talking about the ranch, I knew that, given the old man's stamina, we'd be staying to lunch and maybe dinner if we didn't get moving. I was waiting for an appropriate moment to take leave, but Father Jack did it for me.

"Do you ride?" Haro asked the priest.

"Only as penance for my sins."

"We'll drive, then. I want you to see my cattle. We raise the finest Herefords in the state."

"I should like nothing better, sir, another time. I've imposed on Texana to take me to visit Electra Reaves."

Haro said, "Maybe, Padre, while you're there, you'll perform an exorcism and drive her away from here."

"Please, Grandfather—"

"Be silent," Haro said, giving Alicia a hard look. "That woman's got you bewitched." His voice vibrated with emotion. "The devil doesn't always wear horns."

"Come, Don Federico," Severa Salinas interjected, putting a soft hand on his arm.

Her touch quieted him, and he said, "Another time, then, as you say, Padre." He rose with magnificent dignity, and we said our good-byes.

Alicia escorted us back downstairs.

"As you can see, my grandfather is not himself," she said. "Uncle Carlos upset him badly."

"He's a grand old gentleman, and I'm glad to have met him," Father Jack told her.

"He doesn't understand," she said severely. "For all that he hasn't been to Mass in years, he still resents my Protestant conversion." Alicia looked defiantly at Father Jack.

"It's to be of no church that's dangerous," the priest said without emphasis.

His neutral response seemed to please Alicia, and she managed a smile and wave as we drove away.

Neither of us spoke until we crossed the cattleguard.

"What they need is the miracle of that saint's hand to restore harmony," I said.

"Better to trust in God than in the sort of relics Chaucer mocked in the fourteenth century. Though you're right. That's not a happy family."

"They always have been before. Or at least I thought so. Don Federico's too much of a gentleman to let his feelings show usually. I've never seen him like that. Especially to criticize his family in front of us."

"Old age, even one as robust as his seems to be, has a way of stripping the social veneer from us. We like to think we approach death with courage and grace. Just as often it's bitterness and resentment that sees us out. It's as though the very old can't be bothered with anything but essentials, and the finer emotions are lost to weariness and spiritual ennui."

"Something to look forward to," I said dryly.

"Think how it makes me feel. If a doctor makes the worst patient, doesn't it follow that the priest makes the worst petitioner before God?"

"Alicia would certainly think so."

"Yes. I'm afraid she may have a convert's zeal without the winnowing of a mature sinner's understanding of human weakness, and that makes for an unforgiving nature. A dangerous time for one's soul."

Ahead the blue mountains rolled away into Mexico like clouds building on the horizon.

"Don Federico doesn't think much of the evangelista," I said. "I wonder what she thinks of him?"

"I'll bet she'll tell us," he said.

"I never bet against a priest. The odds, surely, are in your favor."

SIX

WE TRAVELED BACK DOWN the canyon in a brief but violent thunderstorm. Fingertips of clouds dragged against the mountaintops, and neon strips of lightning illuminated the surrounding slopes, vibrating the air with an electronic tingle.

With straining engine, whining gears, and mud spewing, the four-wheel drive got us across the Arroyo de la Aura at the open end of the canyon. This was the cutoff point for Electra Reaves's place, a concrete-block house on sixty-nine acres. As we topped the ridge, I stopped, got out, and used my hand to clear the worst of the mud from the windshield so the wipers could finish the job. Father Jack cleared the other side for me. I got a bottle of water from the toolbox and we rinsed our hands. From where we stood we could see the small corral and house two miles in the distance. Rising behind it and extending for twenty miles or more was a chain of sawtooth peaks on which the fast-moving storm battered itself out. Already, above our heads, the sky shone clear and blue, and the air was fragrant with the mingled scents of desert plants and the smell of damp earth.

It took us fifteen minutes lurching and sliding on the water-filled ruts of the trail to reach the house. On the way we glimpsed a coyote so intent on catching rodents driven out of their burrows by the flash flood that we were almost upon it before it vanished into the scrub.

Electra Reaves had heard us coming. She leaned against the doorframe, a pistol in one hand, finger on the trigger.

A reasonable precaution in such a remote location. A golden Great Dane named Max waited with her to see who the company was. I waved, parked close, and saw Electra step back into the house. When she emerged, her hands held nothing.

We stepped out of the truck into complete silence. I turned and looked back at the vast and empty canyon. The only evidence of man was the trail, first made by wagons hundreds of years ago. In such moments the present pours itself into the past, so that I almost heard the creaking wings and saw the shadow of a pterosaur sweeping across the canyon floor, sensed the unseen presence of the Apache and Comanche mounting raids from here into Mexico, envisioned the blue-clad cavalrymen winding down the canyon leading the harnessed camels that were to become a failed experiment in this desert.

"See something interesting back there?"

The astringent voice shriveled imagination.

"Admiring the view," I said, turning to greet the *evangelista.*

Stepping from the porch, she gave my hand a brief touch, courtesy on a tiny scale. "Nice to have company," she said. The dog watched us intently, alert but not threatening since his owner had greeted us.

Electra was fortyish, small, and thin. I guessed her weight at 115 pounds, tops. Standing next to her, I felt like a giant. She wore a loose green sweater over brown wool pants tucked into high-top boots. Her graying hair hung in a thick braid pinned up on the back of her head. Her brown skin and prominent cheekbones emphasized the green eyes under unplucked brows. A broad nose, a slightly downturned mouth finished the face.

She glanced at Father Jack, who stood jingling the change in his pockets. He roused himself from his thoughts, glanced down the trail, and said, "I guess you don't get any accidental visitors up here at the end of the road."

"You'd be surprised." She went to a wooden box on the porch and rummaged in it. Lifting out something, she walked back to us, and held it up so we could see. The doll had a crudely painted face with red lips and glass eyes. Red paint had been dribbled on its torso, and ocotillo circled the head. Thumbtacks held the hands and feet to a cross made of two sticks tied together with twine.

Father Jack touched his finger to the ocotillo. "The crown of thorns."

Electra said, "I found it nailed to my front door last week when I got back from across the river. It's the third one in as many months."

"That's not what I'd call an accidental visitor. Anything but." He handed the crucified doll back. "Perhaps you should move into Polvo."

"That wouldn't suit me just now."

"Doesn't it worry you?" he said, looking at the doll.

"I'm handy with a gun. Max is handy with his teeth."

"Let me introduce you two," I said.

Her lips flexed in what might have been a smile when I mentioned Jack Raff's vocation. He hardly looked the part, dressed casually as he always was, his open manner as casual as a ranch hand's, including occasional cussing.

"You've heard I'm a Gospel-trumpeter, I suppose," she said, peering close enough to his face to suggest nearsightedness. "Do you view me with alarm and aversion?"

"On the contrary," he said. "With a spirit of hope and brotherly commiseration laced with admiration."

"How very generous of you. Not everyone I meet from your side of the altar is so open-minded. I always say there's plenty of work on the other side for all of us, no matter the denomination."

"And what is yours?" Father Jack said, blunting his inquisitiveness with an enlarged smile.

Electra returned his smile, tooth for tooth. "None. Pure Gospel all the way. I hand out tracts on the sayings of Jesus. That's what I teach."

"It must be pleasant, not worrying with dogma and tacked-on theology," the priest said.

"What a sweetheart you are." Electra pushed her sleeve back to look at her watch. "Lunchtime. You'll eat with Max and me." She turned and headed indoors.

"Gives orders like a bishop," Father Jack murmured as, meek and mild, we followed behind the trotting dog.

The house had three rooms, no electricity, no telephone. As we passed through what had been intended as the living room, with windows overlooking the trail, I noticed that the pistol Electra had been holding as we drove up had been placed, ready and waiting, on top of boxes of religious tracts stacked on a small table by the door. We passed through a short hallway and into a wide kitchen.

The room was cold and clean. The couple that had briefly occupied it had painted it adobe orange with green trim. That seemed to be as far as the improvements had gone. I knew from her shopping trips to the trading post that Electra lived out of cans and cooked on a propane stove run from a portable tank outside the kitchen window and piped in through a hole drilled in the wall. She washed dishes in a plastic pan with water hauled from the well near the tiny orchard. Near the back door, a tin bathtub hung on a nail driven into the exposed ceiling joist.

As she started pulling out a skillet and pans, I offered to help, but she shook her head, saying, "It would take me longer to tell you where things are than to do it myself."

Father Jack and I sat at a long wooden table polished so

thickly it looked almost fake except for the fine patina beneath the layers of wax. Before Electra started preparing our lunch, she scooped dry food into Max's pan. While the dog crunched, the *evangelista* poured oil into an iron skillet, struck a match, and lighted the flame under it. She used a manual can opener, dumped the contents into another pan, and fired the second burner.

Watching her, I wondered, as I had the few times we'd met before, about her background. On her visits to the trading post, she rarely made small talk. No one seemed to know where she'd come from or anything about her personal life. The cabin and the few acres that went with it had been abandoned for several years. Then one day nine months ago a cowboy saw smoke curling from the stovepipe on the roof and reported that someone had set up housekeeping in the abandoned Conver house, as it was called. The owner of the adjoining ranch had sent one of his hands to check, thinking illegals had made camp there. The rider found Electra Reaves sitting in a rocking chair on the front porch, Max by her side. She told the cowboy she'd bought the place from the couple who'd owned it. That fact and her vocation were all anyone knew about her. Mindful of our own privacy, we respect that of others when they make it plain that's what they want. Electra had made it pretty plain.

"We came down from La Noria," I said conversationally.

"How is the old man keeping himself?" Electra asked.

"Don Haro's vigor is amazing," I said.

"He'd show you vigor if he knew you intended coming here," she said, opening drawers and getting silverware out. "The mention of my name is enough to set him off."

"Why is that?" Father Jack asked.

"He thinks I'm a witch. He believes that's how I got Alicia as one of my converts, by using magic."

Father Jack said, "I wouldn't have thought of him as a superstitious man."

"Take it from me, he is," she said, her back to us as she peeled potatoes with a butcher knife. "He went so far as to call in a curandera from Ojinaga to lay hands on Alicia. That old woman prayed over that girl, rubbed potions on her, swept her with a broom and egg. If you don't know about such things, that's a double measure of healing to rid the girl of evil spirits. Híjole! They tried everything." Electra rinsed the potatoes in a pan of water and started slicing them on a cutting board. "Alicia's mother sent her out here from California, you know. She'd got tied up with some cult or other out there. It didn't take me five minutes to put her on the right path. When she can get away, which isn't often, she goes over to the ranchos and ejidos with me. That really burns her grandfather up. That old man will get bilis if he's not careful, letting his anger eat on him. All that bile makes the whole body sick. The curanderos are right about that." The hot oil sizzled as Electra dropped in the potatoes.

We dined on french fries, red beans from the can heated with chopped onions, and tortillas, all washed down with instant coffee. During the meal, Electra questioned Father Jack about his ministry, how he liked the borderland, and where he'd lived and worked before coming here. Dessert was bananas in condensed milk. When we finished, Electra scraped the leftovers into the dog's pan.

"It's nice, having company," she said, clearing the table and stacking things in the dishpan. "Do you get over to the other side much, Padre?"

"Yes. I say Mass at far-flung pueblitos, baptize babies,

and marry a lot of couples that have been, uh, waiting for a priest to come along.''

Electra gave a sharp laugh. ''Living together with their six kids, you mean. The poor souls do the best they can, though, don't they? Bless their hearts. The trouble with Mexico is it needs to learn to read before it learns to pray.''

''You mean, then they could read the Bible for themselves?'' Father Jack said.

''That's exactly what I mean.''

''I find I deal mostly with two kinds of people,'' the priest said. ''Those who hunger for the sacraments, and those who think religion is for babies and women.''

''It must be hard on you. I can see that. Your kind carry a lot of baggage. Not you personally, of course, but the Catholic Church. After all, Mexico's 1917 constitution calls the clergy the most baneful and perverse enemy.''

''And that's only the opening sentence of that paragraph,'' Father Jack said. ''Still, we've come a long way since Graham Greene's whiskey priest.''

''You do the best you can, like me. I suppose it's a problem for you, with so many Protestants making headway in the villages. Used to be, they concentrated on just the cities and the Indians. Not that anybody can really convert the Indians. Not even the Jesuits did that. All those crosses in Chiapas are erected on the sites where they worshiped the old gods, you know. I've seen foreign nuns there carrying on about how wonderful it is the Indians are so pious. That's how little they know, bless their hearts. And it's becoming the same all over Mexico, the more the Indians move north.''

''I acknowledge the persistence of the Indians in mixing violence and religion, the actual crucifixions that occur in some Easter pageants, the penitentes who lash themselves until their backs bleed. Surely in your work you encounter some who are sincere after so many generations of mission work by Dominicans, Franciscans, and others?''

"I'll show you how sincere your converts are." She jumped to her feet, left the room, and opened the only interior door in the short hall.

"Take a look," she said.

We got up and went to the door. The room couldn't have measured more than eight feet square, and must have been the original bedroom. The wooden floor had vanished beneath a deep pile of religious artifacts. Plaster, pottery, and wooden statues of saints, reliquaries, and candlesticks had been heaped with crucifixes of every size, not the sanitized figure of Christ found in American churches, but the dehydrated, emaciated, bloodied Christ of Mexico, the cruel mockery of the crown of thorns on his bowed head. Around the room, propped against the stucco walls, life-size angels and saints leaned like drunks at an all-night party. I recognized Saint John, Saint Jude, Saint Martin de Cabellero, and others. Cardboard boxes overflowed with smaller items. Wooden chalices looking ancient enough to have been carved by Saint Joseph himself were tumbled with those of silver and gold, medals and medallions, candlesticks.

"Woman, have you been looting our churches?" Father Jack demanded.

"I pay from fifty cents to ten dollars for each item the gente bring me."

Her choice of words implied a comfortable familiarity with the Mexican villagers. *Gente* means the people and has many uses in many senses in Spanish, but most often for family, and around gringos, race. The people. We versus you, the non-Mexican.

I pointed at the treasure trove. "What do you do with all these things?" I said.

"I sell them and buy Bibles and food and clothes for the

villagers on the other side. Most of them are dirt-poor. They come from the south to Mexico City to find work. There's no room for them there, and they're discouraged from staying where they have to beg or starve. So they shift north with a couple of goats and the clothes on their backs. I pay them so much for coming to Bible study. The ones who find out about me bring others.''

Father Jack said, "Those statues. The reliquaries. The chalices. Those never came from any poor village. Those things have been stolen from churches.''

"Dear man, don't upset yourself," Electra said. "If they have to relocate, the gente always take their saints and relics with them. I don't ask for provenance on what someone brings in. I'm busy fighting against their poverty. The money I pay goes to clothe and feed their families.''

Father Jack's face flushed. "You must see what you're doing. The commandment Thou shalt not steal is absolute—''

"I don't ask them to steal. I don't know that they are stealing. Neither do you. I've been in villages where when things were going bad—crops lost to drought or goats drowned in a flash flood—the gente would carry out the statue of their patron saint and bury it upside down as punishment, then get them a new saint who'd bring better luck. Maybe these are all bad-luck saints.''

A spasm of painful emotions shifted across the priest's face but he said nothing more.

"We'll be on our way now, Electra." I took Father Jack's arm and moved him toward the door. "By the way, I brought you some dog food. It's a free sample of a new brand the salesman gave me.'' On her infrequent visits to the trading post, Electra never failed to buy dog food as well as feed for her horse, a big gelding she called Doc.

Electra came with us to the door, Max padding along

eager-eyed and tail wagging, as if he understood he was to get a present. Electra accepted the twenty-pound sack of dog food I lifted from behind the front seat. She propped it between her knees, patted her pockets, reaching into one and handing me what she had taken from it.

"That might clean up nicely," she said.

"This isn't necessary..." I began, looking down at a tarnished, unusual chain from which dangled a blackened medal.

"It's just another religious trinket someone gave me."

Not wanting to reopen that subject, I slipped the chain and medal into the pocket of my jacket. There didn't seem to be anything more to say. I opened the door of the pickup and got in.

Electra looked up at Father Jack and said, "I hope you'll understand how I feel. The statues aren't important. It's the people who bring them to me I help. I'd hate to think you really object to getting people a better way of life, whatever the cost."

Father Jack said, "Would you allow me to bless you?"

She looked surprised. I know I was, not at the words, but at the tone of voice that held a gravity I had never heard from him.

Laughing lightly, she said, "Thanks all the same. Unlike Señor Haro, I don't believe in curses or blessings."

For a long moment, Father Jack gazed at her. "Then I'll say que le vaya bien."

"Good luck to you, too," Electra told him as he got in the passenger side. "Real good to meet you, Father. You do God's work. We're both on the same side, just different vantage points. You take care now."

As we drove away I glanced in the rearview mirror. The evangelista was striding toward the corral beyond the house.

The canyon track necessitated my keeping my eyes straight ahead and concentrating my mind on staying in the ruts. Father Jack kept his thoughts to himself as he fingered a rosary he'd taken from his pocket.

When we turned out of the canyon and onto the lava-rock surface of the road that paralleled the river all the way to El Polvo, he slipped his beads back into his pocket, saying, "I wonder if Don Federico still prays the rosary the way his godparents taught him. Sometimes when I'm troubled I rub mine, like worry beads."

"Are you troubled now?"

"Too much sugar for the pound."

"I beg your pardon?"

"Sorry," he said. "I was thinking aloud. Electra, all that 'bless their hearts' business from a woman who doesn't believe in blessings."

"Some people say such things out of habit, without thinking."

"Without meaning might be a more appropriate way of putting it. A lot of contradictions there," he said thoughtfully.

We fell back on silence as I negotiated a broad sweep of loose shale. I had my eyes on the road. Father Jack faced the panorama to the south, a broad valley slipping down toward the Rio Grande.

Feeling safer on the firmer ground we soon reached, I stated my opinion. "Electra shouldn't have rubbed in her anti-Catholic feeling by showing you those statues."

"There are too many people in the world who seem to worship God for spite," Father Jack said, his tone so woeful that I thought it best to make no comment.

Electra had certainly unsettled him. I found her an awkward but well-meaning woman, abrupt in manner to the point of curtness, which sometimes happens to those who live alone with no one much to please but themselves. I had no idea of what success she'd had with her proselytizing to the villages except for the load of church artifacts she'd managed to collect, and after all, a few American dollars went a long way in Mexico. To keep the income flowing, some people might go along with her. It didn't necessarily mean they believed in her view of religion. Necessity moves mountains, too.

We'd hit the blacktop before Father Jack spoke again. "A soft, yielding mind is a dangerous thing."

"Yes," I said vaguely, unsure of his point.

He elaborated. "I was speaking of Alicia. Going through life trying on religions like new clothes can leave one naked at the worst time. It's so easy for a priest or minister to drive someone from the Church. A wrong word or mistaken attitude, the failure to speak or do the right thing when someone needs spiritual help, and the person turns away from the Church forever."

"You're appreciated here, you know. And loved."

He turned and smiled at me and said simply, "Thank you." He checked his watch. "Drop me at my house, will you?"

"You left your pickup at my place, remember?" The used Chevy was his third vehicle since his assignment here. The priest never kept track of oil changes, engine tune-ups, or other vital parts of automotive maintenance.

He said, "I'm expecting visitors. I'll hitch a ride with someone to the posada and collect my pickup."

Mentally I sagged. In all the anxiety of yesterday's events and the hurry of today's business, I'd forgotten the first party of the Christmas season was at my place. I drove past the double line of flat-roofed adobes and the trailers that make up the main street of El Polvo, wheeled around the blindingly white church and the adjoining cemetery to

Father Jack's house. The small adobe sits on a rise above the cemetery and had once belonged to Dona Aurora, a fortune-teller. After her death the house had remained vacant for a year, and then her children had offered it to the Church. Father Jack had moved into the adobe gratefully, having lived first in a trailer, and later in the warehouse donated for the failed goat-cheese cooperative.

He stepped out, slamming the door. ''Thanks. See you tonight.'' He waved and turned away.

I headed home, feeling tired and a little out of sorts, knowing all that I had to do in order to ready the trading post for the *posada*. The dash clock read 2:05. I had less than five hours until I'd be welcoming the whole town at my door. Thank goodness Clay would be there to help me. I only hoped his day had been shorter and less hectic than mine.

I overflowed with relief when I saw his van parked by his office. With his help, I'd get the decorating for the party done in short order and have a little time left over to relax. I parked near the backdoor beside Charlie's Cadillac, a fitted tarp cover protecting it from the elements.

I dumped my jacket and boots in the mudroom and padded to the kitchen in my socks. Phobe came bounding from the front, greeting me with a chirrup, then running madly all over the house, her way of letting me know she was both glad to see me and resentful of being left alone all day. I heard the hum of the washing machine from the utility room and noticed an empty tumbler on the counter beside the lesser brand of whiskey I sell in the trading post. Going to the bedroom, I peeked in, heard the shower running full blast, and sighed. When a vet has to wash the clothes he wore and himself, it means the day's work has been messy. When this particular vet has a glass of whiskey before six in the evening, it means the job has been an unpleasant one.

I crossed to the bath and called through the half-opened door, "I'm home. Everything okay?"

Over the throb of the shower head, Clay said, "I just finished helping Jerry bury twelve horses."

"Oh, Clay," I said, shocked. Then, knowing he probably hadn't eaten since breakfast, I told him I'd fix something right away.

"Make it easy on yourself," he said.

I went to the kitchen, washed my hands at the sink, and made two peanut butter and jelly sandwiches and a pot of coffee. Clay came in, sat down heavily at the table, and picked up one of his sandwiches, saying, "Perfect. High energy, low effort. I'm starving." He looked gray and drawn. I drank my coffee and asked no questions while he ate or after he finished, instead suggesting that he stretch out on the couch.

"That's a great idea," he said. I washed the plate and mugs, and before I could dry them his breathing had deepened and slowed. I tiptoed to the storeroom for the box containing the Christmas decorations I'd bought a month ago in Presidio.

I was on the ladder looping the rope over the rafter and raising the burro piñata to hang head high when Clay came in, looking rested but still tense. He looked puzzled for an instant, not yet fully awake; then awareness struck and he said, "The posada. I forgot it."

"So did I until Father Jack mentioned it on the way home," I said, coming down the ladder. I'd already hung the paper streamers, set out the folding chairs, and put out the paper plates and napkins on one end of the display table. Now cleared of sale goods and draped in four alternating tablecloths of red and green, it would serve as our buffet. I stepped back and admired my work. The whole space looked festive.

"You shouldn't have let me sleep," he said. "This is too much for you to do all by yourself."

"You looked dead on your feet, and I wanted you awake for the party." I studied the grime on my hands. After the holidays I'd have a go at cleaning the tops of the cross-beams. "What happened with the horses? Could you save any of them?"

"None. Three were dead by the time I got there. I walked into the corral and one seized up and lay over, thrashing and quaking so much her legs cut furrows in the ground. Three others took a few steps and went down the same way. As soon as Jerry showed me what they'd eaten, I knew I couldn't save them. By then the rest had collapsed, so I finished them."

"What was it?"

"Strychnine. It contracts the muscles. Poor beasts were suffocating."

"But how—"

"Gopher poison. Pellets of milo-covered strychnine."

I pulled out one of the chairs and sat down. "What happened? How'd they get into poison like that?"

Clay sat down, too. "Sometime before daylight somebody poured out the pellets along the fence just inside the runs by the stables. We found footprints. The horses thought it was feed, of course, since milo is a feed grain."

"You mean someone did this deliberately?"

Clay rubbed his tired eyes. "Don't see how it could be anything else. We called the sheriff and the insurance company. That's what took me so long. The insurance agent asked me to do the autopsies and send in the tissue samples and stomach contents to the Veterinary Medical Diagnosis

Lab at A & M. It'll take about two weeks for them to verify my findings and send a report to the insurance agency.''

"The ranch had its remuda insured?" I asked.

"No, no, these weren't the working stock. These were Bascom Davis's cutting horses, his breeding stock."

I shut my eyes. I hadn't known the man owned that many. I had seen three mares, beautiful creatures with coats like polished amber. The pregnant animals had been Davis's initial purchase when he decided to move into breeding as well as showing cutting horses. For years he'd ridden a gelding named Ironsides in amateur and charity competitions. Jerry had taken delivery of the mares last spring, asking Clay out to check them over as soon as they stepped out of the trailer. It was unbelievable to think someone had poisoned them.

"Has Davis been told yet?" I asked.

Clay nodded. "Jerry talked to someone at Davis's office. He's worried sick he'll lose his grazing lease over this."

"At least they were insured. That's some comfort."

"Not to Jerry. And I doubt to Bascom Davis. Three months ago he paid three hundred thousand dollars for a stallion named Dancing Dan for show and breeding. The stallion died, too. The poisoner put the pellets in a bucket and set it just inside the stall."

"Andalon and his deputies will have their hands full investigating this," I said.

"The insurance company is sending their own investigator. From the sound of it, our friend Andalon will be expected to cooperate as needed and otherwise stay out of the way. I expect he'll be grateful, considering a big-name politician is involved." Clay glanced up at the decorations, shoved back his chair, and stood. "Not a word of this to anybody tonight."

"Rumors will be flying already, but I know better than to talk about this."

"Not the animal deaths from predators or human neglect that I usually deal with. I'm kind of glad we have the party to stop me worrying about it."

"I guess it will get into the papers."

"I'm not worried about that. I'm worried that whoever did this might develop a taste for it."

"But surely" I stopped.

Clay put my thought into words. "Yeah. Most likely it's somebody with a grudge against Davis."

"What a lot of money to spend on a hobby," I said, trying to imagine a three-hundred-thousand-dollar horse.

"He stood to make money with the stallion. Come to that, if the insurance pays, he's not out a penny. That investigator will be after him first."

"You think so?"

"There are two kinds of politicians. The kind who like to show off what their money can buy, and the kind who like to hide how much they have. Since we're six hundred miles from everything, having a ranch in Presidio County means Bascom Davis is the hiding kind. Or was until he bought that stallion. I expect the insurance agent is going to be very interested in why a man buys a show horse in what is working horse country. Now, what do you want me to do for the party?"

"Shave."

SEVEN

DRESSING FOR THE PARTY, I had no presentiment of near-disaster. I zipped up an ankle-length skirt, buttoned up the matching red overblouse, a western cut in silk with delicate beading on the collar, and slipped on flats. Don't get the wrong idea. My five-foot-nine height has never bothered me. I wear low-heeled shoes most of the time because I like comfort. As a finishing touch I pinned on one of my favorite pieces of jewelry, the triangular face of an Aztec god carved in turquoise and set in silver.

Taking care of last-minute chores, I stacked the extra platters, put out utensils for serving the covered dishes the guests would bring, and checked my contribution, a double-crust chicken pot pie warming in the oven. I adjusted the temperature setting down to 250 degrees. Finally, I coaxed Phobe into the laundry room. She curled up on her bed of feed sacks and I brushed her fur to settle her down. Phobe is not a party animal. The presence of too many people overexcites her, and can invite disaster. Like the time she pounced from a high shelf onto the back of one our guests unaccustomed to bobcat play. Quite naturally, the woman had run screaming, frightening Phobe into tightening her grip. If Clay hadn't come in by the front, blocking the woman's path, she'd be running still. Needless to say, she'd never returned for a second visit. Since that episode Phobe has been dropped from the guest list. At the moment she was lovably quiet, all soft fur, golden eyes, and throaty purr. As her eyes closed, I put down the brush, got to my feet, and eased out, shutting the door behind me. I checked the bedroom for Clay, heard him moving around out front, and went to see what he was doing.

He had set up the Christmas tree and was hanging the ornaments. "Nice job," I told him, and together we finished decorating the bare branches of the mesquite tree with handblown globes we'd bought in Chihuahua on our third anniversary, kiln-fired clay animals made by a neighbor, and icicles that were the cut-glass drops from a chandelier we'd found at a garage sale in Alpine. As a finishing touch, Clay added the hummingbird's nest of spiderweb and lichen that he'd found in the brush.

I put the boxes away under the counter, and Clay flipped on the exterior Christmas lights to welcome our guests. As if by signal the silence of the night vanished as the first vehicle in a conga line of pickups and cars pulled into the parking lot.

The leader was Pete Rosales. He sat astride the iron seat of his antique John Deere tractor pulling a rusting, open-topped cattle trailer loaded with three generations of family members. The grown-ups sat on hay bales placed around the sides, and the children bunched in the middle. As the prolific Rosales clan climbed down, pickup doors slammed, footsteps grated on gravel, and the excited squeals of children mixed with voices of teenagers and the more modulated greetings of the adults. From infants to great-grandmothers, everyone attended the *posadas*.

Clay and I stood on the porch, a receiving line of two. As the guests filed inside, I noticed a woman in a pink dress and a man in a white shirt and black pants arguing by their pickup.

I nudged Clay with my elbow, and between hellos he caught a glance of the situation.

Ruben Reyes reached for his wife Claudia's hand. She yanked it free, then slapped the back of his hand. Ruben said something we couldn't hear, but managed to look both angry and pleading, then nodded in our direction. Claudia turned, our eyes met, and I experienced an uncomfortable feeling that I voiced into words.

"I think she's upset with me," I said softly to Clay.

"Egoist."

I ignored that, and said, "Should we do something? Go talk to them?"

"No."

Irene Pick, the schoolteacher, breezed up the steps carrying a foil-wrapped baking dish held in both hands. She was accompanied by her son's girlfriend, Elvia, holding my fourteen-month-old goddaughter in her arms. I gave one last, worried glance at Claudia and Ruben. Elvia had already gone in, but Irene caught my look and turned in that direction.

Impulsively she called out, "Claudia," the syllables trailing off as she realized the situation. "My goodness," she said to me, "a family squabble." She shook her head and pushed through the door.

Clay took my elbow, and we followed Irene and joined our guests.

Inside, noise and laughter and warmth flowed as freely as later would the beer iced down in the 1947 Coca-Cola box. For now, we awaited the arrival of the other half of the town in a candlelight procession representing Mary and Joseph's journey to Bethlehem.

By tradition we wait until we hear the singing before looking out in surprise, but this was the first of the novena of *posadas* culminating on Christmas Eve, and the children, after running to see what piñata I'd chosen, had crowded together at the windows in anticipation.

I went to the kitchen to see if anyone needed any help, but things were well in hand. I returned to the front with a bowl of salad in one hand and a dish of tamales in the other. As I set them on the table one little boy shouted, "They're here! They're here!" The small talk ceased, and we flocked to the porch.

The pilgrims walked in a loose group, each holding a flickering candle. The combined glow bathed them in light as they came along the road and turned into the parking lot. Making their way slowly along the lane the drivers had left, they stopped at the foot of the porch steps. In front, two teenagers carried a small litter on which rested the clay figurines of Mary riding a burro led by Joseph. Behind them stood the figure of an angel, white wings touched with pink and gold. In voices with the fidelity of long practice, the pilgrims sang:

> "We bid you good evening,
> we ask you for a bed.
> A pallet of straw will do,
> on which to lay our heads."

We responded:

> "We do not know you,
> nor do we strangers trust.
> You may be thieves,
> intending to rob us."

The pleadings continued back and forth:

> "We come not to steal
> nor do we ask for your best,
> but only some small corner
> for my poor wife to rest."

"Go farther down the road.
You'll find a place to stay.
There's an inn that takes in wayfarers
by night and by day."

Finally, after more pleadings, we welcomed them:

"Come in, come in, Mary and Joseph,
The babe stirs in her womb.
Let the doors be opened.
For the King of Heaven we make room."

We stepped aside, and the pilgrims came up the steps and entered. The litter was placed on a table near the door. We clapped, the new arrivals greeted the others, and everyone lined up for the buffet.

"Nice table, Texana," a woman's voice whispered in my ear. I turned and smiled at Gwen Masters, a rancher from just up the road, which is to say she lived within twenty-five miles of Polvo. Gwen is sixty-five, soft-tempered, and outspoken. She ranches on sixteen thousand acres, largely working alone except when she rounds up her cattle for shipping.

She piled her plate with short ribs, corn bread, and Jell-O salad. "I hear there's trouble at Red Mountain. I like Jerry Ayrs. He's the only man I know can work cattle without whooping and hollering and scaring them to death."

It amazes me how fast word passes in our area, especially when you consider we're spread thin—there are only about two of us per square mile.

"What kind of so-'n'-so goes around poisoning animals!" she said. "Might as well poison a child as kill an animal that trusts you."

Around us at least twenty pairs of ears tuned in to

Gwen's husky voice. Never shy, retired Border Patrol agent Hub Jackson, standing across the table from us, asked the question for them all.

"Who are you talking about?"

"Don't know who," Gwen said reasonably, spooning salsa onto her plate. "That's the point. Clay was there. Ask him."

Hub spotted Clay leaning against the counter, a forkful of food halfway to his mouth. "Hey, Clay," Hub called.

Poor Clay. Exactly what he'd hoped to avoid. I decided to be needed in the kitchen.

I walked in on Claudia and Ruben Reyes. Relieved to see their argument hadn't kept them from joining the party, I smiled. Claudia didn't. Ruben gave me one nervous glance and shifted his eyes to his wife with an uncomfortable look.

"Texana," Claudia said. Not a greeting but a challenge.

"This is not the time," Ruben said to her.

Claudia looked furious, but clamped her lips together.

"What's wrong?" I said, looking from one to another.

Claudia's dark eyes fixed on my face. Harshly, as if the words hurt her throat as they came out, she said, "How is it you walk away while my primo hermano is taken to jail?"

Primo hermano. Literally brother-cousin, the term meant as close as a brother, a part of the extended family that is the heart of Mexican life.

"They are saying you were in the cab with the dead man," Claudia said, her words bunched tightly together. "Only after that did Oscar arrive. Yet you're free, and Oscar's wife has not seen him or his taxi since."

Ruben put his arm around his wife's shoulders, looked apologetically at me, and said, "We spent the day in Ojinaga with Oscar's family. His wife and children can find out nothing. I gave some money to a lawyer who promised to approach the comandante's office, but..." He shook his head.

Ruben knew as well as I did the futility of the gesture he had made, probably to calm his wife's family. A lawyer would get nowhere with the military.

"Claudia, I told the comandante what happened," I said. "Now I'll tell you. I went to the dentist. I wanted a taxi to drive me to this side. I went to one that was empty and I found the man dead. I made it clear to the comandante that the taxi driver came up afterward and was obviously as surprised and shocked as I had been to find a man had been murdered in his cab."

"They let you go. Why? I was told this comandante himself drove you back to the zocalo," Claudia said, the accusation plain. If I'd been released, I must have cooperated with the authorities. Cooperating implied betrayal, and there was only one person I could have betrayed. Nothing I said was going to convince Claudia that I hadn't denounced her *primo hermano* in order to save myself.

Behind me a throat was cleared diplomatically. I turned. Pete Rosales stood just inside the door. He is a bushy-haired, stocky man, and a friend. Blunt-speaking on most occasions, he swallowed whatever words had been in his mouth, silenced by the tension ricocheting among the three of us.

Claudia made a sound of disgust, marched past Pete and out the door. Ruben blinked and followed her.

I managed a smile for Pete, but he wasn't fooled. "You look like you just lost your best friend."

"A friend, anyway." I didn't want to explain now just how much Claudia's words had stung. We'd never been close, but I'd known her all my life and had taken her goodwill for granted because I liked her.

Pete said, "Hey, cheer up. Everybody knows you're one fine lady who puts her heart into things. An entrona. Whatever Claudia's ticked off about, she'll get over it. Her temper is ahead of her heart, that's all."

"I hope you're right, Pete," I told him. Pete is intensely loyal to those he considers friends, and given to voicing outrageous promises of physical violence to those he doesn't. If he has ever carried out such threats, I don't know about it, and I've known him all my life, too. Just like Claudia. Would he react like Claudia when he found out what had happened? And how many more people in Polvo would take the Reyeses' side and believe I'd betrayed an innocent man? Maybe think I'd gotten away with murder? Suddenly I saw myself on the outside, an outcast from the sense of community I'd shared with these people.

"Gee," Pete said, "I forgot what I'm here for. Clay says it's time to break the piñata."

"It's a little early, isn't it?" I said, snapping back to current events. "Has everyone finished eating?"

"Don't think so. They're gabbing too much about this poisoner on the loose to chew their food. Clay wants to shift their attention."

My heart wasn't in it, but I accompanied Pete to the front room. Talk about babble: "I think it's political…somebody after Jerry's job…gonna lock my dogs up…reward and they'll catch him…bound to be somebody with a grudge against Davis."

I didn't have to look for Clay. At six foot one he stands literally head and shoulders over most of Polvo's citizens. Looking as wrung-out as I felt, he was listening patiently to Irene. I veered to the vintage phonograph in the corner, positioned the needle on the record, and adjusted the volume to high. The guaranteed high fidelity promised by the album's jacket produced a scratchy chorus of "Jingle

Bells" that drowned out conversation and brought the kids running. "Me, me," they shouted. In turn, Pete put his hand on the heads of five children, alternating girl, boy. Disappointed groans from those not chosen; squeals and laughter from the chosen as they jumped up and down.

I handed Pete the scarf, and he tied it over the eyes of child number one, put the plastic bat in her hands, spun her around, sending her off in the wrong direction beating the air wildly as the piñata was swung out of reach by Pete tugging at the opposite end of the rope.

As the record advanced through "Frosty the Snowman," Irene worked her way to my side, bent her head close to my ear, and spoke over the music. "Claudia collected her family, and they all left except for the granddaughter over there to mind the kids. I guess whatever's wrong, she wanted the little ones to enjoy the piñata."

I nodded, letting her think what she wanted, hoping she'd ask no questions. Everyone would be aware something had happened. By tomorrow the story would be out.

The record spun on through "Deck the Halls." Each child took a turn while the onlookers called out directions. "Swing higher," one would shout. "No, lower," another would call. A direction to aim left would be countered by a cry of, "No, right." Finally Pete lowered the piñata into striking range. The last child gave a mighty swing that landed square on the papier-mâché donkey, bursting it, and showering the children with hard candies and tiny plastic toys that they scrambled to collect.

Pete tied back the rope holding the remnants of the piñata, and I exchanged the Christmas album for a big band recording. Pete grabbed his wife's hand, and soon everyone was dancing, literally in the aisles.

I approached Clay. Though he doesn't enjoy dancing, I love it, and he gave in to me with good grace.

As we did a foxtrot between pet foods and glasswares, he said, "It's been an eventful day. I don't like eventful days. How about you? The party is a success, I'd say."

"Remember what I said on the porch about Claudia being angry with me? Well as much as I normally enjoy being right, I wish I hadn't been this time."

"What's her problem?"

I explained.

Clay said, "Time for this night to end."

The record finished, and the needle, stuck in the last grove, made a whishing sound over and over again until someone nearby lifted it. Parents started rounding up children and wiping their sticky faces and hands before helping them into their coats. The men who had retired to the porch came back inside smelling of cigarettes and beer. A volunteer cleanup crew started to clear the table. Our *posada* was winding down.

By ten o'clock it was over. With plenty of helping hands the leftovers had been wrapped to be taken home, the dishes washed, dried, and stacked, the floor swept, the chairs folded and put away. Clay and I stood on the porch waving goodbye to the last of the departing guests. The wind had picked up, blowing from the northwest. A car door closed with a blunted sound. Laughter and conversation carried back to us from a group of teens who'd convinced their parents to let them walk home. There was a moment of quiet; then from the solid dark beyond the glow of the Christmas lights I heard an androgynous voice saying, "Suerte y mortaja del cielo bajan." Fortune and death come from above.

I shivered, whether from cold or premonition I wasn't sure.

EIGHT

WEDNESDAY I experienced fortune and misfortune. Both stemmed from the same incident.

Clay had driven out to Red Mountain Ranch immediately after breakfast to meet with the insurance investigator who was flying in that morning. The ranch had a private landing strip, and Bascom Davis himself was expected sometime during the day.

Like Davis, I had insurance woes. I called the agency that had always carried our vehicles.

"You parked it on the street?" the agent said in the tone an attorney must use with a client who admits making a full confession of a crime to the police before calling him.

"It wasn't as if I'd left the keys in," I said. "And it wasn't on the street. I left it where people park if they want to walk across the bridge and into Ojinaga."

"Was it a secured parking area?"

"There are no guards. But it's in plain sight of the border checkpoint. You live in Marfa. Haven't you ever been down to Presidio?"

"I never go to the border. It's another country down there," he said. I heard paper shuffling, then his dry voice again. "Statistically, you live where it simply isn't wise to own a four-wheel-drive vehicle, let alone leave it unattended."

"Maybe I should move," I said, restraining myself from making reasonable comments about terrain, distances, and necessity.

"That would be an excellent idea," he said, taking my sarcasm as a serious suggestion.

I decided it was time to get to the point. "When may I expect a check?"

"I'll need a copy of the sheriff's report of this theft," he asked.

I promptly confirmed his opinion of me as an idiot by admitting that I hadn't gotten around to reporting the theft. He suggested I do so, and said he'd be in touch after the paperwork had been completed. As soon as we disconnected, I called Andalon.

"Might as well go ahead and send your extra set of keys to Mexico," he said, "but I'll file the report for you." I gave him my vehicle identification number and other data.

As I hung up, I heard engine noise and a car door slam in the parking lot. A customer! I thought joyfully. It was ten o'clock. I'd been open since six and had spent the time putting the sale items back on the table we'd used for the buffet and giving Phobe her morning exercise by letting her chase and shred each paper streamer as I yanked it down. The register had been open once to put in the cash and change in mixed dollars and pesos.

I settled behind the counter trying not to appear overly eager. The closing of our border crossing combined with the expenses of Christmas for most families had slowed my cash customers and increased those who wanted a credit line. Trouble was, I had no one to give me a credit account in return. My suppliers wanted cash.

The bell above the front door jangled, and Claudia walked in, wearing one of the bright, loose dresses she preferred, a self-conscious expression on her face. This would be not a further confrontation, I sensed, but rather a real conversation designed to repair the damage done to our friendship by misunderstanding and false assumptions. I smiled and stood to greet her. The bell jangled again.

I didn't know the middle-aged Mexican man who came

through the door. He wore a cowboy hat that looked as if only the band held it together, a checked shirt that had seen many washings, threadbare jeans, and boots so worn down that the leather had split at the creases. Stopping a few feet from the counter, he removed his hat and said, "Buenos días. One of you is Señora Jones?" His eyes darted between Claudia and me.

"I'm Texana Jones."

He swept his arm toward the parking lot and at the same time made a graceful bow to me.

"Comandante Zurita sends his greetings, and wishes you to know that thanks to his supreme vigilance he has recovered your stolen vehicle. He vows that the thief will suffer the most serious punishment. The comandante has personally entrusted me to return this nice vehicle to you with his compliments and a full tank of the finest Nova gasoline."

He briefly suspended between two fingers a key ring with my brass T initial charm and the keys to my pickup, placed them on the counter in front of me, and smiled so broadly I could see the gaps from missing teeth.

Claudia stiffened, drew in her breath, and hardened the expression on her face. I said, "Claudia, I don't—" She turned away and walked out. Dismayed, I rang up no sale on the cash register, took out a five, and handed it across to the man, who widened his smile and pocketed the cash as I said, "For your trouble, señor. I'm grateful."

I picked up the keys and followed him to the door, half in disbelief that the pickup would really be mine, half in expectation that if it was mine, it would have a cracked windshield, crunched bumper, no seats, missing radio— you get the picture. It was untouched, unless you count the fact that it appeared to have been freshly washed and polished. I circled it, examining it carefully. I unlocked and opened the toolbox, found not so much as the towrope missing. I looked at the man. Had he stolen it? It would suit the *comandante's* sense of humor, I thought, to make the thief return the vehicle.

I surveyed the parking lot and road. Seeing no other vehicle in sight, I asked the man how he would get back to Ojinaga.

He shrugged. "No problema. I walk."

"All that way?"

"It is nothing. There is no hurry." And with that, he placed his hat on his head and departed.

I checked the truck inside and out once more before calling off both Andalon, who chuckled at the shift in events because he understood that nothing in *la frontera* is out of the ordinary, and the insurance agent, who implied that I'd intended to defraud the company and had chickened out. I decided I'd better start shopping immediately for a new agent.

For the rest of the morning I had not a single customer, not even for gasoline. I thought of telephoning Claudia, of going to see her. I did nothing. What was the point? She had heard the man's explanation, the why and how of the truck being returned. I didn't bring up Ghee's name in explanation of how I squeaked out of being arrested like her cousin for fear of cementing her notion that I was involved in something I shouldn't be. So firmly in Mexico was money equated with corruption that Claudia would be suspicious of the very name of a man so powerful as Gordon Suarez. And I admitted my own resentment of her attitude held me back, too. We'd spent many hours together cleaning the church in our turn, talking of family and friends in the way of close neighbors who know one another's minor sins well enough to understand forgiveness. Claudia had decided against me.

To take my mind off things I could do nothing about, I

took Phobe for a romp outside. The sun shone, the breeze was light and cool, and the air smelled fresh and clean. It was a smug sort of day, as if Nature preened, pleased with its own perfection. It could not last. I pulled a strip of rope for Phobe to chase. She would pounce on it with her paws, worry it with her teeth, then drop it, looking up expectantly at me, waiting for the game to begin again. When she tired of this, she rolled in the sand, then hunted down and sniffed the scent markings of whatever varmints had passed through her domain since her last outing. I pondered not for the first time what life was like seen, heard, and scented through such sharp senses. I looked around to see her sitting at the door expectantly, ready to go in. As we did, the telephone rang.

It was Carlos Haro, calling to tell me he'd finished the Christmas gift for Clay that I'd commissioned.

I looked over my shoulder at the wall clock. Twelve noon. Clay had cooked us a full breakfast in anticipation of his busy day. Tonight we had the second *posada,* another heavy meal. I'd skip lunch and leave immediately. I'd have time to pick up the gift, then stop on the way home to visit my father, find out how Charlie was, and take him a change of clothes.

I left Phobe in the front to have the run of the trading post, wrote a note for Clay, locked up, collected Charlie's clothes from the suitcase in the trunk of his Cadillac, and drove to Marfa, taking the scenic route through Pinto Canyon. The first fifteen miles of gravel road climbs steadily, crossing several creeks and many cattle guards before the last thirty-eight paved miles into town. Not surprisingly, I passed no other vehicle along the way, only a scattering of pronghorn antelope.

Marfa sits comfortably on the plains in the wide upper point of our triangular-shaped county. I cruised down Highland Street toward the domed courthouse, slowing to avoid the two kids throwing a Frisbee across the wide street lined with one- and two-story buildings that preserve the town's frontier look. The Haro Silverworks is housed on a side street in one of the former gun sheds of Fort D.A. Russell. Carlos Haro had put in long tables and benches, and set up shop. He stood at one of the tables, observing as an apprentice used a small hammer, tapping and shaping a silver bowl over a wooden mold. Carlos glanced up and gave me a quick smile. Two of his three permanent employees worked at other projects. I liked the shop. It was a good room, with the beauty that the utilitarian workplace of the artisan sometimes achieves. Silversmith's tools hung in neat racks on the brick-lined walls, and skylights bathed the mesquite tables with light. I sat on one of the stools and waited. In a few minutes, Carlos left the apprentice on his own and came forward to greet me.

A stockier version of his father, Carlos is a man of boundless energy who asserts his personal identity with a graying mustache that bristles like a scared porcupine. We shook hands, and Carlos removed a tray from beneath a nearby counter. In the old days, when he'd first started work as a silversmith, he'd sold items locally by displaying them on a bench on the street in front of his shop. To this day he has no formal display area. The difference is that now he doesn't need one. His work has achieved the status of art, and is done primarily by commission or for resale in specialty stores and galleries in places like New York, Dallas, and Los Angeles. Like his nephew, Henry, he was making the Haro name known.

Trained as a sculptor, he'd perfected his own style of jewelry making using handmade tools and hand processing. His signature pieces were large pins, rings, and bracelets of simple lines. He didn't stop at jewelry, but also created bowls, pitchers, and vases with complex Indian motifs in bas-relief.

I watched his small hands as he smoothed out a velvet square on the tabletop, lifted a soft cloth bag from many on the tray, loosened the drawstring closure, and turned it upside down. Two items dropped onto the velvet. The silver dollar-sized one had been engraved with Clay's initials surrounded by a finely done line of various animals, marching nose to tail in minute but perfect form. The second piece, shaped like a flattened bullet, showed a snake entwined around a staff with a raised V, emblem of the American Association of Veterinary Medicine. Like charms, each had a small hole in it.

When I'd ordered the gift, I'd given Carlos a twelve-inch ribbon-width of soft, tanned deerskin. Carlos brought it out, used a leather punch to make a hole at each end, and then deftly attached the small silver links to hold the silver pieces to the leather.

"Like them?" Carlos asked.

"It's perfect." The bookmark was for Clay's vet manuals. "I'm so pleased, Carlos. I'm going to show this to my father this afternoon. He gave me the hide and suggested it for a bookmark." I turned the pieces over in my hand and saw the Haro Silverworks mark on the back of each, and the script initial with which Carlos marked the pieces he made himself. The job was so small, I'd been sure he'd assign it to one of his employees, maybe even an apprentice. The personal mark of the master silversmith made even these small items more valuable.

I gave him a grateful look. "Clay will be thrilled."

"It was local people who supported me when I was getting started," he said. "I don't forget those who helped me."

He reached under the counter again, brought out a square blue box with the business name embossed on the top. "We've had such a good Christmas season, I'm out of every size box except for this. I can fold the leather loosely. It's so soft, I don't think it will crease, and you can unfold it when you get home."

"I like it. It will fool Clay into thinking it's a watch."

Carlos polished away my finger marks from the silver before placing the bookmark in the box. "We do everything but gift wrap," he said, presenting it to me. I dropped it into my jacket pocket, and my fingers touched the chain the *evangelista* had given me.

"Will that cloth clean something really tarnished?" I asked him.

"What have you got?"

I brought out the medal.

Carlos gave me a surprised look, took the medal from my hands, and held it gently. He examined it, beginning with the flattened irregular links of the broken chain, and following that to the blackened medal. He reached beneath the counter, took out a jeweler's glass, and looked at both sides of the medal. He put the piece down on the velvet square and rubbed lightly with the polishing cloth, first one side of the medal, then the other, bringing up the color to a smudged gray. He touched one link of the chain with the tip of a stubby finger, then ran the cloth along the length until it showed silver-gray.

"I don't want to wipe away all the patina. Feel the weight of it, and the almost ridged rim. This is handmade, and old. Have you seen the design?"

"No," I said, bending over the medal. The cleaning had revealed a half-torso figure of a woman, the eyes of her face downcast as if in humility, her hands folded to her breasts as if in prayer. A spiked crown encircled her head like a halo, and around the bottom rim of the medal ran three short words.

I frowned. "What is it? Do you know what it means?"

"It's a religious medal. 'Vota vita mea.' My life is devoted."

I turned the medal over, but the back was smooth.

"I collect old religious medals," Carlos said. "I'd like to have this. In return you can pick out any piece of jewelry in the store, and no charge on Clay's gift."

It was a generous offer. I fingered the medal thoughtfully. "I'm not sure the person who gave this to me realized how old it might be. I think I'd better offer to return it."

"In that case, let me box it for you."

As I wrote out the check for the bookmark, Carlos said, "I heard about the trouble at Red Mountain."

I must have looked surprised.

"Talk of the town," Carlos said. "You know how it is. We lead quiet lives. Something like that, everybody starts to speculate."

"What exactly are they speculating?"

"It varies. Everything from carelessness to insurance fraud. We'll probably know soon enough. I hear a special investigator's coming out from Dallas. I guess this will bring my nephew home."

"Why's that?"

"Henry has a vested interest in anything to do with Bascom Davis. Political bedfellows, isn't that the term?" Resentment in the tone, faint but distinct, but whether for his nephew, for Davis, or for the philosophical whoring of politics in general, I couldn't tell. He handed me the box. "If the owner doesn't want this back, my offer still goes."

I slipped it into my pocket with the first box, thanked Carlos, and left. Sitting in the pickup, I took out the box and looked once more at the medal. A trinket, Electra had called it. Maybe she wouldn't want it back. Carlos had a necklace I had been coveting for some time. Still, if the medal was valuable—I opened the glove compartment and put the box inside. I'd leave it there until I had time to go back to Electra's place.

Outside of Marfa the land wore a cover of buff-colored grass stretching up the mountainous volcanic upthrusts on which the rock face lies exposed, eroded by the rushing seasonal rains. On the right is a broken stretch of tilted wooden poles, remnants of the private telephone lines ranch owners once depended on to connect them with the outside world. Now we have a microwave system. The gray pavement ahead was empty. I let the speedometer hit eighty and kept it there. In no time, I'd be at the turnoff to my father's house. What frame of mind would I find him in? I said a silent prayer that this would be one of his good days.

NINE

MY FATHER'S PLACE lies three miles off the highway. The turn is just past the Border Patrol checkpoint on Highway 67 between Marfa and Presidio. Once, the ranch comprised nineteen thousand acres running all the way to the road frontage, but after my mother's death when I was twenty-one, Dad sold all but three thousand acres and the easement to a neighbor.

The dirt road had washed from the recent thundershowers. It took me ten minutes to negotiate before I reached the cattle guard.

The house sits in a wide, concave depression between two hills, protecting it on the north from the biting winds of winter and on the south from the dusty winds of spring. Not until I rounded the first hill did I realize something had happened. My father stood in front of the white clapboard house watching two Border Patrolmen in green uniforms and combat boots as they patted down three Mexican males posed with legs spread wide, hands palm down on the hood of the white Cherokee with a dark green stripe.

I parked by the barn, got out, and stood waiting as the agents loaded their prisoners into the back of the vehicle behind the heavy grille that separated them from the front seat.

I recognized neither agent. One, a Mexican American, was putting three knives into a lockbox. The other, an Anglo, interrupted his conversation with my father to nod and say, "Ma'am," as I approached.

"This is my daughter," my father said. "These gentlemen are helping me with a spot of trouble."

"Glad to do it, Mr. Ricciotti," said the Anglo.

"These guys have earned a free ride back to Ojinaga," said the other, opening the driver's door.

"Appreciate you doing the hard part," the Anglo said, climbing into the passenger side and slamming the door. They pulled out slowly. Behind them, their passengers sat with expressionless faces.

As the vehicle made its slow departure, my father shook his head. "Took the Mexicans probably three days to get here," he said, "and they'll be back on the other side in less than an hour."

"What happened?"

"Tell you in a minute." Turning toward the house he called out, "Okay, Charlie, you can let Woo Hoo out now."

The front door opened, an arm pushed the screen door outward, and a short-legged brown-and-white mutt with floppy ears and a face like a fox rushed out and down the steps. Nose to ground, he circled where the Border Patrol vehicle had been, followed the scent down the drive to the cattle guard, stopped, and gave a staccato bark.

"That's right, boy," my father called, "they're gone."

At the sound of my father's voice, Woo Hoo turned around and came back, following us onto the porch, tail wagging. The dog greeted me with a lick on my hand, then went to lie down on the top step, no doubt guarding his owner against further intruders.

"Take a chair," my father said to me, seating himself in one of the three handmade rockers, one filled to overflowing by a fat gray cat named Willie. I pulled the other chair closer to my father's, scanning his face for signs of tension, trying to read whether I would stay awhile or cut my visit short.

My father's long, expressive face, like mine, reveals his every emotion. His sharply arched, dark brows that have not turned as white as his hair accent the broad forehead that furrows with worry or anger. His full-lipped mouth curls in laughter and turns down in sorrow. His deep-set brown eyes reflect any hurt or disappointment like a mirror. Of all the features of his mobile face, only the Neapolitan nose of northern Italy tells one nothing except his family origin. No matter how much he eats, his taut skin stretches too tightly over his bony frame, as if the calories he consumes feed only the chronic depression that has so limited his life and affected the lives of those who love him. Bursts of energy dominate his actions and his work, broken by long periods of lassitude. He needs solitude as others need air, and endures company seldom, and at great cost to his hard-won peace of mind. I think Charlie is one of the few people who doesn't get on his nerves.

The screen door banged as Charlie joined us. He has thinning brown hair. His pale blue eyes look nearsighted though he doesn't wear glasses. No matter that he lives by doing odd jobs that are mostly calorie-burning manual labor such as roofing, building fence, and any kind of plumbing or electrical work, he remains covered in a layer of fat increasing in thickness as it descends to his thighs. He moves with such slow deliberateness that one is always startled that he finishes a task quickly. His personality is as easygoing as his voice is soft. I have never seen him angry or even anxious, nor heard his voice raised. People feel at ease with Charlie. He may be truly a man who never met a person he didn't like.

"How's Bess?" he asked. A question straight from the heart.

"Your car is under canvas and doing well."

"I'll be down in a couple of days to pick her up. She needs a drive."

"You're feeling better then?"

Charlie nodded, lifted Willie up, sat down in the vacated rocker, resettling the cat on his lap.

My father chuckled. "He's fit as can be. Old Valfre came by, doctored him with yerba de víbora and sotol."

Valfre, known only by the single name, was a traveling barber and healer who made a circuit of isolated houses and small communities on both sides of the river, giving shaves and haircuts, tonics and cures, all for bargain-basement prices.

My father sported the shorn look of a marine recruit. "Nice haircut," I said. His view of a haircut is that it should last as long as possible before the next one.

"Valfre does a good job," he said. "Ought to be eight or nine weeks before I need another."

"So tell me, you two," I said. "What happened with the illegals?"

My father had removed the pistol from the holster at his hip, emptied and detached the cylinder, and swiveled around in his chair to reach for the cleaning kit on the wooden table next to the wall.

"Woo Hoo set up barking about four this morning. I went out and flashed the light around thinking it was a coyote or a coon. The dog started up the hill toward the well, trying to get me to follow. I figured it might be a mountain lion so I went back for the rifle. By then Charlie was awake, so he came along with me. Halfway up the hill we hit a bunch of footprints heading toward the well."

My father ran a copper wire through the gun barrel, then held the piece up to the light. "The way the footprints overlapped, Charlie thought it looked like three, maybe four, so we went carefully. We didn't catch them at the well, but the Mexicans had broken the pipe to the watering tank to fill their jugs.''

"Again," I said.

"Yep. That makes eight or nine times the last two years. I think I'd better put in a faucet.''

Illegals skirting the Border Patrol checkpoint found the well convenient and passed the word along to others about where water could be found on the long trip north. Everyone knew the men coming across the river now could be dangerous. In the old days my father had kept a line shack stocked with canned beans, bread, and a barrel of water for the migrants. Now illegals were crossing in ever increasing numbers, and those who traveled the countryside by dark were feared by the ranchers, a result of too many pulled-down fences, broken locks on gates, butchered cattle, vandalized houses and hunt camps, and the unwary assaulted and robbed. There had been one murder. A rancher, an old man named Tomas Valdez, had fed two illegals only to have them take his gun and kill him with it before driving away in his pickup. They'd been caught, but that was small comfort to his widow.

I said, "You're kidding about the faucet, right?"

My father finished the cleaning procedure, fitted the cylinder into the revolver, and snapped it into place. "I'm not doing anything to encourage illegals coming through. That's why I called the Border Patrol out on these three after we finally caught up to them.''

"Did they give you any trouble, Dad?"

He shook his head. "They'd come across a javelina, killed it with a rock, and roasted it. They were sleeping off the meal when we caught up to them. We woke them up, and they just stood there, looking discouraged.''

Charlie said, "We walked them back and locked them in the shed."

I said, "But that was this morning. What took the Border Patrol so long to get here?"

My father said, "I didn't call them until this afternoon. Before that, I supervised the Mexicans fixing the fence they'd cut between me and the neighbor's place, and, of course, repairing the water pipe they broke. Then I cooked us all a good lunch, and let them have a siesta in the shed so they wouldn't be tired and hungry on the way home. I don't want to encourage them, but I don't want to give them cause to feel vengeful either."

He took aim at the horizon and clicked the trigger of the unloaded gun. "That's my story. What's yours?"

"What do you mean?"

"I hear you're mixed up in murder."

"How did you—?"

"Valfre came through Ojinaga and Presidio on the way up here."

It took me twenty minutes of explaining and answering my father's questions before I could ask one in return. "Did the barber have any fresh news about the murder, like who the dead man was?"

"Valfre says the rumors are that he's either some foreign bigwig in the military or a diplomat." My father looked over at me, emphasizing his next words. "The barber also told us that folks in Ojinaga are saying the woman who owns the trading post upriver did the killing and left the taxi driver to take the blame."

Charlie turned to me and said, "You think the taxi driver killed the guy?"

"That poor man didn't have anything more to do with the murder than I did," I said.

"You don't know that," my father said. "He could have

stabbed him, parked, and left, all so he could pretend to come back and find him dead.''

"Not in his own taxi, Dad. If anything, that's proof of his innocence. Besides, I saw his face when he finally realized the passenger was dead. That was no act."

My father said, "You stay out of it. And keep away from the other side until this business blows over."

I thought of the unpaid bills I needed to collect, many of them across the river, and of my shrinking bank balance. But I dutifully agreed, knowing he was right.

He got up and carried the gun and cleaning kit into the house. Woo Hoo raised his head and followed my father with his eyes. I swear the dog smiled when his master came back out.

I took the Haro Silverworks box out of my pocket and showed the finished bookmark to Charlie and my father. As is his habit, my father muffled his enthusiasm to a low-voiced "Nice." Charlie said he thought Clay would like it. I folded it back into the box and put it away. We sat for some minutes in companionable silence, wrapped in the protective peace of the enclosing hills. The low winter sun turned the bare earth and dead grass gold, and sent the angular shadow of the house inching across the yard. Here there were no telephone or electric wires to mar the immaculate view. An oasis of tranquillity, pooled in light and silence. I understood why my father had kept this place, finding it an anodyne for his depression.

The ranch had been in my mother's family, part of a larger parcel divided between her and her brother at their parents' deaths in an automobile accident. I had never lived here. My mother had died within a year of inheriting it. Until her death, I had not acknowledged the seriousness of my father's condition.

As a child I had been sheltered from an awareness of my

father's moods, as mother had called his ceaseless anxiety that manifested itself in bursts of anger at everything, the weather, a broken knife blade, the pickup that wouldn't start the first time. When he went off alone for extended periods my mother called them camping trips. When he disappeared for days, sometimes weeks, into the privacy of his study, my mother said Daddy was working, and everyone needed time to themselves. I was a solitary child, and I accepted the eccentricities of my family as the norm. Only as a teenager did I begin to understand the enormity of my father's problem, and learn the history of my father's growing reclusiveness.

After college, he had gone to work for the Department of Agriculture. In those days, his depression, phobia, call it what you will, had been more easily managed, but as he grew older he would go into his office and close the door for days, seeing no one unless the job made it necessary. Later he resigned to work as a surveyor. It kept him outdoors and alone, so that for a time, his life became more bearable.

Over the long years of illness, he'd tried various treatments. None helped. Some made him worse. He gave up on doctors. He fought his battle against himself alone, except for my mother, who had tried to protect him from all anxiety by taking it on herself. In the end, it was she who collapsed, dead, the doctor said, before she hit the kitchen floor. My father found her when he came in from work. Her death had pushed him close to the edge of the psychological darkness he had battled against for so long. He had blamed himself for mother's first and fatal heart attack. The ranch saved him. The sale of the greater part of the land had given him a modest income on which to retire early. The remainder gave him a place to live in the solitude that solaced and sustained him. I had asked him once to describe his feelings. He had summed it up in one terse sentence: "I live at the edge of panic without knowing why." The ranch, and a few nearly toothless Longhorn cows, more pets than livestock, and the dog and cat for his only companions worked somehow to keep the panic at bay.

I glanced at my father's lined, gaunt face and saw stillness and an outward calm.

He caught my look, and reached out to put his hand over mine. "Not to worry," he said softly, and changed the subject by asking what Clay was doing.

"He's at Red Mountain Ranch," I said. Thinking of Carlos Haro's words about his brother's vested interest, I added, "What do either of you know about Bascom Davis?"

Charlie said, "The rancher?"

I doubted whether he knew of Davis's political accomplishments. For Charlie the world beyond our borderland doesn't exist. He reads no newspapers, watches no television, and as far as I know listens to no radio except for ranchero music. It probably accounts for his ease of mind. I explained, noting Davis's involvement in Henry Haro's ambitious rise in Texas politics.

Charlie said, "Sounds like Henry will have some big shoes to fill."

"Take out the Odor-Eaters and anybody could do it," my father said.

I knew the cause of my father's caustic attitude toward the land commissioner. West of the Pecos River, much of the territory is "mineral classified," which means that while the surface may be privately owned, the state controls the mineral interest. Two months ago the land commissioner had approved the leasing of over three thousand acres of a nearby ranch, belonging to a woman named Bobbie Utley, for strip-mining for zeolite, a clay derived from weathered volcanic earth.

My father referred to the sore subject now, saying, "Imagine having your place dug up for kitty litter." He looked at the cat and added, "Nothing personal, Willie."

Rumors were flying that similar leases were being sought for strip-mining of the minute amounts of gold and silver locked in the soil. Some landowners celebrated the event, hoping they too might get a lease and the fifty percent profits from the proceeds. Those like my father and Bobbie Utley, who lived on the land and loved it, saw only the destruction of a parched Eden.

Charlie, ever the gentle optimist, said, "Maybe if Henry gets elected he'll change things."

"Can't happen," my father said. "Robbing the schoolchildren of Texas, that's what they'll say, since the state's portion of the money goes to the permanent school fund. Anyway, no government entity ever lets go of money. Their power lies in how much money they control. From what I read, Henry's made his way by being a first-class sycophant to Davis."

"That's just the kind most likely to rebel when he gets a little power of his own," Charlie said.

That was Charlie. He ignored politics, but he knew people.

I saw my father's hands clasped in his lap, thumbs spinning around each other, a nervous tic that signaled fatigue with visitors and conversation.

"Time for me to go," I said, getting up from the rocker. "Charlie, I almost forgot. I brought you some clothes. They're still in the pickup." Charlie got up to walk to the truck with me.

My father said, "Be vigilant." How many times in my childhood had I heard that phrase? It was my father's version of the classic borderland warning. Out here parents don't tell kids to have a good time. They say, "Be careful." That's because it's a hundred miles to a hospital, and if you're lost or injured it can be a long time, if ever, before you're found.

I kissed his cheek and said, "You, too." The dog padded after Charlie and me. Charlie took the folded clothes from the seat, and I got in and started the motor.

I measure the distance home, not in miles, but in landmarks: Chinati Peak; Shafter, an old mining town that rests beneath the Tres Hermanas mountain; then the FFA sign reading Welcome to Presidio. After that, the road drops swiftly into the river valley. The first sight of the broad plain with its line of trees, and I know I'm only fifty miles from home.

My first warning came twenty miles along 170, when I noticed the flying trail of dust kicked up by a vehicle descending Cemetery Hill, a side road that dead-ended at the Campo Santo—the Field of Saints. The leaning crosses and worn stones on the hilltop were all that was left of a small settlement that had once existed between Presidio and Polvo.

My speed was a modest thirty miles per hour, dropping to twenty at the frequent dips. Going faster wore out the shock absorbers that much more quickly. Plus I had a tendency to feel seasick from bouncing along at a speedier pace.

From habit developed over a lifetime of driving our lonely roads, as soon as I passed the point where the dirt road joined the blacktop I glanced in the rearview mirror to see which way the only other vehicle for miles would go. The driver turned in my direction. The vehicle didn't belong to anyone from Polvo. Known as a *comando*, it was a former army four-wheel-drive truck adapted to civilian use. This one looked old enough to be Korean War vintage, which didn't surprise me. In Mexico I'd seen World War II trucks hauling ore, livestock, or twenty or thirty people. With cannibalized parts and few special tools, the mechanics on the other side keep anything with an engine running for generations. I knew the truck came from Mexico because I could see the distinct orange color of Chihuahua State's *frontera* tags.

I slowed down trying to read backward in the mirror the *dicho* painted in red capital letters across the front bumper. These sayings are the Mexican equivalent of personalized license plates and bumper stickers combined. They reflect the personality and philosophy of the trucker. Some are religious, some boastful, some sexually oriented. Still others are merely wiseass. I'd seen one that read *Planchada de Peatónes.* Pedestrian Flattener.

I hit the next dip and decided to forget trying to read the *dicho* and pay attention to what was in front of me before I ran into a cow or a stray dog. Even with the windows up I heard the shifting of gears and the roar of straight pipes as the *comando* accelerated. Reflex action brought my eyes back to the mirror. And to the image of the massive bumper. For an instant my stomach felt like I was falling in an elevator; then the *comando* rammed me. The pickup leaped forward, parts rattling. I clutched the steering wheel, tried to regain control, getting only a sluggish response, as if I were pulling an overloaded cattle trailer. I lifted my foot off the gas, but the pickup accelerated. My eyes darted to the mirror. All I saw was the truck's hood and the top of the grille riding the tail. We'd locked bumpers.

We hit the dip with a booming sound. The rear of my truck folded. The pickup lurched, bounced, wobbled, came loose from the *comando,* and sailed sideways, airborne. The landscape danced around me to the grinding accompaniment of metal crunching metal. Then came a bone-jarring stop, and stillness. I couldn't see, and my head felt as if it was still spinning. I realized I had my eyes squeezed shut. I opened them and found myself wedged against the roof of the cab, the seat belt tight across my windpipe, choking me. A mesquite post and two strands of barbed wire pressed against my driver's-side window. The pickup had flipped, rolled, and landed hard against a fence, resting upside down. I turned my aching neck sideways. The passenger-side door looked undamaged. I fumbled with the seat belt. I wasn't hurt as far as I could tell, but I'd go numb from the neck down if I stayed in this position. The belt released, and my neck and left shoulder took my full weight. I used my hands to push against the steering wheel and toward the passenger side while I twisted my legs around toward my blocked door. Then I sort of inched like a snail until I touched the door handle. That's when the pair of black boots stepped into my view.

The man who heaved the door open leaned over, grasped me by the wrists, and hauled me out. Lying prone on my back on the ground, I had an upside-down view of a broad face with small eyes. The man's hair flowed to his shoulders and a saggy mustache grew into a tattered black beard that reached his chest. Texana Jones meets Wolf Man. Even upside down he looked menacing.

That didn't stop me from shooting off my big mouth. "If you didn't have brakes why didn't you drive off the road instead of—"

I didn't finish the sentence because he bent over, grabbed a fistful of my jacket, rammed his other hand into first one pocket and then the other, stuffing the contents into his own. He rolled me over and felt in the back pockets of my jeans. The hands left my body, and I heard running feet, a heavy door slamming, and the unmuffled motor firing to life. I turned over and raised myself up on one elbow, trembling like a scared kitten. The big truck didn't maneuver easily. It took him several goes to make a full turn without going off into the sand. I had plenty of time to note the mud-smeared license plate, and read the *dicho* on the bumper.

Fear kicked me in the stomach just as I got to my feet, and I vomited.

Thirty minutes later, as I sat with my head on my knees, my back against the pickup, the school bus came along. José Silva, the driver, was so intent on getting home after having dropped the high school kids off in Polvo that he passed me by, brakes squeaking as he stopped. He backed the bus, sticking his head out the window just as I raised my face. The door opened, and José jumped out and came running, shouting, "Are you okay? Are you hurt?"

I told him I was okay, and he helped me to my feet.

"I'll radio for the ambulance."

I shook my head. "I'm fine. Just shaken. If you could give me a ride into Polvo."

"Sure thing. No problema. What happened? You joyriding and lose control?" he said.

"I got run off the road by The Holy Ghost."

José pulled his head back and stared. "Hey, maybe I better call for that ambulance."

TEN

I THOUGHT SHE'D HIT her head, you know. What she said sounded so crazy. After she explained that The Holy Ghost was the dicho painted on the comando, I radioed the sheriff and gave him the description. But that trucker, he had plenty of time to get back to the other side. If I hadn't stopped to talk to my brother-in-law after I dropped the kids off, I might have caught that hijo de la chingada.''

Son of a bitch, in spades. I couldn't have agreed more with José. From where I stood in the bedroom, I could hear the bus driver saying all this to Clay in our kitchen. I unbuttoned my shirt with shaking fingers. By the time I got to removing my slacks, my hands had steadied a bit. I left my clothes in a pile on the floor, and went to soak in the claw-footed tub we seldom use because it takes too much water to fill. On this occasion I indulged myself, and the water lapped within a few inches of the rim when I lowered myself into its comforting warmth.

I closed my eyes and inhaled the scent of the bath beads foaming around me. The door clicked as Clay came in. ''I think you should drink this coffee now,'' he said. He folded a towel, placed it behind my head where it rested against the rim of the tub, and put the warm mug into my hands. I opened my eyes, lifted my head, and sipped.

''Ugh, sugar.''

''It's good for shock.'' He dipped his hand in the bathwater. ''That's too hot,'' he said. ''You could faint.'' He ran the cold water and swirled it around me until the bath felt lukewarm.

"Killjoy. The heat eases the aches and pains."

"See, the sugar in the coffee is restoring you to your usual self. Argumentative."

"Bastard."

"Honey, I was just joking."

"I didn't mean you. I was thinking of that trucker."

"If you can manage anger, I guess you're not going to die on me. So talk."

Earlier, while José hovered and Clay had been checking my eyes for dilation and focus, taking my pulse, and feeling all over my head for dents like some pup that had been hit by a car, I'd explained about the accident but not how the pickup had been returned to me. Now I gave Clay the details I'd left out because of the bus driver's presence, including that Claudia had been there and her reaction.

"She'll get over it," Clay said. "I got out your pajamas. What else can I do for you?"

"What time is it?"

He pushed back his sleeve to look at his watch. "Five-thirty."

"Then I have time for a nap before the posada."

"We'll skip this one. You're going to bed, and I'm going to give you a linament massage. You're going to be more sore in the morning than a roping calf."

"I have to go. Especially tonight."

"Why? Claudia and Ruben are cooking all the food. Even if they weren't, one little covered dish wouldn't be missed."

"Claudia is why I have to go."

"Texana, you can't worry this much over what Claudia thinks."

"It isn't just Claudia." I told him what my father had said about the gossip going around. My worry didn't change his mind.

"Showing up at Claudia's isn't going to change a thing. People are going to think what they want to think."

"If I don't go, it looks like I'm hiding because I'm guilty."

"Too simplistic. If Claudia thinks you deliberately let her cousin take the blame, she'll assume you're brassy enough to show up at her party."

"Then I'll be brassy," I said.

"That's my girl," Clay said, bending over to kiss the top of my head. He straightened and blew dirt off his lips. "You'd better wash your hair. I've called a tow truck. I'm going to wait at the pickup until it comes."

I was out of the tub and in bed but too keyed up to sleep when Clay got back shortly before seven.

"Everything okay?" I asked.

"Fine. José stayed to help me unload when the tow got there and righted the pickup. You know it's totaled."

I sighed. "Our insurance man is going to love this."

Clay dropped something into my lap. "This was in the glove compartment. I think I showed admirable restraint in not opening it so close to Christmas."

It took me a minute to remember that the box couldn't be Clay's gift. That was gone. It had been in my jacket, along with my billfold and checkbook. I opened the lid and showed Clay the medal, explaining how I'd come by it.

"It must have quite a history," he said. He put the lid back on and placed it in the bedside table. "Still want to go tonight?"

I nodded and threw back the cover to get dressed.

Bundled in our coats, we stepped out into the night and by unspoken agreement stopped and gazed up at the star-strung sky. Against the blue-black of the mountains no light showed. We might have been alone on all the earth, suspended between two darknesses.

I felt Clay's hand on my shoulder. "Time to change your mind," he said.

"Let's go."

Clay cut on the flashlight. Tonight, we were to be in the group carrying the litter with Joseph and Mary. Clay and I would take his pickup to the meeting place at the edge of Polvo and walk in procession to Casa Azul, Claudia and Ruben's home and part-time restaurant.

As we rounded the front of the trading post we could see how the wind whipped the trees along the river. "No candles tonight," I said.

Just before the road reaches Polvo it makes a deep curve around a long, narrow mesa, which blocks the view of the little community, so that the sight of the adobes and trailers outlined by the glow of many-colored Christmas lights surprised the eye and delighted the heart.

Very nearly the last arrivals, we parked with the other vehicles along the road. As we got out to join the group clustered together in the middle of the blacktop, the chattering voices ceased for an instant.

Then a welcoming voice rang out, "Hey, you two." It was Elvia.

"How are you, Texana?" Pete Rosales said. "We heard about your accident."

Before I could answer, Father Jack, the beam of his flashlight preceding him, came walking up. His baritone voice carried on the wind like a kettledrum. "Time to get started, time to get started. Where's the Holy Family?"

"In the back of my truck," Clay said.

"And the litter bearers?"

"Here," piped a breaking young voice.

"Then get it, and let's be off on our procession."

The host of flashlights bobbed and weaved along the

road, shining the way for the Holy Family to seek shelter for another night in their journey to Bethlehem.

The Reyeses' adobe has no sign indicating the restaurant other than the vivid blue of its walls, illuminated for the season with tiny white lights. A wreath in the window blinked *Feliz Navidad* over the Dr Pepper logo, and luminarias lined the flagstone path to the front door.

The litter bearers went ahead, and we lined up two by two behind them along the walk. We sang the lyrics requesting a bed for the night for Mary and Joseph. The answer came finally, as it had the night before and would with each successive *posada* over the next seven nights, with the householders bidding us welcome.

The procession filed in slowly, Clay and I last in line, immediately behind Elvia and Irene.

Ruben stood on one side of the door, Claudia on the other. As I stepped forward, her hand moved as if to shut the door in my face. In the room behind her, those nearest watched us with curious eyes.

"Hurry up, you two," Father Jack said, coming forward, his voice hearty, his eyes shrewd and aware. "You're letting in the cold night air. What we want is Christmas cheer, not Christmas chill."

Claudia's face looked indecisive for a moment; then she moved back, and we entered.

"It's party time," Clay whispered in my ear.

To accommodate their guests the Reyeses had crowded in extra tables to join the usual eight in the front room where, on Thursday, Friday, and Saturday nights, diners came from as far away as Marathon and Alpine to enjoy the traditional Mexican dishes cooked by Claudia and served by Ruben. A small courtyard connects the restaurant to the kitchen and the living quarters. In its center stood an artificial Christmas tree, and beneath this the litter bearers had placed the Holy Family. Those in tomorrow night's procession would come here to pick it up and start their journey to the next *posada,* which would be at the school.

We added our coats to the pile on the bench by the door and got in the line of guests that circled the room, ran down the courtyard's portico, and into the kitchen. There Claudia and Ruben loaded food from the hot plates with their seasonal specialty, *barbacoa* in the traditional manner of Mexico. Barbecued *cabeza de vaca.* Head of cow. In this case, many, cooked whole. The preparations had begun days before, with Ruben and his helpers digging a deep pit behind the house and filling it with wood charcoal. Rising before daylight, Ruben had fired the charcoal, waiting until it burned red before placing the foil-wrapped meat in the trench and covering it over with the dirt taken from the pit. After that, the meat cooked for eight hours before being removed to the kitchen. Claudia and her daughters and daughters-in-law would have stripped the meat from the bones and prepared the salsas.

By the time we'd been served, all the tables had been taken, extra chairs squeezed in so people sat elbow to elbow. Five guests jammed together at the side table in the kitchen. Others ate standing up. Clay retrieved our coats, and we joined Elvia and Irene on one of the benches under the portico beneath the dangling piñata.

Father Jack joined us, bringing his own plate plus another piled high with enough warm tortillas for us all.

"Glad you feel well enough to be here, Texana," he said, placing strips of meat into the center of a tortilla and spooning on the salsa. "Did I hear right? You got hit by The Holy Spirit."

"By The Holy Ghost, actually."

"Ah, a traditionalist."

We broke into laughter disproportionally merry in re-

sponse to the light joke. Evidently I wasn't the only one
feeling the tension. I had little appetite, and finished one
filled tortilla before putting my plate aside. From time to
time, as the meal progressed, people passed us on the way
for second helpings. Some stopped to chat, others didn't.
Several asked about the accident.

As soon as Father Jack finished his meal he left us in
order to circulate. Elvia and Irene hugged my sides like
bodyguards, making small talk, mostly to each other because the day's events had caught up with me and I could
barely sit up, let alone make conversation. I think they felt
as relieved as I did when Ruben rounded the children up
for the piñata that swung in the wind on the portico opposite. When the first child had been blindfolded and given
the bat, I touched Clay's arm and said I was ready to go.
As we made our way across the packed front room toward
the door, I looked for Claudia to say good-bye, but didn't
see her. Just as well. I wished I had stayed home.

"That was unpleasant," I said to Clay as we walked
down the front path.

"You're done in. Why don't you wait here while I go
get the pickup?"

I nodded.

As soon as I hit the seat, I put my head back and closed
my eyes. I felt so drained physically that I dozed off on the
brief drive home.

"What the hell?"

Clay's irate words woke me.

He braked, backed short, and pulled up toward the front-
porch steps, switching on high beams as he did so.
"Damn," he said under his breath.

Across the wall and one window of the trading post
someone had spray-painted in foot-high black letters the
words *Gringa Fea*. Ugly Gringa.

Clay wanted to clean the paint off immediately, but I told him to leave it until morning. "If you have to be out on calls, I'll get Charlie," I told him. He was so angry he nearly insisted, but when he saw my face in the light he gave in.

"Bed for you, and a cup of hot milk. I'll bring it."

As if sensing our distress, Phobe greeted us with subdued enthusiasm, settling down almost immediately to sleep near my feet.

Clay brought in the milk, laced liberally with whiskey. He sat on the bed beside me while I drank it, then took the cup and turned out the light. Easing down into the flannel sheets, I heard him leave the room and go through to the front, probably to check the locks on the windows and doors. When he returned he undressed in the dark and got in beside me. Seeking the comfort and reassurance of touch, I reached out for his hand, and he took mine and held it against his heart. Now that I wanted sleep to come, it would not. I thought of the words on the front wall and felt the tears slip across my cheeks to soak into the pillow. I knew I was overreacting, in part because of the earlier events of the day. Nonetheless, the words had stained more than the wood on which they'd been sprayed.

El Polvo had been founded by a handful of families, my father's among them. Franco Ricciotti, his grandfather, had left northern Italy in 1881, part of a group of growers and wine makers welcomed in Chihuahua, Mexico, by the government of Porfirio Díaz. The dangers of the Mexican frontier eventually sent the growers into Texas. Most settled in Del Rio and Val Verde, but the memory of his first sight of the Trans-Pecos region stayed with Great-grandfather Franco, and in 1888 he returned, renting a room in Marfa while he scouted out a place to settle. Within a few months, he paid the state of Texas a dollar for a section of land and hired workers to build the trading post on the wagon road running along the slight rise above the floodplain of the Rio Grande. The Luna family had been living at the Polvo site since 1879, along with the Ybarras and the Risas. Because of the proximity of the trading post, other families, like the Masterses, moved into the site nearest the river crossing. These families knew each other as friends whether their name was Luna or Masters or Ricciotti.

Each generation of children in Polvo grew up as a part of the community, schooled together, played together, attended Mass together, intermarried. Except for college, I had lived away from the borderland only once, during a brief first marriage that ended, not in animosity, but in mutual relief. I had returned home sure in the knowledge that I wanted to be in this place, among these people always. At night when I locked the door of the trading post, it was never against my neighbors. Every memory of my life was bound up with the community, and it is shared memories that bond us, one to another.

Tonight for the first time, seeing the scrawled words on the trading post my great-grandfather had built, recognizing the hatred and resentment that lay behind them, I felt cut off by suspicion and distrust from all I had thought I belonged to, and from everything I believed in. I dreaded the morning.

ELEVEN

THE TELEPHONE'S shrill ring woke me. I rolled over with a groan of discomfort. Seven-thirty. Clay had let me oversleep. I sat up, groggy and stiff. The more I moved, the more I hurt. In the bathroom, examining myself in the mirror, I discovered bruises on my cheekbone, hip, and knee. Since the marks were all on the left side, I assumed I'd banged against the door and window as the truck rolled over.

I seldom wear makeup but I spread some over my cheek, toning down the discoloration but not hiding it. The knee was the most painful and swollen, and for comfort I opted for a skirt instead of my usual jeans. I was fully dressed when Clay brought in breakfast on a tray.

"I appreciate the indulgence, but eating in bed twice in one week is too much," I told him. "I'll come to the table. If I don't move around, I'm afraid I'll stiffen in place." I showed him my knee, and he went to his office and returned carrying a cold pack. After he taped it around the joint, he fetched two aspirin from the medicine chest and told me to take them.

We sat at the kitchen table and ate the scrambled eggs and toast. After two cups of coffee with extra half-and-half, my self-pity ration, I noticed Clay looking at me, watching to see when I'd be ready for conversation.

"What?" I said.

"I was thinking of that trucker. Why didn't he grab everything from the glove compartment? The door was wide open. Not a very thorough thief."

"I was bigger than he was. Maybe I scared him. I hope so."

"If you're feeling vindictive, you must be better. You feel well enough to manage alone for part of the day? I'm expecting the insurance investigator."

"Of course I can. I'm not an invalid. You've waited on me quite enough."

"He needn't disturb you. I'll be out on the porch, and I'll take him around to the office as soon as he gets here."

That was as close as Clay had come to mentioning the spray-painting. He wouldn't have said that much if he could have avoided it. He knew without my saying how much the incident disturbed me.

"When are you expecting this man?" I asked.

"I have no idea. Jerry Ayrs telephoned the news a while ago. He sounded worried. He said not to let on he'd called."

"Then we won't. What's this investigator like?"

"His name is J. Frank Causley. He's a retired Texas Ranger."

"A baseball player turned detective?" I said.

"The other Texas Rangers. The guys with the boots and badges."

"Oh. Bigfoot Wallace and Jack Hays."

"He's thorough. He interviewed Jerry, took him over every moment of the day it happened. What time he got up, how long it took him to get dressed, where he sat when he ate breakfast. Causley measured the exact distance from Jerry's trailer to the stables, knew the direction of the prevailing winds, and already had a weather report for the night the poisoner visited. He inspected everything. Stables, barns, house. Even Jerry's trailer."

"Jerry let him?"

"It wouldn't have looked good if he'd said no. Anyway,

Bascom Davis owns it, so Causley was only being polite asking permission. Like all good lawmen, he subdues his personality, but that's like saying a Colt .45 is quiet until it's fired.''

''Was Bascom Davis there while all this was going on?''

''He flew in about one.''

''Anybody come with him?''

''Not that I saw. I was ready to go about the time he got there, but I waited for him, in case he wanted to ask me anything. We talked for a couple of minutes, if that. I got the feeling he was so upset he could hardly speak.''

''What does this Mr. Causley want with you? Didn't he talk to you yesterday?''

''Took me through a drill just like he did Jerry.''

''And Jerry didn't know why he's coming here?''

''Didn't know or wouldn't say, which is unusual for Jerry.'' Clay got up and started clearing the table. ''Probably I'm reading too much into Jerry's anxiety. Causley must need a little more information and is saving me a trip.''

I offered to wash the dishes so Clay could get started on the paint removal. He went out the back door to feed the kenneled dogs and check on a burro he was treating for mange. I remained at the table, staring out at the desert. By the time I'd unlocked the front doors and flipped the Closed sign to read Open, Clay was scrubbing at the window glass. I made coffee in the machine, wiped the thin film of dust that had accumulated on the customers' tables the day before, and took my seat on the stool behind the counter, my sore leg resting straight out on the edge of the shelf where I kept the paper bags. As much as I needed the business, it suited me if no one stopped until that paint was gone.

Ask little and much shall be given. Within five minutes

two pickups stopped to pump gas, and a third pulled in and parked.

The sign posted out front on the right-hand porch rail states that no firearms are allowed on the premises, but that doesn't apply to Deputy Sheriff Dennis Bustamente. He strolled in, his Combat Masterpiece .38 in its leather holster, bullets slotted in the gun belt, looking carefree and unconcerned as always. His efficiency as a law officer exists in inverse proportion to the sloppiness of his appearance: wrinkled khakis, scuffed boots, and blond hair in need of a trim. Even his badge has lost its luster and gained a dent.

Off duty, there was nothing lusterless about his personality. Among the ladies of Presidio he had a reputation as a heartbreaker. On the job he was all seriousness and attentive quiet.

He had come, he explained, to take my statement about the accident, and to report that The Holy Ghost truck had crossed into Ojinaga before the bus driver's call came in, though Dennis had broken the speed laws getting to the crossing. The customs agents would keep an eye out and notify him if it came to this side again, but if the driver had any sense, he'd stay well away. The sheriff had reported the accident and robbery to the Ojinaga police, and had actually received a return call to inform him that one *tránsito*, traffic cop, had seen the *comando* run a stop sign on the far side of town. The Ojinaga police official who called had assured the sheriff that the vehicle had been seen on the road to Chihuahua.

"Fulfilling his obligation to us, while at the same time exempting himself from further responsibility," Dennis said. "This comando, you think maybe that he came down the hill because he was waiting for you."

"I thought he couldn't stop. I mean trucks like that never seem to have brakes."

"And the ones that do drive like they don't," Dennis said. "Still, a person parked on Cemetery Hill could see any vehicle coming from either direction along that road from a long way off. Maybe this guy was looking to rob somebody. Lots of crazies out there, just most of them don't live around Presidio and Polvo." After he took down my statement of how the accident happened, he said, "I need a list of the items stolen and a description."

The men pumping gas came in to pay. I knew them both, one a rancher upriver, the other a cowboy with a ten-year-old pickup hauling his horse to a day job for the rancher. Dennis waited until they'd gone out the door before resuming our conversation.

"You were going to tell me what the trucker took," he reminded me.

"My billfold. No credit cards, my checkbook, and thirty dollars in cash. And a Christmas present for Clay." I described it for him and told him the price, $178.

"You sure that's all? He didn't take tools or the spare tire? Sometimes, an accident like this, you're so shook up you forget things."

"Clay checked. Nothing was missing."

"I'll give Carlos a call," Dennis said. "Ask him to valuate the bookmark in writing." He put away his pad and slipped the pen into the pocket clip. "I talked to Clay about the graffiti. He said you'd be the one to decide about filing a complaint."

I shook my head. "I don't want to do that."

"Your choice. But let some kid get away with this, and it might happen again."

"It has never happened before. I have to think it won't be repeated. You saw what it said?"

He nodded.

"It's very personal, wouldn't you say?"

"Could be," Dennis said. "Or it could be some kid, knowing everybody is at a posada, decides to cause trouble."

"In that case, why stop there? Why not more graffiti? Why not break in and trash the place or steal something? This way, it seems the message was the whole point."

"You're afraid it might have something to do with the Ojinaga business?" Dennis asked, putting my fear into words.

"Oh, Dennis, I hope not. What's being said?"

"Not as much as you think. It's just that with Presidio having an almost nonexistent crime rate, a murder on the other side is news. People get a little excited." He paused. "I think this will make you feel better." He pulled a folded newspaper out of his back pocket, handed it to me, and pointed to page one, saying, "Right there, underneath the story on the economic talks in the border cities."

I unfolded *The International,* Presidio's weekly newspaper.

German National Murdered in Ojinaga

OJINAGA, Chih., Mex.—Sources in the Mexican Defense Department, Secretaria de la Defensa Nacional, have reported the death of Col. Herbert Heinkel, commanding officer of the German Air Force pilots flying training missions out of Holloman Air Force Base in New Mexico.

The sources, who requested anonymity, reported that soldiers under the command of Comandante Augusto Zurita detained a man believed to be responsible for the German's death. It is reported that Col. Heinkel died after a puncture wound to the heart.

It is believed that the detained man, an Ojinaga cab driver, is a member of a group of 25 armed insurgents operating in a region known as Cordellera de El Mulato, close to Ojinaga.

According to the informant, the group is similar to those operating in the south of Mexico in Chiapas and Guerrero. Their presence is the reason for the recent increase in the military installation in Ojinaga.

Chihuahua's leading newspaper, *El Heraldo,* reports that a military attaché of the German embassy in Mexico City will work with the Mexican judicial police in Ojinaga.

"Feel better?" Dennis said as I put the newspaper down on the counter. "I don't think anybody is going to think you had a reason to kill this German—unless you did it to stop the flyovers, and no grand jury around here is going to indict you for that."

I smiled, and thanked him for bringing me the newspaper. In truth, I didn't know what to think, except that the Mexican military were doing what they often did, calling the cabbie an insurgent to inflate the propaganda value of their arrest. The ice pack on my knee dripped down my leg, and I excused myself to Dennis, went to the kitchen, removed the pack, and dropped it into the sink.

I got back to the front as Gwen Masters came in to pay for gas. She put down two twenties, saying, "Don't you let that nonsense"—jerking her head in the direction of the porch—"get you down." And to Dennis, "You oughta stop whoever's kid did that."

"Yes, ma'am," Dennis said.

Gwen departed, and Dennis turned back to me. "I'll be around more often, keeping an eye out. Maybe we'll get lucky and this trucker will be foolish enough to cross into Presidio again. I'll be sending you a copy of the accident and robbery report for your insurance carrier."

Something else to look forward to. A second conversation with the insurance agent. Plus I needed to call the bank about my checks.

Dennis left, but I noticed he stopped on the porch, and Clay came down the ladder to talk with him. I went through to the kitchen, lifted the receiver on the wall phone, and punched in the bank's number. They agreed to stop any checks after the one I'd written to Carlos. That taken care of, I rang the agent.

I managed to keep my temper under control and my explanation short, informing him the sheriff's report had been taken care of. He had nothing to say beyond a sarcastic *"Another* incident involving your pickup," which left me certain we'd change agents at the next renewal date.

I returned to the front to find Elvia rushing down the aisle calling, "Comadre, comadre."

Elvia's face, with its dark eyes under perfect brows, high cheekbones, and full lips, glowed with health and the expressiveness of her personality. She had a thoughtful manner, given to quietness broken by bursts of personal confidences. At the moment, she was angry.

"What is this nastiness someone has written on your beautiful old building?" she demanded, her temper flaring the color in her skin. "I hate this for you, comadre."

"I'm not crazy about it myself." I invited her into the back, leaving the interior door open so I could hear the bell. We sat at the kitchen table. Not wanting to hash over the spray-painting again, I diverted her with a question about the baby.

While she chattered, I thought about the first time I had seen her, standing in the yard of a penitentiary in Chihuahua. Seventeen-year-old Elvia had been earning three dollars a day cooking and doing laundry for several prisoners, including Irene's son Kyle. She had come into the crowded prison yard looking for him, but he had waved her off, fearful his mother might see her. As we left, only I had witnessed their embrace and the obviousness of her pregnancy. After Kyle's release had been arranged and he had returned home, he'd tried to put everything that had happened in Mexico behind him, but he told his mother about Elvia. Irene had returned to the prison, located Elvia, and after talking with her over a period of time, arranged for her to come to Polvo. Irene had not pressed for a hurried marriage between her immature son and the mother-to-be of her grandchild. Instead, she offered Elvia a home, and promised to teach the girl English and the other skills needed in order to earn her GED and become self-supporting. In Mexico Elvia had gone to school through *primaria,* sixth grade, when the grandmother who raised her had died, and she had been left on her own. Kyle, who had never planned an hour ahead in his young life, had been persuaded to go back to college. Irene wanted to give them both time to adjust to the situation and decide about whether they had a future together.

The baby had been born in the hospital at Alpine; Elvia had named her daughter Esperanza, which means hope. She had asked Clay and me to be the baby's godparents, a serious personal and financial responsibility in Mexico. This is why Elvia called me *comadre,* co-mother.

Ecstatic about life in the United States, Elvia had adapted to American culture by cutting her long black hair very short, living in jeans and T-shirts, and learning to drive. She watched American movies on video and read voraciously from my library. Her English skills improved with the ease of a natural linguist. Irene, married out of high school, a mother by nineteen, divorced by her husband on her fortieth birthday, was encouraging Elvia to go to college. I knew she hoped for Elvia, whom she had grown to love as a daughter, to be financially independent before committing herself to any relationship.

"Comadre," Elvia said sternly, "you're not listening to me."

"I'm sorry. What were you saying?"

"About these mean words on the storefront. You must pay no attention to them. You act like nothing has happened. In Mexico appearance is everything—how you hold your head up. Nothing else is anybody's business." She frowned deeply. "First your pickup is stolen, then wrecked. You are robbed. Now this spray-painting. I think you must have a bad enemy."

Elvia said all this so fast I lost my breath just listening to her. I didn't know what to think of her combination of fact and melodrama. I didn't want to encourage her idea that I'd become someone's target.

"There's no evidence any of these things are connected. The trucker probably didn't have brakes, and his robbing me was opportunistic—"

Opportunistic. Elvia's lips formed the word silently. "Taking advantage of a situation? Is that what this word means."

"Exactly." I said, pleased at her quickness. It was part of her charm, this instant understanding.

She blinked, bit her lip, and dropped her eyes. "Oh, comadre, I think I have been opportunistic."

"I'll fix coffee and we'll talk about it."

She looked so unhappy that instead of coffee I got out milk for hot chocolate, her favorite drink. I popped the mugs into the microwave. When the milk had heated, I stirred in the instant cocoa, added the spoonful of extra sugar Elvia liked in hers, topped it off with two marsh-mallows, and rejoined her at the table. I didn't press her with questions, and after a few minutes the story poured out, in a roundabout way.

"I love America. I love this culture. I could never go back to Mexico. My mother left when I was a baby. My mother's mother, my abuela, sold vegetables in the street market. Every day she took me with her and kept me on a blanket beneath the stall. One day an old man saw me, and he made a cradle and gave it to my abuela. She would rock me with her foot while she bargained over price with her customers. She was a good woman. When I was older, she saw to it that I was clean and went to school. She said she didn't want me to repeat the mistakes of her daughter, my mother, and go off with some salvaje, some savage, who knows nothing but to drink, and smoke, and go with other women. She said once my father went after my mother with a machete. She said all men in Mexico are savages. They marry a woman only so she can serve him. They expect a woman to be abnegada—I don't know what this is in English."

"Self-sacrificing."

Elvia nodded vigorously. "Yes. Good only for bearing children, that is what my abuela told me. When she died, she had only two possessions, her metate for grinding corn and her molcajete and tejolote. What you call a mortar and pestle. I will keep them always. After she died, I told myself I would be wise, like my abuela wanted. Never would I marry. Then I fell in love."

A tear slipped down Elvia's face and she sniffed. I handed her a paper napkin.

"I met Geraldo in the market where I took over my abuela's stall. He and his brother shined shoes, one at each end of the plaza. I was fourteen."

I said gently, "Elvia, are you trying to tell me you married this boy?"

"No, no." She shook her head. "But I loved him, and we—you know."

"Yes, I know."

She sniffed and wiped her eyes, then spoke very fast, as if the words propelled themselves. "I have an angelito, a little angel in the grave in Mexico. The midwife said he came too soon. For three days I held him. Then he died. I put out candles for him in the church. Someday when I have my education and a job to pay my way, I will return to his grave. I will burn incense, and put out pan de muertito and paper flowers in a fine corona, and I will sit with him and eat the bread and tell him how much I miss him."

"What happened to the father?"

She looked out the window. "When I told him we were going to have a baby, he said he must go to the United States to get work to support us. He promised he would send for me and the baby. I never heard from him again." She turned to face me. "What should I do, comadre? I am afraid when Kyle finds out he will think I pretended to love him only to come here. He might even think I wanted to look for my angelito's father."

"Is any of that true?"

"No." A whisper. "A little. At first, I smiled and made jokes with him because he was an American. Because I wanted to come here. Then I loved him because he was so nice. He carried the heavy laundry basket for me even though the other men laughed at him because he did this. He gave me extra pay. When I cooked for him, he asked me to eat also. Truly, comadre, I loved him."

"Past tense?"

"Yes, comadre. He seems different here. So young. Younger than me. When he comes home he talks of fraternity parties. Such things are very important to him, but they are so silly. So childish. Never does he plan for the future or worry about his grades. He's like a little boy. A lovable little boy, but only a boy. What am I going to do?''

"You have to tell Kyle. You've changed. That's quite true, you know. Before you speak to Kyle, talk to Irene. Believe me, she'll understand." And approve, though I didn't say it aloud. Irene loved her youngest son, but she had few illusions about him.

Her hands tightened a little, but her eyes remained steady. "Yes, you're right. I'll tell Irene first. I owe her everything."

"Whatever happens, you have friends here."

She rose, came around to my side of the table, and bent to kiss me on the cheek. "You're wise, comadre."

I laughed. "Don't count on it. I feel like I know less and less every day." I let her out the back door and waved her on her way.

I checked the clock. Almost eleven. I was taking things out of the refrigerator to fix a quick lunch when the front bell jangled.

I didn't know the man standing in the aisles gazing up at the row of antique tools displayed above the high upper shelves on three sides of the trading post. Half-turned away from me, he nonetheless caught my entrance into the room and acknowledged it by removing his hat. It had a roper crease. With that, the jeans tucked inside his boots, and the white western shirt, I took him for a stockman.

"Morning, ma'am."

The moderately deep voice suggested intelligence, the benign expression implied goodwill. A big man, tall and broad-shouldered, only a slight thickening around the waist hinted that his years might add up to more than fifty. His hair, somewhere between blond and white, swept back from a wide forehead, and the deep blue eyes showed smile lines at the corners. Too much sun had mottled his fair skin, and too much drink had thickened the flesh of his nose, robbing him of the undoubted handsomeness of his youth, but adding the interest of contrast to the otherwise even features.

He walked toward the counter with a toed-in gait.

I smiled a warm welcome. I needed new customers.

"How may I help you?" I said.

"I'd like to look at your horse supplies."

"Let me show you where they are."

He ambled along behind me to the far end of the room, where the equine supplies take up both sides of two full-length shelves and most of one wall.

"I have a little of everything, as you can see. Grooming supplies, health care, saddle pads and blankets, stable equipment, tack…" I waited while he took his time looking the shelves over. "If there's something you need that I don't carry, I can order it. Generally it will arrive within a week."

"This is what I'm looking for," he said, nudging a fifty-pound sack of range cubes with his boot.

"How many would you like?"

"Just the one will do for now."

I got the dolly, rolled it over to the shelf, and slid the feed onto it. I rolled it up to the counter, where he stood waiting. It takes the best part of a twenty to pay for the fifty-pound bag. I have to charge more because I don't buy enough quantity to get wholesale prices. He didn't complain about the price, but asked for a receipt for his records. Every time I do this, I swear I'll give up the old brass register for one that will at least print a receipt, but even when I have a little extra money, I seem to find other uses for it.

I glanced down at the tax form to fill in the name. "I appreciate your business, Mr...?"

He carefully placed the bills in his wallet, extracted a business card, and handed it to me. J. Frank Causley, Insurance Investigator, Dallas, Texas.

He folded the wallet, replaced it in his back pocket, said, "Mind loading that for me?" He led the way to the front door, opening it for me. I rolled the dolly out. An older, green pickup sporting new tires was backed up to the steps, tailgate down. I righted the dolly and hoisted the sack into the truck, sliding it into the pickup's bed and closing the tailgate.

I faced Causley to find him observing me with a bland look. A poker face if ever I saw one. I bet he never gave away a hand. However, this play was obvious, though he'd set me up for it nicely.

I said, "Now you know I can lift a fifty-pound sack of range cubes by myself. What would you have done if Clay had met you out here?"

"Well now, I made a little arrangement to avoid that happening after I drove past and saw him on the ladder. I always like to survey the territory before I visit."

"What did you do? Kidnap him?"

"Paid a kid down the road to bring in his puppy for a full medical examination and all his shots."

"As long as you're paying for the shots, too," I told him.

"He did," Clay said, coming around the corner and onto the porch. "The bill was thirty-five dollars. The kid pocketed the change."

Causley nodded. "Fair enough. I didn't have time to check up on the cost so I gave him a fifty."

"You underestimated our neighborliness," Clay said. "Chucho described the man who paid him to bring the dog in. I'm much obliged for you helping with animal health. That's one less unvaccinated dog for me to worry about. You don't strike me as a charitable organization. What's this about?''

"Mr. Causley bought a sack of cubes from me. My guess is he didn't ride his horse down here from Dallas.''

"No, ma'am, I didn't. I'm not playing tricks. This is serious business.''

"Then why don't you state it,'' I said.

"I'd like to know if you could tell me how an empty fifty-pound bag like the one you just loaded into my pickup and stamped Texana's Trading Post came to be filled with gopher pellets.''

TWELVE

IF CAUSLEY HAD intended the words to shock, it worked.

"I stamp all my stock. Everything I can. It's the only advertising I do," I said.

"If we're going to talk, let's get off this damn porch," Clay said. The profanity was a sign of stress.

"I see you've had a bit of trouble here, too," Causley remarked, looking up at the graffiti.

"I scrubbed at it all morning without making much headway," Clay said, opening the door and standing back for Causley to enter first.

"Try sanding it, then stain the whole wall with a colored wood preservative," Causley said.

Clay said, "Speaking from experience?"

"Some. Not everybody loves a badge."

As Causley moved down the aisle ahead of us, a shift of light and motion from the side caught my eye. Before I could warn him, Phobe pounced at his back in her stalker game. As she landed, Causley moved forward in one smooth motion, reached a hand behind, grasped a handful of fur at the back of her neck, and flipped her over his shoulder, catching her weight with his free hand beneath her belly and lowering her to the floor. Disoriented, Phobe froze.

Causley chuckled. "Surprised you, didn't I?" Phobe turned in his direction, blinked, made some remarks in her meowing-Siamese voice, and tilted her head as if to ask if there was more play coming. When Causley bent, scratched her ears briefly, then walked past her, she looked disappointed. As we passed into the living quarters she continued observing the intriguing newcomer by peeking from behind the door.

"Where'd you learn that trick?" I asked him.

"Used to have a tame cougar named Miss Kitty, played the same kind of game as your bobcat, only she'd nip my neck like I was a deer she was going to bring down. Course, I've been jumped by a few wild varmints in my time since I worked mostly as a field man. My first Ranger posting was with Company E out of Midland. I spent a lot of time all over the Trans-Pecos. I even made it this far up the road once or twice. Hotter than twelve yards of hell in the summertime, I remember." He gave the room a casual look, though I have no doubt he took in details he'd recall perfectly if he ever needed to. "Mind if I sit down?" he asked. "My feet are killing me."

I gestured to a chair and offered to fix coffee. Causley declined, and Clay shot me a look that said clearly, this is not a social visit. As if I didn't know.

"Do you mind telling us where you found this feed sack you mentioned?" Clay said, sitting on the edge of his chair.

"Couple of hundred yards from the compound at Red Mountain. Caught on a maguey plant. Could have been windblown from where the poisoner dropped it after dumping the contents out at the corral. Might have flown out of the bed of a pickup. Most ranchers toss their empty feed sacks into the back of the truck."

"It might have been dropped," Clay said, "by somebody going across country on horseback."

Causley said, "Lots of possibilities. Point is, it came from here, and it has strychnine and milo residue in it." He turned to me. "Who all do you sell these feed cubes to?"

"Anybody who wants them," I said. That sounded flippant, even to my ears, so I explained. "I sell mostly from one to five bags at a time to people who own one or two horses for riding."

"Any exceptions?"

I paused too long before answering. Causley leaned forward. "Who?"

"La Noria Ranch. They do almost all their business with me. Alicia Haro keeps paint horses, and the ranch buys for the remuda, the workhorses, too."

"I know the term," he said. "They buy from you recently?"

"I made a delivery the morning Jerry called Clay up to Red Mountain."

"So they had run out?"

"I don't know. Lalo, he's a ranch hand, called and ordered twenty bags, along with a long list of other items."

"When was that?"

"The date of the call? Maybe three or four days before. I'd have to look at the order book to be sure."

"Would you do that for me?"

I went out to the counter, pulled out the ledger, came back, and showed him the date, order, and amount.

Causley jotted it all down in a little notebook. He kept it out, and wrote down my answers to a succession of questions, including what time I got up the day the horses died, when I left the trading post, how many sacks of cubes La Noria usually bought, did I know where this Lalo kept the feed on hand, did either Clay or I know of any bad feeling between the Haros and Bascom Davis? Lalo? Other ranch hands? Jerry Ayrs and either of the ranchers?

Clay said, "None," volunteering nothing about the symbiotic Davis-Haro political relationship. But then, if Causley read the papers, he'd know that for himself.

"Ayrs ever work for the Haro ranch?"

Clay said, "He's cowboyed for any number of ranchers. When it comes time for rounding up and working the cattle, most ranchers hire day help." Clay paused, then added forcefully, "I've known Jerry a long time. I've seen him handling animals. I can tell a whole lot about a man by the way he treats animals. Ayrs is a good man."

Causley just smiled, and said, "Good enough to say no if, say, his boss asked for a favor?"

"You might as well think I did it as suspect Jerry," Clay said in a low tone.

"I checked into that. You're clear because of the timing. There's no way for you to have put out the poison, come home to deliver pups at the post office, and then take the call and get to Red Mountain while any of the horses were still alive."

Clay re-formed his pinched lips into a grin. "You've already talked to Lucy, I see."

"At the beginning of an investigation, everybody is equally suspect," Causley said.

I watched as the big man relaxed physically and glanced out the window toward the endless desert. His sudden sense of ease gave me the impression that he had abandoned us as serious suspects.

He said, "That sack might have been left for a purpose." He turned his gaze back on me. "Mrs. Jones, anybody mad enough at you to want to try and ruin your business by doing something like that?"

My reaction was a defensive, "No."

His poker face was unyielding to any hint of expression. "Your pickup is stolen. You're run off the road. Somebody paints a rude comment across the front of your business. Seems like you're snakebit when it comes to luck lately. Anything you want to tell me? Any squabbles with customers? It could be something big or something small, blown up in somebody's mind to a real grievance.''

"There's nothing like that. I'm on good terms with my customers. I've known a lot of them all my life. Most of them I like. The ones I don't, I treat with courtesy. They help pay the bills, too.''

"What about that three hours Mr. Jones was out. You could have been anywhere.''

"I've already given you an account of that day. Ask me anything else you want.''

"Ever stock any gopher poison.''

"No. And I never had anyone request it.''

Causley got to his feet. "Would you be willing to write out a list of the names of folks that you've sold even one sack of cubes to? Say, in the last six months?''

I nodded, went back to the ledger, flipped back six months. He took notes as I read out names. In fifteen minutes, we'd finished.

Causley flipped the notebook closed and slipped it into his pocket. "Appreciate your time, folks. I'll show myself out.''

We took him at his word and sat there. When we heard the door close, Clay said, "How about that coffee now? I'll make it.''

"What do you think?'' I asked him a few minutes later as we drank the brew.

"I think he's fair. I think he's smart. And I think he won't quit until he catches someone.''

"What about that feed sack?''

"Don't worry about that. He's shaking the bushes to see what flies out. My guess is he's eliminating so he can close in on Bascom Davis for insurance fraud. That would finish his political career and Henry Haro's with him.''

"That reminds me.'' I went to get *The International* from

the counter. "Read all about it," I said, handing him the paper. The headline caught his eye immediately, and I sat quietly until he'd read the story twice.

"Well, what do you know about that?" he said, putting aside the paper.

"You know," I told him, "I wasn't much in the party mood, but now, I'm looking forward to tonight's posada. It might be interesting."

Clay frowned. "If you mean what I think, I wouldn't get my hopes up."

"This story is bound to stop Claudia thinking I had anything to do with this German colonel's death."

He gave me a look of pity.

I said, "Go ahead. Say it."

"The dead man's identity won't make a difference to Claudia. She blames race for what happened to her cousin."

"But race worked against me. The comandante had every reason to prefer to blame the murder of one foreigner on another."

"When it comes to family, people go with their hearts, whether it's love or hate. Claudia doesn't care who killed the German. You got free, her cousin didn't. In fact, she may be more sure, with two non-Mexicans involved, that something is going on, some kind of plot with her cousin as the fall guy. It's too bad the Mexican authorities decided to use this as an excuse to blast the rebels, and I'm guessing that's exactly what they did. Politics is politics, whether it's Washington or Mexico City. The truth and what's proffered as the truth are seldom one and the same. After the body blow Mexico's ruling party took in the last election, the military are twice as anxious to curb sympathy for the insurgents. It means they'll hold on to that cabbie as an example to scare others."

"The cabbie probably doesn't know any more about the rebels than I do."

Clay patted my knee. "Cheer up. As Pete likes to say, *let it happen*. We can handle whatever it is."

"I feel beat," I told him. "I think I'll take a nap."

"You're going to the posada, aren't you?"

I thought of what Elvia had said about holding my head up. "Absolutely."

THIRTEEN

AFTER CAUSLEY LEFT neither Clay nor I had much appetite, and we decided to skip lunch. I knew without his saying a word that my husband worried for my sake, hating the circumstances that, however tenuously, linked my name with another crime.

A little after two, Clay got a call from a rancher whose son's calf, raised to enter in the county livestock show on Saturday, was off its feed and running a fever. Clay took the mobile lab van, leaving his pickup for me in case he couldn't make it back for the posada. As it turned out, I was the one who missed the party.

Restless and bored, I wanted to do something. When I'm worried, I take solace in activity. Not a customer had passed through the doors since the insurance investigator walked out. I felt like a pariah, and it was making me crazy. I needed something to occupy my mind besides my own troubles. I flipped the sign on the front door to read CLOSED, changed from the skirt to a pair of slacks that fit loosely enough not to put pressure on my swollen knee, dropped the gift box with the *evangelista's* medal into my jacket pocket, along with my pistol. No more carrying it in the glove compartment since the *comando* rammed me. I collected the extra set of keys and went out the back door. I drove Clay's pickup around front and topped off the tanks. A few hours, and I'd know whether or not Electra wanted the medal back. If she didn't keep it, I'd see if Carlos could duplicate Clay's gift in time for Christmas, or I could pick out something else, maybe a silver link hatband or a watchband. Either way, the silversmith could have the medal. As I drove, running an errand with a purpose, I felt better with each passing mile.

I had reached the Arroyo de la Aura cutoff. The thin afternoon light stretched from cliff to cliff, and no cloud marred the rich blue sky. I made good time on the dry track, and parked in front of Electra's house. This time she did not stand on the porch, nor did I see a glimpse of Max. She's on the other side, across the river, I thought, reaching into the glove compartment for a pencil and paper to leave a note on her door.

As I straightened, I saw it. I stepped out of the pickup, and walked stone-footed toward the barn. From somewhere nearby, taking delight in the warmth of the sun, a mockingbird sang its erratic song.

Against the unpainted wood of the double doors the crucified figure hung, head lolling on one shoulder, boots dangling loose only inches from the hard-packed ground. I recognized the green sweater and brown pants as the clothes Electra had been wearing on my last visit. Twenty feet away I stopped and consciously breathed for the first time in as many seconds when I realized what I was looking at. Not the *evangelista*, but a life-size straw figure, dressed in her clothes, with a pair of light work gloves for the hands and a knitted cap on the head.

I edged closer. The person who nailed it up might still be close, watching me. I slipped my hand into my jacket pocket, withdrew my pistol, and cocked the hammer. If someone was watching, I wanted the person to know I would defend myself.

The neigh of the horse nearly unnerved me. The gelding had been standing so still on the far side of the corral I hadn't noticed him against the brown hillside.

"Hello, Doc," I said. The big animal shied nervously

and snorted, but stayed where he was by his feeder. Next to it, the water trough, operated on a float system from a larger enclosed tank, nearly overflowed, but except for a few strands of hay, the feeder stood empty. The hay was in the barn. The grotesque figure had been nailed across both doors, so that to get feed for the horse, I'd have to pull it loose to get inside. I felt an aversion to touching it, but if the *evangelista* didn't get back while I was there, I'd have to take the figure down anyway. I couldn't leave it for her when she arrived home alone. It had shocked me badly, and I didn't live here. I wasn't the one being terrorized. I marched to the barn door.

The original landowner had built the barn to last, for holding feed to get cattle and horses through drought or bad winters, for storing tools and supplies for fence repairs, and everything needed to work cattle from ropes to branding irons. Though small, its deeply pitched roof gave an illusion of size. Even without upkeep, it would outlast the cabin by many years. I took one last look behind and around me. Nothing moved on the hills.

With my free hand I reached out and yanked one glove off the nail, and the figure sagged to the ground, hanging by the remaining nail. Someone had gone to a lot of trouble constructing the dummy. The gloved hands had been tied with twine to the straw-stuffed sleeves. The boots had been tightly stuffed with cloth and straw to keep them on. The clothing had been arranged to hide every inch of the straw body, and the cap added to cover the drooping head. So much care merely to convey hate, I thought. Still mindful of strangers who might be lurking, I held my gun, barrel pointed down, finger on the trigger, and opened the left-hand door.

One step and I hit the heavy mix of odors like an invisible wall that stopped me in my tracks. Reacting to the smell, my stomach gave a pitching roll like a dinghy in a hurricane, but it was the sight that caused me to involuntarily contract my hands—and thus my trigger finger. The shot sounded like the big bang that unleashed the universe. It resounded against the walls and sent wild echoes flying down the canyon.

Yet my eyes were so locked onto the sight before me that I didn't flinch at the noise. The barn had been roofed in used tin, and sunlight poured through the hundreds of old nail holes so that the body strung upside down from the rafter seemed suspended in golden rain.

The rope had been tied around the *evangelista's* ankles, tossed over the broad rafter, and after the body had been hoisted upward, tied off on a post of a stall against the back wall. Her throat had been cut so deeply that I couldn't see her face. Her long braided hair, the end touching the floor, had acted as a wick for the total volume of her body's blood, which had soaked into the floor, turning the packed soil to mud in a large, irregular stain beneath the body.

My muscles unlocked, and I made about three leaping steps to the outside before I collapsed to my knees, my whole body quaking with the palsy of fear. I moved instinctively, getting to my feet, putting one foot ahead of the other in the zombie fashion of those in shock, heading for the truck. The horse whinnied. I turned and ran to the corral. Carefully, and with trembling fingers, I put my gun down on the ground and opened the gate to the corral, letting it swing back. Doc galloped out, making a wide circle around the barn and hitting the track down the canyon at a full run. I didn't worry about him. He'd feed on the winter-dried grass, and eventually find a herd of cattle to mix with. Some rancher or cowhand would bring him in.

Though I felt incapable of motion, I remembered to pick

up the gun. I made it to the pickup, dropped the gun on the seat beside me, and started the motor, ignoring the buzzer alerting me to buckle up. I was halfway down the track before I was really conscious of where I was and what I was doing. It was at the turn into the main canyon that I felt the steering wheel pull against me as the truck wobbled right. As little as I wanted to, I had to stop. The front right tire was flat.

I set the emergency brake, got out the jack, fitted it under the bumper, found a rock to put under the back tire as an extra precaution against the pickup rolling downhill, and set to work loosening the nuts. The physical exertion took the edge off the shock and restored me to a calmer state of mind, but by the time I finished changing the tire the long light of sunset shafted across the road. I put my window down as I drove and breathed in the sweet air. By the time I reached the next turn, the gray shades of twilight had turned black, and a soft half-moon rested against the deep hollow of the sky.

The Christmas lights of Polvo had never looked so welcoming. The *posada* had begun, and the pilgrims gathered in front of the schoolhouse steps with the litter carried by two girls. I parked and almost leaped out, stopping to hold on to the truck for a moment, trying to quell the panic that I could feel rising once more in my throat, so that I wanted to run inside yelling my head off. I could hear the singing, the voices floating on the rush of a light wind. I looked for Clay's van but didn't see it as I made my stumbling way around to the back door. I closed it behind me and leaned against it, reveling in the security of light and sound and the presence of too many people crowded into the two rooms of the school. One woman turned around, touched the arm of another, who turned also, until by ones and twos the inside group stopped singing to stare at me.

Lucy Ramos, the postmistress, came forward, followed by Irene and Elvia. They grasped my arm. One of them told me to sit down while another put a chair behind me.

"Get her some aspirin and some of the fruit punch," a calm voice said. "She's in shock." The visiting nurse from Marfa, whose sister lived in Polvo, knelt beside me. "Have you been attacked? Are you injured?"

I shook my head and heard my own hoarse voice saying the words, "Call the sheriff. The *evangelista* has been murdered."

After that, Irene and Elvia kept the party going for the children in the schoolroom, and the adults came and went getting a look at me where I sat in the chair, the nurse by my side with her hand on my shoulder, until Clay arrived, was told what had happened, and bundled me off home, saying that the sheriff would find us there when they wanted to get my statement. The nurse slipped him something and spoke to him briefly. At home, after he had helped me out of my clothes and into bed, he gave me a glass of water and the sleeping pill she had handed him. As I fell asleep with Clay stroking my hair, my last thought was to wonder why the nurse carried around a sleeping pill.

FOURTEEN

THE LITTLE GREEN CAPSULE did its job. I woke with a bitter aftertaste in my mouth, but feeling rested and alert.

The sheriff arrived at nine-fifteen, having already been back to the murder site that morning. One look at his sleep-robbed face, and Clay offered to make a fresh pot of coffee. Andalon accepted, and kept the conversation on the upcoming livestock show until we had finished the coffee as well as all the cinnamon rolls Clay had taken from the freezer and thawed in the microwave.

"That was great, thanks," Andalon said, leaning back in his chair and looking at me across the kitchen table. "You feel like telling me about yesterday?"

I nodded.

"It might make you feel better to know that Ms. Reaves was unconscious before she was killed. Somebody hit her hard on the back of the head with a shovel. We found it propped against the wall of the house right near the back door."

I closed my eyes and passed my hand over my mouth. "I'm glad. I hated thinking…"

"She'd been dead for some time. Probably since early the afternoon before. We know she ate lunch. We found empty cans in the trash. She'd fixed a meal and washed up the dishes, but the pans she cooked in hadn't been cleaned up yet. She'd used the iron skillet to fry something, poured the oil off into a can, and sprinkled salt to soak up the residue and scrub the skillet with, but she hadn't done it yet."

"Someone interrupted her?" Clay said.

"Looks that way."

I waited a moment, keeping silent, thinking Andalon intended to add something more, but all he said was, "Tell your story any way you want to. I'll ask questions later..."

I started with the visit Father Jack and I made, and the *evangelista* telling us about the crucified figures.

Andalon said he'd found one of the small dolls in the house. "A real ugly warning, I'd call it. I'd say the life-size figure was a step up in intimidation except the woman is dead, and that's the ultimate in intimidation."

"Did you find Max?" I asked him.

"No sign of the dog. I understand he was a pretty good guard dog, so I expected him to be dead somewhere around the house. We called and searched for a couple of hundred yards around that place. One odd thing, we didn't find any personal effects in that house. It's like Electra Reaves lived somewhere else and was just camping out at the cabin. So far, no one can tell me where she came from before she showed up here."

"Ask Alicia Lagos. She told me she went with Electra sometimes to visit the ranchos and ejidos. Maybe she can tell you more about her. She might know about relatives or friends to notify."

"Mr. Haro's granddaughter? I wouldn't have thought she'd be the type."

I laughed. "To be a Protestant, you mean?" Andalon is a staunch Methodist.

He grinned. "Mr. Haro is so old-world, you know. I guess I thought the whole family was. I met the granddaughter once at a horse show." Andalon's wife, Marta, is a horse enthusiast, often joining trail-riding events held for charity.

After I recounted my finding the body, Andalon took me

over a few details, but there was nothing more that I could recall that might help him, and he left intending to visit Father Jack and get his impressions of the *evangelista*. My thoughts kept returning to the straw figure and why someone had gone to so much trouble to prepare and place it. It was as if two different minds had been at work. I dismissed it, and left the fact-finding to Andalon. In spite of his easygoing persona, he had an acute intelligence, and very little got past him.

Clay insisted on my remaining in bed for the rest of the morning, and this time I didn't argue. While he manned the front counter with Phobe for company, I spent the slow hours watching a video of *The Thin Man*. Over the charmingly brittle dialogue of Nick and Nora Charles, I heard the bell jangle again and again. People coming in to hear the gory details, I thought, half-smiling.

I slept through the beginning of a second movie, waking only when Clay clicked off the TV and Phobe launched herself onto the bed.

"How are you feeling?" Clay asked. His voice stayed low-key, but his look was full-blown anxiety.

"Okay," I lied. I yawned and stretched, flinching, the muscle soreness from my being tossed around in the pickup more painful today. "What time is it?"

"A little after one."

I threw back the covers.

We sat on the couch while Clay told me who'd been by for gas or groceries, or a pack of gum in order to have an excuse to ask about the murder. "Father Jack telephoned to ask how you were, and Pete came by. He said to tell you he had a surprise for you when you were feeling better. Oh, and if you're hungry, Irene and Elvia brought three plates of leftovers from the posada. I put it all in the refrigerator."

"The cinnamon rolls filled me up—"

The telephone rang, and Clay answered it. I heard him say, "Hello, Justice," and wondered if my father had heard about my finding the *evangelista*. Mostly Clay listened; then I heard him say, "I'll leave now."

"Problem?" I asked after he hung up.

"Elizabeth is down. He doesn't want to shoot her himself. I told him I'd come now. Once you make a decision like that about an animal you love, it's best to get it over fast."

"I'll get dressed and go with you," I said.

"Good. I don't much like the idea of you staying here by yourself. Too many odd things going on." I didn't say so, but I felt the same way. Never had I felt uncomfortable in my own home before.

My father waited for us in the pasture beyond the hill above the back of the house, kneeling beside the longhorn cow he called Elizabeth. A wiry Mexican man wearing a knitted cap, jeans, and a hunting jacket with a pack of cigarettes poking out of the pocket sat cross-legged on the ground a few feet away, a leather bag beside him. Parked nearby stood a pickup the color of sand.

My father rubbed his hand down the long face of the red-and-white-splotched cow. "You've delivered many a fine calf, old girl." I could see the pain in his eyes as Elizabeth's ears flicked toward the sound of his voice. He got to his feet, nodded at Clay and said, "I'll leave you to it." I took his arm, and we walked together toward the house.

He talked as we went, at the same time listening for the shot. "I could open the back door and call her and here she come running, just like a dog. She was so old and crippled she'd been having trouble getting around for a couple of months now so I knew this was coming, but I kept putting it off. When she didn't come up this morning for feed I figured it was the end. She was over twenty years old, you know, but until this year she produced a fine calf every time.''

"She had a good life on this place," I said, taking his arm. We both winced as the shot rang out.

"Sabino is going to mount the skullcap and horns for me. I never did that with any animal before, but she has a fine set of horns.'' He paused. "I kind of want to keep a part of her around. I told him to leave the rest of the carcass for the buzzards. It's nature's way. I want her old bones to dissolve into the earth here. She was born on this place, you know."

We walked to the house. Clay joined us in a few minutes, driving the pickup back and parking in front of the porch where we sat. My father got iced tea for us, and nudged Willie from his rocker so Clay could sit down. Woo Hoo, released from inside the house, settled at my father's feet.

"Where's Charlie?" I asked.

"He took my truck into Presidio to buy groceries for me. He said he owed me for all he ate. I'd have told him that was nonsense, but you don't argue with a man who feels indebted."

"Sounds like he's ready to leave," Clay said.

"He's pining for his car." My father looked at his watch. "He ought to be back pretty soon. Maybe you could wait and give him a ride?" The unspoken request was for a return to solitude. My father knows his limits and protects them to protect himself and those he loves.

"Sure thing," Clay said.

I thought about my shrinking sales receipts and said, "It's a good thing Charlie will work for room and board." Charlie knew everyone and collected gossip effortlessly. Knowing he'd return with the tale of my pickup being totaled and my discovery of the *evangelista's* body, I told my father what had happened, including all about Electra Reaves, Alicia Haro, and the proselytizing.

"I was wondering about that bruise on your face," he said when I'd finished.

"That's the worst of it," I assured him, pushing back my memory of the sight of Electra's body.

My father said, "I think I'll ask Charlie to act as bodyguard for you."

I was tugging nervously at my hair as I grasped around in my mind for a subject to deflect my father's worry. Clay and I have been married more than long enough to read each other's body language. He broke in deftly with a series of questions. "Justice, do you know anything about Electra Reaves? Any tales going around from Valfre? Anything like that?"

"None. I never even heard of her that I recall. If Valfre comes by here on his way back down to Presidio, I'll ask him about her. Never knew old Haro's granddaughter was living with him, either. I don't blame him for not liking the girl's traveling on the other side with this woman, though. That's asking for trouble. For some, it's a short step between religious fervor and religious fanaticism. If she's been preaching against the Church on the other side, she might be next. Nothing like Mexico for a schizophrenic relationship between Church and State. Half of them blame the Church for Mexico's troubles, and the other half make pilgrimages crawling on their knees for miles to pray at some shrine."

I looked at my father sideways. "Fine talk for a citizen of a country that started out with In God We Trust on our coinage and ended up banning prayer from school, and has televangelists who rake in more cash than the Home Shopping Network." I made my remarks half-jokingly, but my father's comment about Alicia disturbed me. I hadn't thought of her being in danger because of her association with the *evangelista*.

"I wonder if Don Federico will try and get Alicia to go back to her mother in California for a while."

"Good luck to him," my father said. "She sounds as bullheaded as you."

"I prefer goal-oriented to bullheaded."

"Haro can afford to hire security guards if he's worried," my father said. "If he'll part with the money," he added, touching one hand to his elbow, a gesture in *la frontera* that indicates a person thrifty to the point of stinginess.

Clay said, "How did Haro make his money?"

My father laughed. "Some say he found some of the gold Pancho Villa's men are supposed to have buried. Others claim he found the Lost Butler Mine."

"I never heard of that," Clay said.

"Butler was an old prospector who worked this whole region during the early part of the century. Around 1924 he came high-stepping into town claiming he found a chimney of gold, a seam that gets pushed up out of the earth. He had a little gold with him, high-quality nuggets they say, but no one really believed the old man because he'd told one tale too many. They laughed him out of town. No one ever saw him again. Some say he couldn't relocate the chimney and was ashamed to come back. Others say he was followed and killed. Legend has it the gold will be found with his bones. No one had any idea of even the direction of the mine, let alone its location. For years people on both sides of the river have searched for the lost mine, and a lot of money has been made from selling bogus maps of the location. The myth says whoever finds the lost mine will have bad luck."

"That leaves out the Haro family," I said. "They've had enough good luck for three families."

My father looked at me pityingly. "The luck of the devil. I do happen to know the true story of how Haro made his money, though most folks around here don't."

"So tell us," I said.

"The Texas veterans land scandal mean anything to you?"

Clay knew instantly what my father referred to, but I remembered it only vaguely as something studied and forgotten from Texas history class in high school.

My father explained. "Right after the war the land commissioner, a man by the name of Giles, proposed a constitutional amendment to provide veterans with land. The deal was the state would buy the land at market prices, then resell it to veterans for low interest and a long mortgage. The state legislature appropriated a hundred million dollars to subsidize the purchase of land. You have any idea how much money that was in the early fifties? A piece of pie that big just begged fraud, and that's what happened. Suddenly a handful of businessmen started entertaining black veterans at private clubs. Bottle clubs they called them in those days because public bars were illegal. Some of these big suits recruited a few Mexicans to handle part of the swindle by bringing in the Mexican American veterans. One of those working the scheme was Federico Haro. I'm not saying he knew he was helping commit fraud and rob people. He may have believed what the big boys told him. Whichever, he helped dupe the veterans into signing applications for state loans to buy land. The racketeers bought up big parcels of land cheap, subdivided it into tracts, and resold it to the state at inflated prices for resale to other veterans. I don't know the details, but Haro must have gotten his money up front, or in land. When the scandal broke,

Land Commissioner Giles admitted taking bribes to push the amendment and approve the inflated valuations of the land. He resigned along with three of his staff. There was only one criminal indictment and that was thrown out on a technicality. In my opinion they should all have gone to jail.''

''How did you find out Haro was involved?'' Clay asked.

''I took an interest because a couple of my friends from the service signed over their land rights. Most of the land was in South Texas, by the way, where Haro came from originally. I figure the big rancher he worked for was in on the deal. Of course, Haro already owned his land here in Presidio County before the land fraud. Anyhow, when his name came up in one of the articles in the Cuero newspaper that broke the land fraud story, it jumped out at me.''

One crooked land commissioner. Now there was another land commissioner involved in trouble over expensive horses mysteriously poisoned. Was that a swindle, too? Insurance fraud? Is that what J. Frank Causley thought? I wondered how his investigation into the horse poisonings was coming.

Clay was saying something to me, and I had to ask him to repeat it.

''Show your dad the medal. It's still in your jacket pocket, isn't it?''

I handed my father the box and let him open it. He lifted the medal out, turned it over in his hand, and peered so close he might have been smelling it. He needed glasses but he'd wait until life was a blur before he'd do anything about it.

''Have you ever seen anything like that?'' I asked. He shook his head. ''But it reminds me of something I came across the other day. Just a minute...'' He jumped to his feet in one of his sudden spurts of energy and went inside.

We heard sounds of drawers being opened and shut in rapid succession. In a moment my father returned and dropped something into my lap.

I held it up so Clay could see, too.

"It's a heart," Clay said. It was indeed. A perfect heart, about an inch and a half at its width and an inch and a quarter deep. Made of silver, it had been engraved with vines and flowers on the front and back.

"I found that sometime in the late sixties, when I did a survey for the Nells Ranch on that section of land they bought from La Noria to straighten out the fence line and give the Nells a water well that Haro never used. I remember it like it was yesterday. It was right at the bottom of the cliff in the sand, looking as if somebody dropped it yesterday. I figured the cattle must have turned it up with their hooves like they do sometimes with arrowheads. I gave it to your mother, but she said she'd keep it for you. I came across it in that old bureau of ours when I went looking for an extra button to sew on my shirt last week. I cleaned it up a little. You take it with you. Make a nice locket, that milagro."

"Is that what it is? An offering to a saint?" I said, holding the heart cupped in my hand. "I've never seen one like this."

"It's old, like that medal of yours."

I leaned over and kissed my father on his cheek. He patted my hand absently, watching the road. I looked, heard the soft hum of a well-tuned motor. In a couple of minutes my father's pickup came over the hill and down the gravel drive, Charlie behind the wheel. Before he ever got out of the truck, he had his head out, saying, "Have you heard the news?"

"They already told me about the evangelista," my father said.

"No, not the evangelista. There has been another murder. On the Haro ranch."

"Alicia?" It came out louder than I intended.

Charlie was extricating himself from behind the wheel now. No easy task for one of his bulk.

"No, somebody shot Eliseo Silva in the back of the head. When he didn't come in for supper, his son went looking for him but couldn't find him. Finally, the ranch hands woke up Señor Haro, and he ordered them to borrow the hunting dogs from the Nells Ranch. They found Eliseo in one of the old line-shacks."

My father put it into words for all of us. "What the hell is going on around here?"

Clay and I helped Charlie carry in the seven bags of groceries, but my father insisted on putting them away. "Or I'll never find anything," he said. We sat on the porch listening to him bang cupboard doors, saying nothing more about the murder at La Noria until my father joined us. There was little more Charlie could add, except that Andalon had left a deputy on watch for the night.

"Charlie, Texana and Clay stayed to give you a ride back," my father said. "If you don't have pressing business, I wish you'd hang around the trading post."

"I can do that," Charlie said, knowing without being told why my father made the request. He got up from the rocking chair, went inside, and came back with his one change of clothes folded neatly over his arm. He shook my father's hand, patted Woo Hoo on the head, gave Willie's ears a quick rub, and said, "I'm ready when you folks are." He picked up a paper bag he'd kept apart from the groceries. "I bought some polish and a dustcloth as a present for Bess," he said.

On the way home Charlie caught us up on the news from Presidio, including the fact that the taxi driver had confessed to the murder of the German colonel and had been sent to await trial in the *penitenciaría* in Chihuahua.

FIFTEEN

CADILLAC CHARLIE opened his baby lips, scooped in a spoonful of caramel custard, swallowed, and said, "Everybody sure seems tense. How long have things been like this?"

I looked around the room at Claudia, her family, and the Corteses, the Munozes, the Acalas, and others grouped to one side, and Clay and me, Elvia, Irene, Gwen Masters, and an almost equal number of friends on the other side. While not entirely divided by race, since Pete Rosalas and his numerous family members filled in the middle ground, and Father Jack changed sides with every refill of his plate, a line had clearly been drawn. It hurt my heart to see resentment and suspicion separating us. Somehow we'd lost our sense of trust and harmony, our tolerance for differences, our appreciation for commonalities.

Clay and I had brought Charlie with us to the rectory *posada*. Since Father Jack's house is too small for a full dinner, it was a special dessert night in which all the best cooks tried to surpass one another in whipping up a specialty. The children loved the event because they could come and go, getting a sweet and returning to help build adobe mud snowmen in the backyard, supervised by eighty-year-old Juan Onda, who had built many of the adobe buildings on both sides of the border.

"Except for the Christmas Eve posada," Father Jack said, his voice carrying over the ranchero music played by the five-piece local band squeezed into one corner of the living room, "I like dulces night the best of the whole season." His plate overflowed with sweets: crystallized orange slices; *gaznates*—cornets of thin dough filled with coconut paste; *bizcochos*—cookies flavored with anise and clove; acid-sweet tamarind candies; and sweetened cream cheese with *queso de tuna*—prickly pear preserves; plus assorted squares of bright jellies and custards.

"I see you're all staring at my plate," Father Jack said. "No doubt you envy my capacity. I have to be diplomatic, you know, and at least taste each dessert, otherwise the cooks feel slighted." He glanced around. "I'd feast on cheerful looks, only I don't see many."

"Too much talking and not enough eating," Gwen Masters said in a disapproving voice. "If they'd keep their mouths full, they wouldn't have time to slander anybody."

"It's because of Claudia's primo hermano's confession. The family's lost hope," Irene said. "I'm glad school was out for the holidays today. Claudia's grandchildren have been upset by the adults' tension. I don't like it when the kids repeat what they hear at home. We've had two fights this week."

I could feel myself flush. Irene saw my face. "Oh, Texana, I'm sorry.... I didn't mean, that is…"

I shook my head. "It's all right, Irene. I know the Reyeses feel I'm somehow to blame."

"Well, you're not," Clay said. "I'm getting a little tired of Claudia's sulking."

"Amen," Gwen almost shouted.

Father Jack said, "I've tried to talk Claudia into a better frame of mind, but anger feeds on itself." He sounded resigned. "Next Sunday's collection will be for money to help support her cousin's family."

Gwen said, "You'd think two gruesome murders on this side would take folks' minds off this taxi driver—"

The band stopped playing just in time for the last half of Gwen's comment to resound across the room.

"What the devil do you mean, you damned old gringa? It's just another Mexican in jail to you, isn't it? That's where you think we all should be. Let me tell you, it's you Anglos who are the outsiders here. Mexicans lived here long before whites moved in."

"You shut your mouth, Tommy Lopez," Elvia shouted. "You've been here five months. What do you know about it?"

"I know more than some mojada in a hurry to marry an Anglo college boy so she can become gringafied!"

"Sí, hombre, el mexicano…" Elvia let loose a string of pure gutter talk, *calo,* picked up from working in the prison, no doubt. The insults she hurled went well outside my experience of border talk, but judging by the look on Tommy Lopez's face he understood.

"Tía Taco," he shouted, the Spanglish equivalent of calling a black an Uncle Tom. The whole room buzzed with comments and shifted with movement.

Elvia shouted back, "Hijo de puta," son of a whore, and Tommy Lopez hurled himself at her.

Father Jack shoved his plate into my hands. In one stride he stepped between the two combatants. "Enough!" he shouted.

The entire room fell silent. The priest's fierce blue eyes swept the small space, catching every eye, searching every face. "We've had too much talk and not enough understanding, too much accusation and not enough forgiveness, too much hate and not enough love. Hate kills, though no one cries murder, but the sin is mortal to the one who hates. Now, collect your children, take them home, and put them to bed. Then get down on your knees and ask God's forgiveness and the light of His understanding, that this community might be healed."

Elvia and Tommy stood there, either afraid or too embarrassed to move.

Around the rest of the room, eyes dropped, heads bowed, feet shuffled. People got their coats, mothers and fathers went to collect their children, women hurried to collect the dishes they had brought, and a handful of teenagers giggled nervously and were shushed loudly by their parents. In family groups Polvo departed and awakened the silent night with slamming car doors and accelerating motors. Tommy, standing alone, gave Elvia a long stare, someone handed him his coat, and he grabbed it and left.

Clay put his arm around me on one side and Elvia, who had finally moved back to us, on the other.

"Let's go to my house and have coffee," Irene suggested. We nodded agreement, and Irene explained that they had to stop and pick up the baby. "We left her with old Mrs. Peña for the evening, but my door is open. Go in and make yourselves at home. I'll go get our coats."

While Irene went to the bedroom, Elvia went to Father Jack, touched his arm lightly, looked him in the eye, and apologized.

He smiled down at her. "Dear child, I've had more bouts with the old devil temper than I care to think about. Take my advice, when you want to make a point, stay calm. Otherwise, all anyone will remember is how mad you were. There's no strength in anger."

Someone knocked at the door. Father Jack answered it, and I recognized Andalon's voice as the priest welcomed him in. He looked around the room and said, "I guess I missed the party."

"We closed out a little early," Father Jack said.

Irene and Elvia left to pick up Esperanza, but Andalon

asked Clay and me to stay a minute. Father Jack invited us into the kitchen, fixed the sheriff a sandwich as thick as a building, and brought it to the table where we sat.

"Just what I need," Andalon said, looking down at the contents of his plate. He lifted the sandwich and took a manful bite. Then he caught our intense stares. "What do you want to know first? Why I'm here, or what I've learned about the murders?"

"We had some unpleasantness here this evening," Father Jack said. "Most on our minds is the German colonel's murder. It's stirred up the whole community. Have you heard anything about what's going to happen?"

He shook his head despairingly. "There's nothing new there, and there won't be. The federales have a man who confessed to the crime. Whether he really is guilty or was persuaded to be, it's over. I understand the German consulate in Mexico City is satisfied, and I know the Mexican authorities are. That ends it."

Father Jack said, "So the poor man goes to jail for who knows how many years so the authorities can close the case."

"It happens in this country, too, Father," Andalon said. "Not nearly as often and not so obviously, but it happens. Justice and the law don't necessarily have a lot in common."

Father Jack said, "I know, Andalon. It's a good thing for us your brand of law enforcement carries the weight of both. Now enjoy your food and we'll leave you alone."

"Actually, I came to the posada for more then a free meal, though I admit I missed lunch, and home and food are a long way yet. I have some good news for you, Texana. I'm speaking out of turn, maybe, and what I say stays in this room, but I found something in the line shack besides Eliseo's body. There were four empty five-pound containers of gopher pellets. You can buy them at garden centers. I know the insurance investigator talked to you about the feed sack he found with the trading post name on it, but it looks to me like somebody used the line shack to store the pellets and refill the used feed sack from your place.''

"Does Mr. Causley know about this yet?" I asked.

"He does. I called him as soon as I found the containers. Somebody had tossed some burlap bags over them, but otherwise they weren't hidden. Causley spent most of yesterday with me going over that shed. I'll say this for him, he knows his business.''

"So Texana is in the clear?" Father Jack said.

"Causley doesn't confide in me, but he headed straight for La Noria headquarters to talk to Lalo last night, and he was expected at the main house this morning when I stopped to get statements from the rest of the hands and the family.''

I said, "Thanks, Andalon, for telling me about this." Clay got to his feet. "We'd better get going. Irene will have that coffee made by now." We left Andalon finishing his meal, and Father Jack showed us to the door.

"Be careful," he said as we left. "Something ugly is happening around here."

Outside, the moon backlit thin clouds like a lamp draped with a veil. We drove to Irene's house behind the school, but not even the Christmas lights of Polvo alleviated the dark tension of my mind. I believe in evil, in its power to grow and corrupt and destroy. Something evil had come among us, here, where the term "good neighbors" had always been more, much more, than mere words.

Irene opened the door to welcome us in before we'd even gotten out of the pickup. We had coffee and brandy, I cuddled my goddaughter in my lap, and for the rest of the evening I felt the joy of shared experience, the bond of friendship, the love that pushes back loneliness and makes life bearable.

SIXTEEN

On Saturday the Presidio Livestock Show was held at the Agriculture Center on the fairgrounds. Most of our community celebrations and events are held during the days of fall or winter, when the morning dawns cold but more often than not warms with the rising sun to moderate temperatures.

Clay had left at five a.m. to help receive the animals and organize the judging. For me the livestock show meant good gasoline sales for the day. Most of Polvo would drive in. Even those whose children weren't showing livestock would be related to or a close neighbor of some child with a calf or donkey or goat to exhibit. It was a major event, with rides, cotton candy, corny dogs, and music. The day-long event meant Polvo would have no *posada* that evening. Given the state of tension in the community, it came as a much-needed break.

By midmorning, when Irene came in, I'd had thirty-nine customers for gas. We'd been so busy Charlie and I both had worked the counter. Now I took a break and invited Irene into the back.

Striking in a purple broom skirt and a blouse of red and purple in a swirling print that suited her fair skin and the mass of gray-streaked, unruly hair, she folded her legs under her on the couch. She was a woman of generous proportions, not so tall as I, but not so angular either. Rubenesque was the word. In the year and a half I had known her, her strength of character had become apparent. After her divorce, she had earned her college degree, her teaching certificate, and had gotten her first job. Like so many middle-aged women who had married as teenagers and begun a family, Irene had found herself after forty.

"Thank you for talking sense to Elvia."

"About all I did was listen. Elvia did most of the talking," I said truthfully. "You're feeling okay with it then, her doubts about marrying Kyle?"

"Okay!" Irene whooped. "I'm ecstatic. Kyle is a nice boy. Someday he'll be a nice man. But ready for marriage and responsibility he's not. He thinks Esperanza is a cute toy to hand over to me or Elvia when she cries or has dirty diapers. Elvia's twice as bright and heaps more mature than my son."

"Kyle will come into his own one day."

"Now that sounds like a remark I might make trying to be diplomatic to the parent of a backward student. Don't look embarrassed. I know my son and I love him, but he's totally self-absorbed, like someone I used to be married to."

I dislike hearing stories titled "The One Hundred and Ten Ways I Hate My Ex." The tales all sound alike. I think rehashing past miseries is an exercise in negativity. Whenever someone dredges up the bitterness of a former relationship, I always find myself wondering why the person didn't pack a bag after the first month. I dodged this one by asking Irene how she thought Kyle would take Elvia's decision.

"He'll be hurt and resentful. He'll spend the entire holiday trying to change her mind. Then he'll head back to college in a sulk. Once he's been there awhile he'll realize he's relieved."

"So it works out best for both of them."

"Absolutely. Now, I have something else to tell you, the real reason for my visit." She leaned forward. She lowered her voice though there was no one to hear except Phobe, perched on her box in front of the window and staring out into the desert. "Elvia and I have been discussing this, and we think we know who spray-painted your storefront. Tommy Lopez."

"Because of the things he said last night?"

"Because of his attitude. I suspected him when it happened. Normally I would never reveal confidential information about a student, but I realized last night that this situation is getting out of hand. His grandmother has guardianship because of problems in the home environment. I made some calls to the junior high school in El Paso where he was enrolled last year. He has a history of arrests for truancy and defacing public buildings. What got the kid removed from his home was the frequency of these problems plus the fact that he stole a car belonging to the principal, spray-painted gang symbols all over it, and left it parked in front of the school. The rival gang members cruising the neighborhood shot at it until it looked like a sieve."

"I see."

"There's more. He stirs up trouble at school among the other children. He enjoys setting them against one another and then standing back and watching them start to distrust one another. He's the classic case of the kid who instigates all the trouble but manages never to get caught. He has even tried to start a gang here. Can you imagine? Thank goodness he'll go to high school next year and be some Presidio teacher's problem and not mine. I'm going to tell Dennis about Tommy and let the deputy keep an eye on him."

I heard a tap at the door, and Charlie stuck his head around it, saying, "Excuse me. Pete is here asking for you."

Irene got up, smoothed her skirt, and said she had to go anyway. "I'm on my way to Presidio to see my students' entries in the livestock show." We walked out to the front together.

"Hey, ladies, a fine day, isn't it?" Pete said with a grin broad enough for two on his face. "Come outside and see what I've got. You, too, Charlie."

How could we resist?

Pete held the front door open, and we walked out and stood on the porch looking at his prize.

The Jeep was used, dusty, and had tires that looked older than I am.

"Isn't it something?" Pete said. "I got it at the sale in Presidio."

Charlie said, "Pete, it still has the Border Patrol stripe on it."

"That's okay. They painted over the emblem."

"Are you giving up the tractor as transportation?"

"Not on your life. But I figure while the border closing is in effect this vehicle is going to keep me out of trouble. You know what they did? Put a barricade across my foot bridge. My own bridge I been using for twenty years at least. If I drive to the crossing upstream, everybody knows my tractor. In this Jeep nobody will notice I don't belong on this side."

"Aren't you afraid you might get shot at driving it on the other side?" I said.

"Only once or twice. Word passes. After that, folks on the other side will start hitching rides with me. Maybe I'll charge a fee. Become some big rico and build me a swimming pool."

Irene laughed, said she'd see us in Presidio later, and left. Charlie offered Pete some polish for the Jeep. Pete looked at him in astonishment, saying, "Man, that's nice of you. But what for? It just gets dirty again.'' Charlie looked as baffled at Pete's attitude as Pete was at his. Two more customers pulled in for gas, and Charlie went in to ring up the sale.

Pete said to me, "I'm going to drive you around the other side and help you collect what's owed you." I didn't ask him how he knew about my stagnant sales. Pete notices everything, including an empty parking lot and sale items twice reduced.

"Thanks, Pete. I drive up in a Border Patrol Jeep, smile, and ask for money. Right. That will work." I know Pete well enough to pull some sarcasm occasionally.

Pete put his foot on the bottom step and wagged his finger at me, saying, "You know in Mexico we ride the money. You give me credit for thirty days, I say, not to worry, I'll pay you. *When* is something else. I'll ride the money for as long as you'll let me." He made a fist with one hand and struck the open palm of the other hand. "Time to get tough."

"I don't even have a rancho or pueblo name for some of my credit clients, just a description, like dead tree canyon. We'll get lost."

"I got that fixed. The Letter Man is coming with us. He knows where everybody lives. Even the really hard to find ranchos. See, we scare them a little with the Border Patrol vehicle. They come out thinking somebody in the family has been caught and personally escorted home, and the Letter Man steps out. They see him, they relax, they're relieved. Everybody trusts the Letter Man."

"When do we leave?"

"I'm at your service now."

"You sure those tires will make it?"

"Saint Rita will protect us. Also I have a fine spare and a portable tank to fill leaks."

"I'll get the accounts book, a few groceries for the Letter Man, and tell Charlie where we're going."

We picked up the Letter Man at his lean-to shed a few hundred feet on the other side of the river from the crossing. Except for a cot bed and a box of clothes, most of his shed housed chickens. He sat outside in a broken chair under a salt cedar. A yellow tabby cat as bony and thin as its owner rubbed against his ankles, but ran for cover as we drove up.

The Letter Man's real name is Glafiro Paredes. He is old, but like many in Mexico he doesn't know his age because he has no birth certificate. His job is delivering the mail that arrives marked general delivery, El Polvo, for people living in the backcountry on the Mexican side of our border. He does this once or twice a month for a few pesos per letter. In exchange the recipient of each letter gets a religious tract thrown in for free. A Church of Christ in El Paso provides the tracts. Glafiro preaches the Gospel by example, and thus is respected. And no one knows the backcountry better.

As Pete stopped the Jeep, the Letter Man pushed himself up out of the chair, his smile bright with gold fillings. He put on his straw hat, worn winter and summer because it is the only one he owns, and proclaimed himself ready for our adventure.

"How do you like my new transport?" Pete asked him as we started out.

The Letter Man rubbed his hand over the seat covers, looked around the interior as another man might check out a hotel suite, and declared it to be a fine vehicle for border travel. His own mode of transportation hardly qualifies for the term, a truck that runs more on the power of prayer than on gas and is as worn by time as its owner.

"Señora Jones, you tell me the names of those you wish

to visit, and I will direct you where the family lives,'' the Letter Man said.

I showed him the list; he nodded solemnly as he read the names, and directed Pete to first go due south on a seemingly abandoned road that rambled like a cow path toward the horizon of blue mountains beneath a clear sky. Our first stop came three miles out at a square adobe sitting in the middle of acres of bare earth. The curious sight of a Border Patrol vehicle on this side of the river brought the family of five outside, parents and children lined up unsmiling, as if for an execution. The Letter Man stepped out and went to speak with the father of the family, and after polite greetings presented my bill. The husband spoke a few words to the wife, who disappeared inside, returning with a tin box which the man then opened, counting the cash into the Letter Man's hand.

This routine was repeated along the miles at single jacales made of scavenged lumber and tin, clustered adobes of the *ejidos,* and one home built in a cave, its opening now faced in adobe bricks, the windows outlined in bright red paint. However modest the dwelling, with few exceptions the dirt yards were swept clean, the children were dressed neatly if in many-times-handed-down clothes, and some attempt had been made at decorating for the Christmas season with homemade crèches, the Holy Family figures of straw that reminded me of the figures left to frighten the *evangelista.*

At most homes we had no trouble collecting the bills. Families with fathers or sons working in the U.S. usually tried to make it home at Christmas and Easter, and so had cash on hand. At one spot at the end of a rutted road stood a house built of old lengths of boards so thin and flimsy it looked as if the winds of spring would blow it away. A strong-looking woman emerged, and after the Letter Man explained our mission, she told us, "My husband has abandoned me." She offered us a fat puppy as payment. I tore up the bill and gave her the bag of canned goods I'd brought to leave with Glafiro. She said God would bless me.

Glafiro looked at the last name on the list and told me, "This ejido I do not know." We asked the woman for directions.

"That place is over a day's walk from here," she said, then explained the signposts to look for, a large boulder shaped like a camel, and a narrow canyon with no way out. We would find the *ejido* at the end. "It is very remote, and they do not welcome strangers."

SEVENTEEN

THE EARTHEN-COLORED Ejido de los Santos mounted the rock-strewn hillside one adobe at a time, like giant building blocks. Goats, pigs, and chickens roamed among the houses. Perched at the top of the hill, blindingly white against the blue sky, was a twin-towered church. Barefoot children played on a rusting swing set at the foot of the hillside. A little boy in plaid shirt and pants rolled up to fit his short legs pointed out the house of the *presidente* of the communal ranch, the third from the top of the hill. Single file we climbed the narrow path that wound around the adobes. Not one face appeared at a window to see who we were.

The whitewashed house of the *presidente* had one door, one window, and a life-size painting of the Virgin of Guadalupe in vivid red, green, and yellow, her figure framed by a sunburst, her feet resting on the quarter moon supported by an angel. Glafiro stopped five feet short of the door and called out, "Hola, amigo! Buenos días!"

The door opened and a man stepped out. Short, dark, with a rounded face, he wore a Dallas Cowboys cap, a white undershirt, brown pants, and leather sandals.

Glafiro greeted the man with a smile and the handshake of northern Mexico, a palm to palm hand-wrestling position with a light touch. He explained that we had come a long distance to speak on a business matter.

The *presidente's* name was Jesusito, and he invited us in. The one room was spotless; a curtain hanging over a rope hid what was probably the sleeping area. A table draped in oilcloth and covered in santos, family pictures, candles, a mosaic cross, and flowers served as a family altar. A few wooden chairs, another table, and a shelf for dishes completed the decor.

The *presidente* invited us to sit down and offered us water. Speaking for us all, Glafiro said, "Gracias, but we have no thirst." The Letter Man was being tactful. Most village wells are polluted, and we had brought along our own water in the Jeep.

Glafiro asked after the health of the *ejidatarios* and the well-being of the *ejido* in general before mentioning the reason for our visit. One of the largest owed me, the bill amounted to six months' worth of charges for lamp oil, flour, sugar, coffee, salt, lard, and other staples. Glafiro presented it to Jesusito.

He looked at it, shook his head sadly, and pushed it back across the table toward Glafiro, saying, "Dios se lo pague."

God will repay you. Meaning the *ejido* could not.

Jesusito told us, "This man Raul, who did the buying for the ejido and who signed his name to this paper, has robbed us as he has robbed you. This thief took not only the money we entrusted to him to spend wisely for supplies, but he stole also the great and good santos from our church, many of them older than living memory. All because he became greedy after listening to an evangelista who came to this and other villages to steal souls. She preached from the back of a pickup. She said the statues were an abomination to God and we would prosper only when the idols were gone from the church. She offered money for the statues to show her good faith and God's blessing. I denounced her as a bruja. The people threw stones at her to drive her away, but I could see the greed and weakness in the eyes of some, and I knew that she had put a spell on them. She is evil, this young woman. The santos are our souls and are not for sale. If she returns I will not answer for what may happen."

"Young?" I said. "You say she was young? You're sure she wasn't middle-aged, a small woman with long gray hair?"

Jesusito looked startled. My abrupt interruption of the male conversation in this place was a breach of good manners. He didn't lose his.

"She was a young woman who should have been at home with her children."

"You have been very generous with your time, señor," Glafiro said, rising to signal our leaving. I picked up the bill from the table, folded it, and held it out to Jesusito. "It is paid in full," I told him.

He accepted it, hiding a second time his surprise at my forward behavior. "Are you a Catholic?" he said.

"I am jubilado—retired."

"You will come back," he said. "In the end, we all come back. The Church is our mother."

Pete, who had remained uncharacteristically silent throughout, waited until we were outside the adobe, then said to Jesusito, "A word with you, señor?"

The *presidente* nodded and the two stepped aside. Glafiro and I made our way down the steep path followed by bleating goats and stepping over sleeping pigs. In a few minutes, Pete joined us in the Jeep, started the motor, and headed out into the desert, a look of relief on his face.

Finally he spoke. "This thief Raul, seems he came back to ask his sweetheart to run away with him and make a new life in America. The girl's father saw him and the ejidatarios chased him down."

"What happened?" I asked.

Pete took a deep breath. "They tied him to a tree, poured gasoline on him, and struck a match."

"God forgive them," Glafiro said.

"To them, it was justice."

We said little on the way back. Knowing that the sort of religious fervor that could result in such an event was something one ran into all over Mexico didn't make it any easier to understand or accept.

Pete dropped off Glafiro, then left me in Presidio, where I ate lunch, did some shopping, and caught the winner's presentation at the end of the poultry judging, the last event of the stock show. Afterward, I located Clay, and as the sun set we sat on a bench in Saint Francis's Plaza watching the living Nativity, eating corny dogs dipped in hot mustard, and listening to the carolers sing "Oh Come, Emmanuel" in Spanish. Between bites, I told what I'd learned that day about the *evangelista.*

"So Alicia showed up at the ejido alone," Clay said, licking mustard from his fingers. "That doesn't prove Electra Reaves sent her. Alicia might have gone on her own."

"Yes, she might have, but she was inspired by Electra, whether she did it on her own or at Electra's request. It was dangerous enough if they'd gone together, but to let Alicia go alone..."

"Are you worried that Alicia may still be carrying out the evangelista's mission now that Electra is dead?"

"I don't know. I'd like to ask her about it."

Clay said, "Old Eliseo's funeral is Monday afternoon at the ranch. You can ask her then. Speaking of the Haros, I picked up some gossip. Rumor is the old man is going to leave most of his estate to the grandson Henry."

I stopped wolfing down the corny dog long enough to say, "How'd you hear this?"

"The usual way. General gossip. Carlos and his father have been arguing over this for some time, Tina the cook overheard, and she told her family, and her brother who owns the hardware store here suggested at a businessmen's lunch meeting that they should invite Henry to speak and explain some of their needs because he was going to be important to the county not just politically, and that with the kind of money Henry Haro would come into, he'd make a name for the county and bring in more business. After the meeting someone asked how he knew Henry would get the money. Now everybody knows."

"Or thinks they do. If it's true it would explain some of Don Federico's remarks the day Father Jack and I were there."

We finished our food, wiped our hands on the paper napkins, and took our trash to the garbage barrel.

"I have some more news," Clay said. "The military garrison in Ojinaga has been beefed up to two hundred and fifty men, and your comandante friend has been replaced with a General Anaya. The Ojinagans that came over today are jumpy as hell about it."

"Is it because of the German's murder?"

"The murder provided an excuse to bring up more troops. Publicly they're saying the buildup is part of ongoing military training. Talk is it's to stop the drugs and weapons smuggling."

"Or to oversee the drug war. Keep the troops in line, so to speak, behind the drug lord the military is betting on to win. I don't like what's happening to the border," I said, my spirits dipping. "Too much change."

"The border is change. That's the norm."

"World disorder is too much for me to cope with. I'll stick to pleasant topics. I caught the last judging. How'd the rest of the livestock show go?"

"Good thing you asked. It reminds me that we need to get out of here before one of those red second-place ribbons finds its way around a rock and comes flying at my head."

"Don't worry. Saint Francis will protect us."

"I seem to remember an earthquake in Italy a year or so ago that destroyed most of his basilica."

"I guess Saint Francis isn't as strong as he used to be. Let's go home."

EIGHTEEN

THE GRACE AND PEACE of God the Father and the Lord Jesus Christ be with you.''

Sunday Mass. We all come back, the *presidente* of the Ejido de los Santos had said, and here I was.

In our small church Father Jack did not need a microphone to make his deep voice resonate to the back pew where I stood, adding my voice to the other fifty-odd parishioners making the response, "And also with you." I spoke the words by rote, much in the same way I come here when the world presses too close. An automatic response from some need deep in myself.

But today the world had intruded even here. As the ritual of the Mass continued, the tension in the church, dense enough to inhale, evidenced itself in knowing sideways looks, backward glances at me from the front pews, and stiff spines and squared shoulders. A movement caught my eye. Claudia Reyes, three rows ahead on the inside edge of the pew, incessantly rubbed her ringed fingers against the polished back of the pew in front of her. Even Father Jack appeared unnaturally aware of each nervous cough and gesture.

Beneath the chasuble, his thick shoulders heaved with a shrugging motion as he grasped both sides of the lectern as if he might hurl it across the church.

"I take my homily from the First book of Kings, the story of Elijah, told by the Lord to go out and stand on the mountain before the Lord. Elijah heard a strong wind tearing at the mountain, but the Lord was not in the wind.

Elijah felt the tremor of an earthquake, but the Lord was not in the earthquake. After the earthquake, there was a fire, but the Lord was not in the fire. Then there was a still voice, and Elijah hid his face before God.''

He paused, leaned over the lectern, wrinkled his forehead in a frown so deep his eyebrows met above his nose, and said, "This community has been torn by the winds of rumor, split by the upheaval of events, burned by the fires of racism. Now is the time for silence and reconciliation so that we, like Elijah, may hear the quiet voice of God.'' He let go his hold on the lectern and dropped his arms to his sides. "I ask you each to sit quietly for a few minutes and meditate upon this.'' He went to his chair.

For a full three minutes not even a drawn breath brushed our ears. The priest rose, went to the altar facing us, and began the liturgy of the Eucharist.

Father, I prayed, open my heart and cleanse my mind of all vain, evil, and distracting thoughts.

"This is the Lamb of God,'' Father Jack intoned as he elevated the Host.

"Lord,'' we responded, "I am not worthy to receive you, but only say the word and I shall be healed.''

Those in the first row moved forward to receive communion, then the second, then the third. Claudia remained seated, her head bowed. Soon it was my turn. I rose and got in line. As I came up to Claudia's row, she stood and left the church down the outside aisle.

Whatever lay ahead, the hurt and misunderstanding remained like a bruise.

That afternoon I opened the trading post, and several of the community members who I felt had been boycotting me stopped to buy gas, canned goods, or a soft drink, make small talk, and pay their bills. Father Jack's words had touched some. At least two dozen children sorted through the candies I import from the other side, taking half an hour deciding whether to buy the mango and chile powder suckers or the tamarind spoons. Charlie, who was camping in the back lot, spent the time cleaning Bess inside and out, and Clay caught up on his reading until Phobe demanded attention. He took her outside for a walk to the river, where she would sit for hours if allowed, splashing the water with her wide paws, chasing lizards, and watching for the alligator gar swimming past.

It was a slow, easy day, and for the first time since the taxi driver and I had been detained in Ojinaga, in spite of Claudia's continuing animosity, I looked forward to the evening's *posada*. Four trailer homes had gone together to sponsor the sixth party of the novena of celebrations. I'd provided all the soft drinks for the event as my contribution, and Charlie had taken them over earlier during the day iced in coolers, so all we had to do to get ready was put on our coats. Charlie chauffeured us in Bess, carefully parking her far enough away from other vehicles that we walked half a mile to the first trailer. After the ceremonial arrival of the Holy Family, sheltered in a shrinelike hut covered with tin in the front of one of the trailers, we congregated around the bonfire built in the middle of the dirt street, roasting hot dogs.

Father Jack made the rounds, greeting each person by name and with a kind word. He stopped by Clay and me, a cheerful smile on his face, and asked how my bill collecting had gone with Pete in the driver's seat. I told him the day had been successful. I didn't tell him about the vigilante justice at the Ejido de los Santos. No point in spoiling Father Jack's convivial mood with news that would hurt him because of the dreadful act that had been committed.

Most people had brought folding chairs. After the meal

and piñata we sat around the fire and sang Christmas carols. I looked for Tommy Lopez, but if he was present he kept well away. I noticed Kyle had arrived home from college. He sat between his mother and Elvia, laughing and holding Esperanza, and I assumed by his carefree attitude that the talk between the two young parents had yet to take place. Apparently the point of Father Jack's homily had taken hold in the community. The divisions of race and friends evident since Claudia had walked out of the trading post during the first posada had vanished. Except for Claudia. She and her family had stayed away. Maybe I had Tommy Lopez's behavior to thank for the general change, as well as Father's Jack's words. The shock of Tommy's hatred had made the virulence of such feelings more evident than even Father Jack's words.

At the evening's close, Father Jack led us in a prayer of blessing for the community, then announced that if anyone from Polvo planned to attend old Eliseo Silva's ten o'clock graveside funeral rides would be available. The men doused the fire with buckets of water and spread the ashes thin. We folded up our chairs and went home.

NINETEEN

THE HARO FAMILY dominated the ring of mourners gathered around Eliseo Silva's grave. Not only Carlos was present, but Henry, the heir apparent, looking so much like his grandfather I felt I was seeing Don Federico in his youth. Beside Henry stood his father, Alberto, from San Antonio. Next came Eduardo, the entrepreneurial farmer from Presidio. I looked around. The two women of the household, Alicia and Don Federico's companion Severa Salinas were absent.

The ranch hands, Tina the housekeeper, our El Polvo group, and José Silva, the school-bus driver from Presidio who was Eliseo's cousin, stood opposite the black-garbed Haros. Eliseo's son Lalo had on a dark suit worn so infrequently that it showed pale dust lines on the shoulders from long months hanging uncovered in some closet. He looked tired and angry as he placed a corona of paper flowers on the handsome heavy casket with brass handles, no doubt paid for by Federico Haro. The old man, handsome in an impeccably cut suit, looked weary and more aged than I had ever seen him.

"Eliseo came to work for me as a boy," he had said in his brief eulogy. "He was a man of loyalty, and I regret his death more than I can say."

Andalon was also in attendance, whether in an official capacity as sheriff or out of respect for the Haro family, I didn't know.

Protected from the winds by the surrounding low hills, the private graveyard covered perhaps an acre several miles from the ranch headquarters and out of sight of the house. Around the scattered graves, the flat land stretched about as far as a football field. Beyond, the blue mountains, only a shade darker than the sky they seemed to touch, made belief in the infinite easy.

The private cemetery predated the Haros' ownership by many generations. Legend had it that the original owner of the ranch land discovered a child's solitary grave marked with a hand-carved rock bearing the name Jessie Ann. Beneath the stone, a faded page torn from the front pages of a Bible bore a plaintive plea in faint script: *Don't leave my little girl here all alone.* Soon after, the man fenced the cemetery in ironwork. Now it held a dozen or so graves, including a formal marker for the little Jessie Ann of unknown origins. One large headstone stood out amid the more modest markers of family members of the earliest rancher. This was the monument to Don Federico's wife, with his name and date of birth already carved beside hers, lacking only the date of death to be complete.

Father Jack made the sign of the cross over Eliseo's casket, saying, "May the Lord bless you and keep you. May His face shine upon you, and may He grant you peace," and the service was over.

The ranch hands loosed the ropes tied to pegs driven into the ground and lowered the casket into the grave. The Haro family stood quietly, waiting as Lalo sprinkled a handful of dirt onto the casket. The ranch hands put on their hats and left to get in their pickups and go back to work. Father Jack, one hand on Lalo's tense shoulder, stood speaking quietly into his ear. Everyone else talked quietly. I walked over to Carlos Haro and touched his arm lightly to get his attention.

"Nice of you to come, Texana," he said.

"I brought this along, if you still want it," I told him,

handing over the religious medal. "The evangelista gave it to me. After you told me it was old and possibly valuable, I thought I should offer to return it to her, but now…"

He looked at the medal as if not quite recognizing it, then took it and slipped it into his pocket. "I understand," he said quietly. "I heard about the thief that got Clay's present. I'm sorry about that. My offer still goes on any item of jewelry from the store. You drop in whenever you want. We'll pick out something special."

By now the rest of the Haro family had formed a phalanx behind their patriarch and were walking slowly toward their vehicles. Carlos followed, catching up to the others. Father Jack was removing the vestments he wore over his habitual jeans and shirt and folding them away in the case in which he carried everything he might possibly need for his mobile ministry. Lalo departed with José Silva and a handful of other men. Charlie stood in conversation with Tina, Don Federico's housekeeper. Clay joined me, and we walked around reading the names and epitaphs on the markers while waiting for Father Jack. The priest had called us at the last minute, asking for a ride to La Noria because his own vehicle would not start. Charlie had looked it over briefly, shaking his head in disbelief that anyone could allow the oil to be both so low and so dirty, and offering to rebuild the motor.

We passed among the graves, some so old the stone had crumbled. "These markers tell the history of this whole region in miniature," Clay said. "Look how they go, starting with the earliest dates in Spanish, changing to a mix of both languages, then to English, and lately a return to Spanish."

"What about this one, I said, pointing down at a flat square stone, neither Spanish nor English.

OSSA HUMILIATA.

"Latin," Clay said. "Something bones."

"The second word looks like humility."

Father Jack arrived beside us in time to hear my remark. "Humble bones," he said. "Maybe a self-effacing family member who died under the weight of some sin, or was just particularly pious." He apologized for keeping us waiting.

Clay said, "No problem. It's an interesting place, this. A peaceful spot to lie for eternity."

Father Jack said, "I wish Lalo felt that way. He is looking to avenge his father's death."

"Can't say as I blame him." Andalon joined us. "A cold-blooded murder, walking up behind the deaf old man and putting the gun to his head."

"You believe the killer came up behind Eliseo knowing he couldn't hear?" Father Jack said.

"That or knew him well enough for the old man to have no reason to be afraid to turn his back."

"Have you had any luck on the evangelista's murder?" the priest asked.

"If it was somebody from the other side there's nothing much I can do. Mexico isn't going to send one of its citizens to be tried over here. Unless they really want to get rid of the person themselves, of course. We're checking out where she came from. Or trying to, anyway. She has turned out to be something of an elusive lady."

I hesitated, then said, "I learned something yesterday that may be connected to the evangelista's death."

I explained about my backcountry bill collecting, the Ejido do los Santos, and what had happened, both to Alicia when she preached from the back of the truck, and to the thief of the santos.

Clay had already heard my story, of course. Andalon

showed no surprise at the events I described, but looked thoughtful. Father Jack looked incensed.

"I knew when I saw those statues in that house something was wrong. That foolish woman. And the Church is just as much at fault. From the beginning the Church did harm to Mexico. We didn't introduce the Indian to Christ, we superimposed Him on their gods and in the places those gods had been worshiped. Now, the intellectuals ignore the Church, the politicians use it when it suits them, and the ignorant mix a violent fanaticism with a faith grounded in a superstitious belief in witches, sorcerers, and curanderos. No wonder so many embrace other faiths..." He put his hand to his mouth. "Forgive me, I'm biting off two sins at once, scandal and despair."

Andalon said, "I think I need to have another talk with Miss Alicia. See you folks later." He made his way around the graves, out the gate, and to his car.

Father Jack looked so glum, Clay patted him on the back and said, "Come on home and have lunch with us."

I heard Father Jack's low, "Thanks, I'd like that. You'd think a man who spends most of his time with people would crave solitude, but the truth is I love company. I'd never have made it as a contemplative." He launched into a story about someone he'd been in seminary with who was now a monk living as a hermit in a desert monastery. I fell behind as he and Clay walked to the pickup. I gave the odd grave marker one last glance, wondering whether anyone could tell me the story behind it. I imagined something romantic and tragic, knowing the truth would probably be more simple and mundane.

By now all the Polvo people had left. As the last one out, I closed the low gate. I assumed the ranch hands would come back later and fill in the grave. Clay and Father Jack leaned on the pickup, waiting.

"What's the holdup?" I said. "Can't find the keys?"

"No, we've lost Charlie," Clay said.

"He was talking with Tina right after the service."

Clay laughed. "I'll bet he rode with her back to the house and she's fixing something for him to eat. Everybody always feeds Charlie. Let's go up to the house and check out the kitchen. We won't intrude upon the family, and Tina makes the best coffee in the world."

The drive took us five minutes. I expected to see Andalon's vehicle, but it wasn't there. The back door of the house stood propped open to let in the breeze, and we stepped inside. We heard several male voices speaking at once drifting down from upstairs. Evidently there was a family conclave being held in Don Federico's room. From the right, through the open kitchen door, came the sound of light female laughter. Women always like Charlie. Clay stood at the door and tapped. Tina looked up, smiled, and motioned us in.

She sat across the kitchen table from Charlie pushing more food at him. The smell of fresh coffee and *buñuelos,* deep-fried flour tortillas sprinkled with sugar and cinnamon, scented the big room, and made my stomach growl.

Tina welcomed us enthusiastically and jumped up for plates and cups. In one minute we were seated around the table enjoying the midmorning snack. We were settling in for second helpings when we heard the voices upstairs grow louder, become shouting.

I suggested it might be time for us to leave. We downed the last of our coffee, thanked Tina, and said good-bye. As we departed, the male voices were still arguing.

Clay got behind the wheel, Charlie rode on the jump seats in back with Father Jack, and I took the shotgun position, meaning that at the gates I got out and opened them. As we drove off, I twisted around to look back at the upper windows of La Noria. Not a face appeared to take notice of our going. I had an idea of what the Haro chat was all about. However long Eliseo Silva had worked for the family, his funeral wouldn't be the reason for grandson Henry to come all the way from Austin. Maybe the rumor Clay had heard about Henry was true, and Don Federico had called the men together to make clear his intentions for the dispensation of his fortune.

Charlie broke into my train of thought with a comment. "Tina says Alicia has gone back to California."

"When did this happen?" I asked.

"Over the weekend. Tina said Bascom Davis sent his private plane and Carlos drove her over to the Davis ranch and put her on board."

"After what happened to the evangelista I don't blame him," Clay said.

"Tina says Alicia has been crying a lot. I guess she didn't want to leave."

"If she were my daughter, I'd want her at home," I said. "I wonder if her mother knows what's been going on here."

"I have more news," Charlie bragged. "Guess who else has been sent home?"

I turned around in the seat to stare at him. "You don't mean—"

Not to be beaten to the punch line, he said, "Severa Salinas, with about ten suitcases of clothes that Tina packed. Don Federico escorted her to the car and had one of the ranch hands drive her to El Paso, where she caught a flight to Monterrey."

"He shipped her back to Mexico?" I said. "Alicia I can understand, but Señora Salinas…?"

Clay said, "Maybe Haro's found someone younger."

We ended our speculation on the Haro family at that and

went on to other topics for the rest of the drive. Even after the sadness of the funeral for a man who died out of time, the day felt somehow peaceful until we arrived back at the trading post and found J.F. Causley waiting for us.

TWENTY

WITH HIS BOOTS propped on the porch rail, the chair tilted back, and his Stetson slanted down over his eyes, Causley looked like an actor resting between takes of a western movie.

He seemed glad to see us, smiling as he shoved his hat back and getting up to shake hands and greet us as we reached the porch, even introducing himself to Charlie without mentioning his investigative status.

Susceptible to the warmth of the moment, I invited him to join us for a late, thrown-together lunch. He said yes.

While I fixed toasted cheese sandwiches, Charlie set up plates, glassware, and silverware buffet style on the counter and made instant tea. Carrots and celery sticks from the refrigerator, and we were done. I added a plate of Oreos for dessert. Father Jack asked about some of Causley's experiences as a Texas Ranger, then told a few tales of his own about his mission work in the inner city of Chicago. Charlie, shy around newcomers, warmed up to Causley enough to recount some adventures of his own across the border. Clay chimed in with his tales of the traveling vet. I think honors were equal all around for hyperbole and laughter.

"Time to hear from you, Texana," Father Jack said.

Clay said, "Tell J. Frank"—we'd graduated to a first-name basis—"about your arrest in Ojinaga."

The event was far enough past for me to appreciate the humor, and I explained, emphasizing my inability to talk because of my tooth, the taxi man's assumption that I was

drunk, and the *comandante's* stolen van and driving habits.
Even Father Jack and Charlie, who'd heard it before in a
more serious mode, laughed, and J. Frank hooted.

When we'd settled down, Charlie offered to drive Father
Jack home, and they left.

J. Frank turned to Clay, saying, "I'm heading home myself tomorrow. I thought I owed it to you, as the vet on the
case, to let you know the results of my investigation. Also
to let you know, Texana, that you're in the clear regarding
that feed sack."

Clay said, "You know who poisoned the horses."

J. Frank looked carefully at us both, one after the other.
"Not to prove, no. But I'm sure, and since it's not the
owners, I think the insurance company will be satisfied."

"I'm glad it wasn't Bascom Davis or Henry Haro," I
said. "I'd hate to think someone would buy such beautiful
animals only to kill them."

J. Frank shrugged. "That happens often enough."

"But not this time," Clay said, prompting him.

"No, not this time. I lifted fingerprints from those empty
gopher-pellet containers from that shed where the old Mexican was killed. I'd already asked for the Haro family to
let me print them and I compared them. I got a match for
the granddaughter, Alicia. Course, she said she sometimes
rode out that way by the shack, even went in because she
kept extra cubes there for the horses. She said she may have
touched the containers, moved them to get at the sacks of
cubes. She said she was in there more than once, but didn't
pay attention to what else was in the shed. Didn't recall the
containers. Weak story, but without a reason why she did
it, it's strong enough to keep her out of jail. Any lawyer
would argue the poisoner wore gloves, while the girl had
nothing to hide, including handling the containers."

J. Frank caught the look Clay and I gave each other and said, "What do you know? What happened?"

Clay said, "Did you tell Andalon about this?"

"I left a copy of my final report with him."

"The rumor is that Federico Haro is going to leave most if not all of his property to his grandson Henry," I said.

"You're thinking that the granddaughter may have been trying to ruin her cousin Henry's political career."

"It's a possibility."

Clay said, "We also found out just this morning at the funeral that Federico Haro had his granddaughter flown out of here on Bascom Davis's private jet Saturday."

"I can't believe it," I said, sitting down. "Alicia. She loves horses."

J. Frank gave a hard laugh. "It looks to me like the young lady may have done more than kill horses. There's Elisio's murder to answer for. Your sheriff friend know she's gone?"

Clay said, "He must have found out this morning, too. She wasn't at the funeral and he went by the house to talk to her. They must have told him she left."

"Sounds like I better go have a talk with him," J. Frank said. "Much obliged to you folks for the food and the information." He looked at me. "I'll show myself out. You sit there and rest easy. You look like you've had a blow."

Clay walked him to the door anyway. I looked up as he came back into the kitchen. "Are you thinking what I'm thinking," I asked him.

"That Alicia never went to California?"

"That's why Severa Salinas packed her bags for Mexico. She's meeting Alicia, to be chaperon and keep her out of trouble."

"More trouble."

"Alicia won't like life in Mexico," I said.

"If she killed Elisio, she'll have to learn to like it."

TWENTY-ONE

"I SEE YOU ARE wearing a milagro," Adelaida, Father Jack's housekeeper, said to me. "You should leave it with the saint, you know, if your heart is to be mended. If it is a broken heart, Saint Abelardo is best. If your heart gives you pain or flutters, curandera Rhea Fair heals with her prayers before God. Look at what she has done for me."

Adelaida held out both her hands, the knuckles swollen, the fingers bent from arthritis. "Before I prayed to Saint Rhea, I could not open my fingers. Now I can twist off bottle caps, and the pain is eased so much I hardly notice it. What would we do without the saints to help us?"

I touched her old, crippled hand gently, and said I was glad for her. "My milagro was a gift from my father, who found it long ago. I don't know who it belonged to or why it was lost."

"Then you should pray for the soul of the person whose heart hurt so much to have it made. Even now it will help."

"I'll light a candle for the person tomorrow."

Adelaida patted my hand, as if I'd responded like a good child. I guess to her eighty-odd years, I seemed young.

She turned away from me to talk to the person seated to her right. We were at the table in postmistress Lucy Ramos's house, one of four homes holding our seventh *posada*. I cut the tender slice of brisket on my plate with a fork, dipped the bite-size piece of succulent meat into the salsa, and put it into my mouth. I tried not to gulp it all down too fast. Good food should be savored, but this was so delicious I was tempted to stuff myself. After the Christmas *posadas* my New Year's resolution is always the same, lose the weight I've gained.

To slow my food consumption down I looked around the lovely room, the adobe walls painted half in green and half in rose with a yellow abstract design stenciled at the chair-rail level. Along one wall, Lucy had tiered shelves on which she displayed her collection of santos, hand-carved and painted saints, and *retablos,* painted plaques, all created to bless the home in which they resided. In Lucy's grouping the Holy Family, depicting Jesus as a small boy holding hands with Joseph and Mary, took pride of place in the center with Christmas lights strung around the figures. Nuestra Señora Soledad, hands clasped in prayer, wore a bright tin crown and a red robe. And my favorite, the Archangel San Rafael, held a staff in one hand and the symbolic trout in the other, making him look like a fly-fishing enthusiast with white wings. There were many others. Lucy had inherited the collection from her mother and grandmother, in whose household the saints had been venerated and prayed to on the family altar. From time to time, she added to it, so that there was no longer room on the shelves for them all.

At the narrow end of the dining room, Lucy's oldest son, a graphic artist working in San Antonio, had painted a map of the Trans-Pecos complete with all the area landmarks, such as Elephant Rock and Cathedral Mountain. All this talk of *milagros,* the figures of the saints, and now seeing the map on the wall—did anyone know where the *evangelista* sold the religious items she bought so cheaply on the other side? She had mentioned selling them, but not to whom.

I was in the crew that cleared the table and washed the dishes while the children gathered for the piñata game. While I scrubbed the cooking pans that had been soaking in warm, soapy water, Lucy dried and put them away. I asked her if she'd heard of anyone selling religious art in the area.

She said, "I saw a wonderful crucifix three months ago. I would have paid so much to have it my husband would have left me. I tell you, Texana, I was so moved when I saw it in Carlos's shop I almost wept. The face of Christ had a look of such suffering innocence I knew the artist truly understood the reality of the sacrifice of pure good. Right there I decided to buy it and give it to the Church." She dried her hands on her apron. "Carlos said it wasn't for sale, but you know me, I can bargain with the best. I thought he was just saying that to drive up the price. That Carlos, he wouldn't budge an inch."

"I wonder where Carlos got it. Did he say?"

"I asked, because of course I wanted to know if the artist might have more, but all he would tell me was that he bought it from a peddler on the other side."

"And he had this on display in his shop?"

Lucy shook her head. "Not really. I was there to buy a quinceañera gift for my granddaughter's coming-of-age party. When I saw the figure it was already boxed like it was waiting for me. Carlos had so many customers that day, I had to wait, but he saw me looking at it and left the man he was helping to come over and tell me it wasn't for sale. He took it out of my hand faster than I could ask him to name a price."

We'd emptied the sink, so we wiped the counter clean and put everything away. In the living room parents helped children into coats for the short walk home. The party was over. I said good night to Lucy, and found Clay and Charlie waiting outside for me. The drive was uneventful.

Charlie said, "Things are getting back to normal. Tomorrow I think I'll work on finishing that sign for the trading post."

TWENTY-TWO

I HAD BEEN to the church to light a candle as I had told
Adelaida I would do. Now I stood watching Charlie fill in
the line of perfect lettering with sure strokes of the brush.
Neither of us heard anything until a faint rub of sound
against the gravel caught our attention and we turned in
time to see the black Mercedes glide into the parking lot.
By the time we walked around the corner of the building,
the driver had stepped out.

Dressed casually in a zip-front leather jacket over a yellow turtleneck, with corduroy slacks and lace-up boots, he
removed his sunglasses and stood assessing the site and
situation. I say this because his expression, though neutral,
radiated intelligence, and he remained motionless except
for his eyes, which moved across the front of the building,
scanned the sweep of hills behind, and came to rest on
Charlie and me, catching us gawking at him because he
looked as out of place here as might the Eiffel Tower.

''He's military,'' Charlie said in a voice only I could
hear. I didn't question his assertion. Charlie is a Vietnam
vet, with an advanced degree in recognizing brass when he
sees it, dress uniform or plainclothes.

At that moment one of the German-flown Tornado fight-
ers burst out of the sky and passed directly overhead, bom-
barding us with surround-sound that pierced the head like
a lance. I clapped my hands over my ears as if such insub-
stantial flesh could muffle the decibel intensity.

The visitor followed the plane with his eyes, a matter of

seconds at that velocity. The sound wave flowed back at us for moments longer, but at last silence returned.

The visitor said, "I appreciate why the good people of the Trans-Pecos object to our military training out of Holloman." The voice was cultured and foreign, a German accent overlaid with the English of Britain.

"Maybe you could put in a good word for us," I said.

He gave a dry laugh, and withdrew a case from an inside pocket, slipped out a card, and presented it to me with a flourish that reminded me of some Continental scene from an Audrey Hepburn movie. The card informed me that he was Colonel Gerhard Max Graf, military attaché with the German embassy in Mexico City.

I felt a flutter of nervous tension. "I think I know, Colonel, why you're here."

"Let me reassure you, I am here only to verify certain details of the death of Colonel Herbert Heinkel. Your name came to me indirectly, shall we say."

I thought of Comandante Zurita. His first report would have contained no mention of me, but when he'd been removed from the command of the garrison, either he'd had an unpleasant chat with a superior, or one of his men had talked. In releasing me, he'd done only what any of his counterparts would have done under the circumstances. Only when a bigger boot comes along is an otherwise acceptable action counted as a mistake.

Graf took my silence for reticence, and said, "A mutual acquaintance vouched for you quite highly."

Would this man call the *comandante* a mutual acquaintance? "Maybe we'd better go inside, Colonel Graf. Charlie, will you take care of any customers?"

Charlie nodded, looking as if he wasn't sure if I'd be safe or not letting the man into the trading post. The colonel, perhaps sensing Charlie's mistrust, suggested we sit on the front porch. I borrowed one of Charlie's unused paint rags to dust off the seat of the chair so the colonel wouldn't get dirty.

"I didn't wish to mention any names in the presence of a third person," he said, his eyes straight ahead, "but Ghee speaks most highly of you."

I hadn't the wits to think of a comment that might not be injudicious, so again I stayed mute.

"I see you are as discreet as he said. Please understand, there is no question of my entertaining any suspicion against you regarding the death. Merely that I wish to ask you to tell me what you recall, particularly before you entered the taxi."

I told him. For the next fifteen minutes he asked questions, and I answered.

Finally, he said, "Was there nothing that struck you as odd or unusual about the scene?"

"No," I said, without thinking.

"This frozen ice treat melting down his shirtfront, for instance?"

"The ice pop? Those are sold all over Mexico. What about it?"

"Did you see the vendor?"

I thought back to the plaza. There had been several vendors, a shoeshine man, another selling bread.

"No, I didn't. The ice pop vendors have small metal pushcarts. I didn't see anyone with a cart."

"I wouldn't have thought there would be much trade in ice pops in winter, even here."

"Of course. You're right. I never thought of that."

"You had more to worry about than seemingly inconsequential details. I believe this is what occurred. Colonel Heinkel was sitting in the taxi, the vendor leaned in the window using this ice pop to hide the knife in the same hand—''

I said, "He'd be talking, too, nonstop, like all the street vendors do, pushing their junk at you, and asking you to buy."

Graf said, "He drops the ice pop, Heinkel sits up straight and looks down at his ruined shirt, and the vendor rams in the knife."

I drew a deep breath at the thought. The colonel was watching me now. Judging my reaction?

"Or I could have done it. Said to Colonel Heinkel, one tourist to another, excuse me, but could you help me? Is that what you're thinking?"

Graf smiled, showing teeth so perfect they looked capped. "Ghee said you were direct. You could have, yes, but I am unable to discover a reason why. There was no robbery. Heinkel still had his wallet and money, and gold cuff links. We are sure it wasn't anything to do with drugs, so…"

"That leaves something personal."

"Yes."

"It wasn't the taxi driver. You should have seen his face when I told him the man was dead."

"I had a talk with the driver, in the presence of the Mexican officials, of course. The man admits to being paid a modest sum to be available on the square at a particular time to insure that Heinkel would be his passenger, then make some excuse and leave, telling the colonel he would be away only a moment, but to remain absent for ten minutes. He was told someone wished to delay Heinkel leaving Mexico for a short time. The driver needed the money. He accepted it. As he walked back to the taxi and saw you getting in, he thought Heinkel must have grown tired of waiting and left. He was truly in great fear when he understood what had happened. It took him some time to grasp that he had been used to facilitate a murder. Not unnaturally, he believed you had been a part of the plot when he learned of your release by the authorities. I tell you in confidence that the kiosk man for the drivers also had been paid to absent himself so that Heinkel could not summon another taxi. The murderer had carefully arranged each detail.''

"Can you tell me why Colonel Heinkel was in Ojinaga?"

"As far as we know, he was sightseeing. The taxi had driven him around the usual tourist sights."

"Is there any hope the taxi man can be released?"

"That is up to the Mexican authorities, but it's doubtful. Wittingly or not, he helped arrange a murder."

"Yes," I said, "I guess he did."

Graf rose. "I'm grateful for your time." He looked toward the river. "This is a peaceful place. I like it. I can see why the colonel wanted to see this land his father wrote of in his letters as a great natural wonder."

"When did the colonel's father visit?"

Graf had a faint smile on his lips. "In 1943. Johann Heinkel came here as a prisoner of war."

"I didn't know."

Graf shrugged. "The sins of our fathers were a long time ago, before you or I were born. It's over."

"Is Johann Heinkel still living?"

"No. He and two others were reported as having escaped from a work duty detail while held here. Two were recaptured. Heinkel was not. His family never heard from him again."

Plainly, from his expression, Graf's mind was already on something else. Maybe trying to decide where to have lunch. I walked with him down the steps. The sunglasses back on, he slid behind the wheel in a motion as smooth as his hair. Charlie came out on the porch and we stood and watched the black car start its slow progress back toward Presidio.

Charlie said, "He wouldn't want to hit the dips too fast in that fine automobile."

I couldn't help thinking, Johann Heinkel's son had come all this way to die. Why? Colonel Graf was wrong. It wasn't over.

TWNETY-THREE

ALL MY LIFE I've hated unfinished business. Leaving Charlie in charge, I drove that afternoon to see my father.

He wanted to go for a ride in his version of an all-terrain vehicle, a paint-chipped Volkswagen with a raised suspension and metal plates on the bottom. My father's proudest possession, it can go almost anywhere on the ranch as fast as forty miles per hour.

We bumped along checking the fence line while I asked him what he remembered about the POW camp at old Fort Russell.

"First off, it wasn't at the fort. It was a few miles out. The prisoners were shipped in, about two hundred, seems like, while I was still training at Camp Polk. They were still here when I got shipped home in 1944. It was '45 before the prisoners were moved out. That's about all I know. The man for you to talk to is Harley Nolan in Marfa. He lives in that two-story brick house near the school."

That's the plus of life in a small town—maybe the minus for some. Everyone knows everyone. It's true in Polvo with 125 people, and it's true in Marfa, with a couple of thousand, more or less.

After my father and I finished the fence-line tour I headed for the county seat and parked in front of Harley Nolan's house. The old soldier and retired plumber waved at me from the second-floor porch and shouted, "The door's open. Come on up."

Harley wore a baseball cap to keep his bald head warm, a sweater over his long-sleeved shirt, jeans, that hung loose over his bony shanks, and a pair of run-down house shoes. I joined him on the porch and sat in the second of two recliners.

"Doc told me I needed this chair to keep my feet up and help my circulation," Harley said.

"I think, Harley, it's time I buy a couple of these for Clay and me."

"Can't beat 'em. What'ya come to see this old man for?"

I didn't mind his bluntness. In some, old age makes time precious and formalities less important. I explained what I wanted to know, and he told me, enjoying the tale of the moments in his youth beside which all that came after was far less exciting.

"The prisoners were all Germans. They came in one bunch, one hundred and eighty-odd, transferred up from Brownwood on November 13, 1943. I was named company commander in charge of the POWs. We kept 'em segregated of course—their own barracks, mess hall, laundry, and recreation area. Kept 'em busy doing repairs around the camp and the military reservation. Only one of 'em was a hard-liner, always making swastikas out of paper, and marking them on the walls when he got a pen or pencil. We shifted him to solitary confinement real quick. Most of 'em was just scared kids wanting to go home. I remember this feller Johann Heinkel 'cause he was one of the officers—there was only two. Heinkel did his best for the others, keeping 'em in line and not letting 'em go slack. A few of 'em we let work out on the ranches, 'cause lots of the owners and hands were in training or gone off to the fronts already. My memory must be failing because you'd think I remember where Heinkel worked, seeing as how he was one of three that escaped, but for the life of me, I don't recall who he worked for."

"Did they get away, these men who escaped?"

"Heinkel did. The sheriff rounded-up the other two over by Sierra Blanca. They claimed they didn't know nothing about Heinkel, that he hadn't come with 'em. Course no one really expected 'em to rat on their officer. We figured he made it into Mexico, and from there back to Germany. It burns me, I can't remember who it was he worked for. Course lots of 'em asked for ranch duty, that's what we called it. Liked being out. We didn't have enough men to supervise 'em, of course. Owners had to do that if they wanted to work 'em."

"Could I find out where he might have worked?" I asked.

"Sure. I'll look over the old records in the county archives. Give me something to do."

"You'll call me?"

"Sure thing," he said, getting to his feet.

"You don't have to go right this minute, Harley."

"I want to. When I take on a job, I like to get right on it."

I left Harley changing his shoes. As long as I was in Marfa, I decided to visit the Haro Silverworks. Carlos wasn't in, I was told, but his assistant told me to look around and select whatever I liked. I saw it immediately, a silver pot that looked as if it came from a pueblo, with a raised design of a ram's head. Carlos never listed prices, saying he adjusted them to suit his clients. In my case, I hesitated to ask, intending to come back when Carlos was in the shop, but the assistant had been keeping her eye on me. "If that's what you've decided on, let me wrap it."

"Okay," I said, before she changed her mind. "By the way, I heard about a most unusual piece that a friend saw here, an antique wooden crucifix. Do you have any other religious art for sale? Angels, saints, that sort of thing?"

The assistant said, "We never have anything like that for sale. What your friend saw must have been something Carlos was buying for his private collection." She wrapped my package and boxed it.

I drove home pleased that I had found something both Clay and I could enjoy.

Charlie had played with Phobe and fed her, swept the wood floor, sold two cases of motor oil, a one-hundred-dollar truck hitch, the only one I had, two automatic dog feeders, and six cartons of soft drinks, plus assorted canned goods. Business was looking up.

Clay came in from his trailer freshly showered and hoping for a quiet late afternoon until the *posada.*

"I always start out really enjoying these parties, but I wind down at about number five," he said, getting a package of salted peanuts and a Pepsi.

"Are you going to put the peanuts in the Pepsi, and drink and eat at the same time, like we used to when we were kids?"

"It's not the same without the bottle. Soft drinks don't taste the same in cans."

"And not chilled in real ice. Nothing was ever so cold on a hot day. Remember Grapette? I loved to drink those."

Charlie said, "Root beer was the best."

"Get one out of the refrigerator. It's canned, but it will have to do. I want to tell you both what I found out today."

"From the military guy?" Charlie said.

"What military guy?" Clay asked.

I told them.

Charlie said, "You should have gotten this military attaché to tell Father Jack about what the taxi driver admitted to so he could tell Claudia and Ruben what really happened. Get them off your back."

"Claudia is a lost cause," Clay said.

I said, "I think Claudia will have to make up her own mind whether or not she believes me. If she doesn't, I'm doubtful anything anyone tells her will change her mind."

Charlie saved the day by making me laugh when he said, "If bodies keep turning up around here, you can make some money by stocking a line of caskets."

TWENTY-FOUR

IT WAS Christmas Eve. Because of the *posada* the night before, I had missed Harley's call, but he caught me over my second cup of coffee, his raspy old voice crackling with so much excitement I missed the first word or two.

"...enjoyed it. I'm gonna go back and do some more research. Did you get the name? La Noria. Johann Heinkel worked for old man Haro at La Noria Ranch for six months beginning in April of 1944. Turns out he trained as an architect before the war, and he helped design the house. Some other prisoners helped on and off. The one who spoke a little English would talk to the Mexican foreman, who spoke some English. The foreman would tell the Mexicans what to do."

"Did the two men who escaped and got caught work there, too?"

"How'd you guess that? The notes in the base historian's logbook says they claimed to have been left unsupervised, so they took off."

"Did Johann Heinkel disappear on the same day?"

"He's listed with the other two as reported escaped by the landowner."

I asked about details, but there were none. Only the scant facts of who, what, when, and where kept in the military historian's log.

"One more thing," Harley said. "The lady here told me that about two months ago old Haro's granddaughter—now what's her name? She searched these records, too."

"Alicia?"

"That's it!"

I thanked Harley, and we disconnected.

I wanted to talk things over with Clay, but he'd gone into town. Phobe jumped into my lap, positioned herself sideways, overflowing into the chair, all so she could look into my eyes as I stroked her fur, an amazingly soothing action for both of us. In a few minutes, she half closed her eyes and raised her head, giving me a direct and intense look. She gave a little grunt of pleasure and dropped her head back, asleep in an instant, sure of her safety with me on guard.

I rested my own head against the back of the chair, my fingers nestled against her soft fur. I closed my eyes and dozed until Charlie's voice called my name. I slid Phobe off my lap and into the chair. She voiced a grumble, but sprawled in comfort.

"The sheriff is here," Charlie said as I pushed through the doors to the front.

Andalon sat at the table by the coffeepot. Looking uncharacteristically rumpled and grumpy, he gave me a quick nod by way of greeting and pushed a color photo toward me.

"Look at that and tell me who you recognize."

I held up the five-by-seven color print. It showed a group of five people in evening dress posed close together and facing the camera. Two men, three women.

"I don't know any of these people," I said.

"The heavyset man on the left is Alberto Haro."

"I met him once, but that's been years ago."

"Look at the woman on the right."

"She's attractive, mature."

"You've met her, too," Andalon said. "Recently."

I looked again. "Where? Who is she?"

"Electra Reaves."

"You're kidding me." I held the photo close. The woman's face, made up like a model's, looked nothing like the *evangelista's*. With her chin tilted upward, her expression pleased and proud, the very shape of her face seemed different from the woman I had known. The vivid red lipstick colored a mouth much fuller than I remembered. The eyes were dark, lustrous even in the flash of the camera. Her black hair, without a strand of gray, had been swept up, revealing her long neck. The artlessly arranged curls on the top of her head softened the line of the forehead. She wore an emerald-colored dress of deceptively simple line, cut low enough to show cleavage, but not so low as to be vulgar.

"I'd never have recognized her."

"That was her intention. Her real name is Laura Riza. She's wanted on a federal warrant for smuggling Asians into this country illegally. And exorbitantly. This picture was taken in Dallas at some charity affair. Riza had a home, make that a mansion, there and in Mexico City. A socialite type, said to be divorced, maiden name unknown."

"What was she doing here? A woman like that, playing at religion. And don't say she had a conversion."

"Hiding. Under the alias Paula Hermana she got caught handing over a bundle of cash, ten thousand dollars to be exact, to a federale stationed at a checkpoint outside Nuevo Laredo. She agreed to turn government witness because undercover agents from the Immigration and Naturalization Service had been watching her for some time and had a pretty good idea of the scope of her operation. Asians from China, Pakistan, and India would fly to Russia, and take a weekly flight from there into Managua, all set up by partners of Riza's in Pakistan and Russia. The going rate was thirty thousand dollars per adult, with children's rates for kids under five. She and her group arranged safe houses, false visas, and transportation into cities like Houston and Dallas.''

"That much money?" I said.

"This is the country of choice for most of the rest of the world. Her smuggling ring moved upwards of sixty people a month into the States. Multiply that by any number of rings that operate in the open all over South and Central America—"

"Why in the open?"

"Because smugglers are admired and respected by people in countries where most of the populace wants to move up here. Anyway, her group had a problem that drew the attention of the authorities. One of her coyotes let a busload of their clients die. He abandoned them in the desert after he decided to use his initiative by robbing them and driving off with the bus. That brought attention to the smuggling, plus the ring got worried that the relatives of the victims might come after them. In fact, the Asian agent disappeared. Either he ran or he was killed. After Riza's arrest, with her real name in the papers and her mug shot, she got scared and in return for protection named some top Mexican Federal Judicial Police officers on her payroll. She told the INS agents she could also give them the names of people in this state who were partners in the smuggling ring, but only if the prosecutor would grant her immunity. While the lawyers were playing games over details, Riza was released on a million dollars bail because of her previous cooperation. She posted it without blinking an eye and then she bolted. Until she turned up dead here and her fingerprints came up a match, they hadn't a clue where she was.''

"How could that happen? Her getting away like that?"

Andalon smiled for the first time. "The agents were a little reticent about details on that point, but I understand one person is being investigated for suspicion of accepting a hefty cash donation toward his retirement.''

"So what was she doing here?''

"As I said, she was hiding out. The feds and the federales would be looking for her, the families of her victims would be looking for her, her partners on both sides of the border would be looking for her.''

"And some of them found her, is that what you think?''

"Right now I'm too tired to think. I guess it doesn't matter, but the feds would like to know, just in case the murder could put them back on the trail of the names she promised them.''

"So they're investigating her murder now?''

"You got it. I'd sure like to clear the case first.''

"Let me get you something to eat,'' I said.

"That would be great.''

I returned with scrambled eggs on toast, fresh coffee, and orange juice. While Andalon ate, I sipped coffee.

When he pushed back the plate I poured him a second cup and asked the questions I'd been thinking over, the obvious one first.

"Alberto Haro is in this picture. Could he have been Electra's—this Laura Riza's partner?''

Andalon tapped the photo still lying on the table between us. "This photo ran in the *Dallas Morning News* two years ago. It was a charity event with four hundred on the guest list, including the well-heeled from around the state. Riza had an active social life, and was in lots of society columns. The feds wouldn't tell me if they had a particular interest in Haro. Of course, the family's connections in San Antonio and Monterrey look promising to the feds, but so could lots of other folks with business in Mexico. Plenty of American companies are taking advantage of the free trade agreement to expand into Mexico. I don't see that the Haros would stand out because of one picture. Whatever else the feds may know about any Riza-Haro connection, they aren't sharing."

"Then why hide out here? There had to be a connection."

"Coincidence. Proximity to Mexico, her second home. She couldn't go back to her house in Mexico City, not with the federales after her. She'd be plenty dead if they got hold of her. Say for the sake of argument Alberto was her partner. Once she'd been arrested, he'd have to know she cut a deal and talked. Why come here right under the nose of the Haro family? Henry's campaign would be over, his entire political career, in fact, if his father was named as a smuggler. If she was this close, and Alberto wanted her dead, he'd have had her killed day one."

"Maybe it took him that long to find her. I didn't recognize her, and Don Federico and Alicia wouldn't have known her as anyone but Electra Reaves."

Andalon laughed. "If Alberto was her partner and she came here, she either trusted him, or had a hell of a nerve." He got up. "I've got to get back to work so I can take time off later for midnight Mass."

"One more question," I said. "Did you find out if Alicia is in California with her mother?"

"I know Bascom Davis's pilot flew her to Santa Barbara. Mrs. Lagos refuses to answer any questions about her daughter's whereabouts. If the insurance company wants to talk to her about the poisoned horses, they'll have to send J. Frank Causley to find her. I've got a warrant to search the Haro house and outbuildings for a gun, but if she killed Eliseo because he discovered the poison containers and suspected her, we won't find it. Mr. Haro got her out pronto. He wouldn't have forgotten to get rid of the gun. Nobody knows how deep the spring is at La Noria. I bet the gun is at the bottom.'' He was halfway to the door when I called another question after him.

"Andalon, is it a crime to dig up an old grave on private land?''

He stopped still, cocked his head, and without even turning around, said, ''Not if you don't get caught.''

I sighed, and watched him go through the front doors. For a half hour after he left, I sat with a pad of paper and pen, drawing names, connecting lines, making diagrams. Trying to place people and events into a pattern that answered the questions I had, the guesses I made about what might have happened.

"You look worried, Texana," Charlie said from behind the counter. "Anything I can help with?''

"Thank you, Charlie, no. I'm just puzzling over questions I don't have answers to. You take a break now. Time for me to do some work.''

"Okay," he said, sliding off the stool and marking his place in one of my books he'd been reading. "I think since it's Christmas Eve, I'll give Bess a wash.''

Father Jack had asked Charlie to participate in the last *posada*, held at the church itself immediately before the *misa del gallo*, the rooster's Mass. The midnight Mass was lovely, a special *posada* in which not only does the Holy Family find lodging, but the birth of the Christ child is celebrated with the placing of the statue of the infant Jesus in the crib of the manger in the church while the people gather around and sing a lullaby. I was going to be sorry to miss it.

First, since Pete Rosales did not have a telephone, I wrote a note; then I telephoned Lucy and asked if one of her grandsons could come to the trading post and deliver a message to the other side. Next I gave considerable thought to how I was going to convince Clay to go along with what I intended to do.

TWENTY-FIVE

CLAY DIDN'T GET HOME until four o'clock. He took some convincing. I primed him with a small whiskey first, followed by a plate of his favorite secret vice, homemade brownies with walnuts, and coffee to offset the whiskey because I needed his full attention.

"That's a job for Andalon," he said after I had explained.

"He'd need a court order. This is all guesswork. There's no proof."

"You can't do it. This is crazy."

"We aren't going to dig up the grave, just make a show of doing it."

"You'll get caught."

"That's exactly what I intend."

"It's a sacrilege, as well as a crime."

"Not if we don't actually uncover and remove the body."

"Lalo won't go along with it."

"Yes, he will. His *father* was murdered."

"What about Pete?" Clay shook his head. "Who am I kidding. He'll love impersonating an officer of the law."

"It's not impersonating. It's suggesting. The Jeep is his and it's coincidental that in the dark it looks like one of the sheriff's department vehicles. Will you do it?"

"Let me have another whiskey. And not that stingy half measure you gave me the first time. Make it a double."

Pete arrived at five o'clock. I found the perfect hat, pants, and shirt for him in stock. He changed clothes, and at dark, we left.

We drove in the shadow of darkness, the mountains around us blocking out the light of the rising full moon.

Pete had his gun belt and holstered pistol slung over the headrest. "Just in case," he said. "You never know how a man's going to react."

He drove slowly. We were in no hurry. Old men sleep little and restlessly. It was nearly eleven when we crossed the cattle guard onto La Noria land, eleven-fifteen when Pete took us to the ranch compound, headlights of the used Border Patrol Jeep on full. Pete stopped at the bunkhouse, left the motor running, got out, walked into the low-slung building, and in a few minutes came out with Lalo still stuffing his shirt into his pants.

Clay and I rode in back, behind the wire screen for prisoners. Lalo slipped into the front seat beside Pete. Clay and I had debated whether or not he should be there, but I said it was important, because his presence made our actions more plausible. Don Federico had to be convinced that Lalo knew something about what had been going on.

It took us ten minutes to reach the cemetery.

Clay had put the shovels in the back with us. I lifted one out. He had the other.

"You want me to leave the lights on?" Pete said.

"Too obvious. We'll use the flashlights," I said. "He'll need some extra time to get dressed."

Clay said, "If you want it to look real, we need to have at least a small pile of dirt by the time he gets here." He dug in the shovel just below the marker. The silvery moonlight shone so bright I could read the Latin inscription without trying.

Pete took the other shovel from me, but I said, "No, you stand with your back to the gate, arms crossed, and look official." I started to dig, but Lalo said, "You'll give it away. There are no women deputies. Let me."

Clay said, "Lalo's right. You'd better sit on this side of the Jeep in the shadow. If we're going to do it, let's do it right."

Clay cut on the lantern, set it on the ground next to the grave, set the shovel, placed his foot on the rim, and put his full weight on it.

Shovelful by shovelful the mound grew, until Clay said, "I think that's enough." He and Lalo rested on their shovels.

Pete said, "I hear something. Somebody's coming, driving without lights."

Clay said, "We better be digging when he gets here." He worked the shovel. "I hit a rock." He heaved, thrusting something up out of the ground. "Just a small one," he said, reaching down to lift it out of the way. "It's a box." He dropped the shovel, held the box in one hand, and wiped the dirt from the surface with the other.

I scrambled to my feet and went to look. The box was metal, a small documents box like the kind you buy at the hardware store.

"Open it," I said. "Can you open it?"

"You know what this is? I thought—"

"Open it," I said. I seemed to be having trouble breathing.

Clay examined the container. The lid was hinged, and there was a keyhole. Clay moved his fingers along the side and the lid came up.

"What's in it?" Pete said, coming closer, as did Lalo.

"It's a wooden box," Clay said.

"It's old. Look at that carving," Lalo said. "It's got a cross on it, and some kind of staff with a sheep."

I said, "It's a goat. It must be. He was a goat herder."

Clay got to his feet and looked at me. "You know what's in this?"

I nodded, and held my hands. Clay gave me the container. I got to my knees and with a trembling hand took out the wooden box and lifted off the thick lid. I heard the startled noises the others made only slightly over the thudding in my ears of my own heartbeat.

The hand was dried to shriveled flesh stretched tight over bones that remained whole. I smelled the scent of incense. It looked smaller than I would have thought.

"This is a joke, right?" Pete said.

"No joke," I said.

Lalo said, "What is it?"

"The saint's hand," I told him.

"The hand of José Zuno."

As one, we turned. Don Federico stood there looking like a dead man about to fall. With an effort of willpower that sent a spasm of pain across his face, he stayed on his feet.

He said, "I will wait for you at the house." He turned and walked slowly back to the vehicle he had parked by the cemetery gate.

Lalo took a stride forward, but Pete had his hand on the young man's arm. He said something to him in a low voice, and Lalo stopped and watched with the rest of us as Don Federico got into his vehicle and drove away, the headlights on this time.

In the long seconds that followed it seemed to me the earth itself lay silent in the midnight air.

Clay found his voice first. "Do you think he realized we weren't Andalon and the deputies?"

I said, "I don't think it mattered."

"What now?" Lalo said. "What does this mean?"

Clay collected both shovels and the lantern, saying, "He said he'd be waiting for us. Let's go talk to him."

I put the lid back on the reliquary and took it with us. I didn't want to leave it behind, and I didn't know what else to do with it. Father Jack would know if there was some special ceremony for a stolen relic, even if he didn't believe in its efficacy.

We parked by the back door of the main house. I put the reliquary on the seat, got out, and walked toward the front. I could hear one of the men knocking on the back door. At the corner a cold wind hit me, whipping my hair back. I zipped up my jacket and stuffed my hands in my pockets. Well below the house, somewhere near the cattle guard, headlights zigged along the road. Don Federico hadn't waited for us.

I heard footsteps. The men had moved out looking for me. I turned back and came face-to-face with Pete.

"Don Federico is driving away," I said. "I'm afraid what he might do. Call the sheriff."

"There's a phone in the bunkhouse," Lalo said.

"Let's go," Pete said, already moving.

I went to the back door. Clay had stopped knocking, when the lights came on inside and out. Another minute and Tina cracked open the door, pulling her robe around her. She stared out with scared eyes, recognized us, and opened the door wide. "I knew I heard a car. What has happened now?"

Clay told her only that we had expected to meet Don Federico at the house and the sheriff was on his way. To be sure, would she see if Don Federico was in his room?

Almost immediately Tina was back, saying, "I don't understand, where could he be? Something is wrong in this house. I heard Señor Haro say he had been cursed. Who knows what the end will be?"

Lalo and Pete came in. Lalo asked Tina if she would make some coffee. Looking miserable, she went into the kitchen. Clay suggested we wait in the kitchen for the sheriff's people to arrive. We sat around the table, drinking coffee, saying little, with Tina watching our faces, trying to read some message of reassurance.

An hour passed, during which I explained to Clay, Pete, and Lalo the story of the saint's hand. After that, there was a long period of silence. I could tell by Clay's eyes he had reached the same conclusion I had. Pete's face gave none of his thoughts away, and Lalo sat stoic, stern-faced.

Pete broke the silence. "It could be daylight before the sheriff gets here."

"You go on home to your family," Clay said.

"No, man," Pete said. "I want to find out the end of all this."

The drone of the helicopter surprised us. We looked at one another, jumped up, and hurried outside.

The whirl of the rotor echoed back at us from the rimrock, making it impossible to determine the direction unless you knew where the chopper came from. We stared toward Marfa. The sound seemed to go on and on, growing in intensity until finally, we saw the lights. We stood and waited until the Hughes OHA-Alpha, a relic from Vietnam now used by the Border Patrol, cut on the quartz halogen lights to locate a safe landing site and lowered itself onto the ground like a dragonfly touching down on the surface tension of pond water.

The rotor whirled to a stop as Andalon stepped out, ducked, and ran clear. Tina had the back door open and we went inside. Without being asked she poured Andalon a mug of coffee. He took it gratefully. "The pilot will be along in a minute," he told Tina, who poured another cup.

Andalon took a swallow of the steaming brew that would have scalded a throat unaccustomed to being mistreated by hot coffee at odd hours, looked at us standing in a circle around the table, unwilling to sit until he did. The Border Patrol pilot came in, accepted the coffee and introduction with a nod of the head. Andalon set down his half-empty cup, took off his leather jacket, draped it over the back of a chair, and sat, his legs stretched full, his ankles crossed, his hand folded over his lap. The rest of us pulled our chairs up to the table, except for Tina, who stayed on her feet by the range.

Andalon said, "Dennis Bustamente is taking care of the search for Mr. Haro. The Border Patrol is helping. Why don't you bunch explain what it is you've been up to."

It was not my imagination that in speaking that last phrase, he fixed his eyes on me. In fact, they all did. So I explained, beginning with what I'd learned about the POW Johann Heinkel, the reported escape of three men and the report of only two recaptured, and their denial of any knowledge of Heinkel. From that, I moved to my assumption that Federico Haro had killed Johann and buried him in the oddly marked grave. I repeated what the German military attaché had said about Colonel Herbert Heinkel wanting to see the place where his father had been held a prisoner of war, explained how I reasoned that the son would have known the name of the rancher his father did work for from the letters Johann wrote to his family from the POW camp before he vanished.

Clay said, "The most natural thing in the world for Johann's son to do would be to come here, to La Noria."

"It was easy for Haro to cover up killing a POW on his own ranch," Andalon said. "Killing a German colonel in peacetime, a man whose name was well known in this area because of all the negative publicity the low-level fights have generated…better to hire it done, and somewhere away from any connection with you."

Pete said, "The old man was smart. He wouldn't use the

federales, who'd know who he was and just how much he could pay. He'd go through someone else paid just enough to be useful without getting suspicious. I'll bet Haro told the guy it was a vengeance killing.''

I took a deep breath, debated with myself whether or not to admit to what else I speculated, and decided if I was going for looking like a half fool, I might as well go for the whole. I said, "J. Frank believes Alicia poisoned the horses. You showed me the photograph of the evangelista, and explained who and what she really was. I thought she must have somehow learned from Alicia about the murder of the POW, or even from Alberto. As the oldest son, maybe Don Federico told him what was in that grave in the cemetery. As children, surely they all wondered about that gravestone and what it meant. Their father would have had to make up some story. I talked to Harley Nolan. He told me about the POW records and the disappearance of Johann Heinkel while he worked here, and that Alicia Lagos made a document search in those records just two months ago. The evangelista was a shrewd woman. I think she made a direct threat to Don Federico, guessing about the murder of Colonel Herbert Heinkel.''

Andalon got up and helped himself to more coffee, taking his time about it. He leaned against the counter, looked us over, and said, "So you decided to dig up the body you thought must be Johann Heinkel's buried under the mysterious marker.''

Clay said, "Old man Haro is the key to unlocking the mystery contained in the grave. Our charade was intended to force him into action of some kind. No law against 'tending' a grave. Besides, Lalo was with us representing the property owner.''

I thought I saw a hint of a smile from Andalon at Clay's remarks. I knew everything was okay when he said, "I've known you and Texana way too long. I'm starting to think this makes sense. Where's this relic?''

"I left it on the seat of Pete's Jeep."

The Border Patrol agent offered to go and get it. In a minute he was back. He handed Andalon the box and turned to Pete, saying, "Nice vehicle."

Pete grinned right back at him. "She's driving real smooth, Joe."

"Good thing," the agent said, "or I'd have to offer you a ride back to the other side."

"Don't you go worrying about me. I'll be home where I belong in no time. I like to visit, but I don't want to live over here. Too dangerous."

Tina's quiet voice interrupted our laughter. "This man you speak of, this German colonel, I think he did come here. Someone foreign did, anyway, an older man in his fifties with nice clothes and a rental car. He and Señor Haro talked for a while, then Señor Haro drove him around the ranch."

"When was this?" Andalon said.

Tina said, "The twelfth of December."

"The feast day of the Virgin of Guadalupe," Andalon said, understanding why Tina recalled the date so exactly. "The colonel died on the fifteenth. One thing is sure, Mr. Haro didn't take off only because he saw you'd found the relic. I'll call the judge after he has his Christmas breakfast in about five more hours and arrange to dig up the grave tomorrow." He picked up the box, got to his feet, and added, "Merry Christmas to all of you. Come on, Joe, let's head back and start the process."

TWENTY-SIX

As IT TURNED OUT, few of us enjoyed Christmas Day.

Pete and Clay and I got to the trading post at 6:10 a.m. Clay microwaved frozen croissants and served them with milk—we were coffeed out. Pete left for home. His family would have a quiet day after *las posadas*. The Rosaleses kept an "old" Christmas, which meant gifts would be given on Kings' Day, January 6, the day the Wise Men reached Bethlehem.

Andalon's ten o'clock telephone call woke Clay who'd been snoring in his chair. I had fallen asleep on the couch, but Clay left it to me to answer, then slipped over to take my place on the couch. Andalon spoke without greeting, knowing we'd be waiting to hear from him. "We thought Haro would head for Mexico since he sent his mistress down there, and most likely Alicia. Instead, he doubled back. He took one of the ranch roads west of Marfa that crosses the Union Pacific line. The engineer on the six-twenty-five saw a vehicle parked on the road with the lights off. At the last minute, the vehicle pulled onto the tracks in front of the train. In the seconds before the crash, the engineer saw the old man's face staring straight at the train, and swore he didn't even blink. Alberto Haro has disappeared from his home in San Antonio. His wife reported him missing when he failed to come back from the office after working late on Christmas Eve, which in itself was unusual for him."

When I didn't say anything, Andalon added, "Carlos is

still at the silverworks. I checked on him myself, and told him about his father. You there, Texana? Say something."

"I...thanks for letting me know, Andalon." I hung up. I felt Clay's strong hands on my shoulders.

"He's dead," he said, knowing without being told. I gave him the details.

"Don't you even think about guilt."

"I shouldn't have interfered," I said.

"We intervened—you, me, Pete, and Lalo. Most important, Lalo—Haro probably killed his father."

"I know. Remember what he said at the funeral about how loyal Elisio was. I think Alicia bashed in the back of the evangelista's head with the shovel, just like J. Frank speculated. Then she must have run to her grandfather for help. He decided to make it look like whoever left the small crucified dolls did the killing. He was healthy and vigorous for his age, but I don't think he had the strength to haul dead weight over the rafter, so he had to have Elisio's help. After that, he couldn't let him live."

"He was cold enough to cut a woman's throat to be doubly sure she died. Haro was a cunning old bastard and a killer."

"He rode with the devil."

Father Jack's voice preceded him into the room, but he caught up with it almost immediately, pushing through the doors. "His own words—remember? I did knock first, as it's a holiday. Did you know your front door is open?"

I blew my nose on a tissue. "I leave the doors open on Christmas Day. Someone always has an emergency, a dead battery or a hangover from too much celebration of the season. Customers can take what they need. If I'm not out front, they drop the money in the bowl by the register." I looked up at him. "Andalon called you, didn't he?"

"About eight this morning. The old man had no intention of being brought to justice. Not in court anyway."

I said, "No wonder, when he still thought he could salvage things, that he sent his granddaughter and mistress away. No telling what the Salinas woman knew about him, and if Alicia wanted to hurt Henry's chances of inheriting their grandfather's money enough to poison horses, she'd have been happy to be granted immunity to corroborate anything that might damage her grandfather. One scandal in the family would bring Henry's political career down."

Clay invited Father Jack to stay for lunch.

"I'm on a postposada diet. I'm tipping the scales at two hundred and thirty-odd. Got to get back into fighting shape. By the way, Charlie stayed in the extra room at my house last night."

"I wondered why we hadn't seen him, but when he's ready to take off on his travels, he just goes. Is he okay?"

"I think he had a near-death experience. Someone scratched the word *chafa* on the door of his Cadillac."

I couldn't think of anything more likely to upset Charlie than marking up Bess with a slang expression that was the Spanish equivalent of "junk."

TWENTY-SEVEN

FRIDAY MORNING Clay had a call to help with a bad calving. By lunchtime he hadn't returned. The day after Christmas is a slow business day for the trading post, and I got out drop cloths, dustpan, and beeswax and did a thorough cleaning job of the rafters. Phobe loved it, playing under the tables that had turned into tents, and climbing the ladder behind me.

I was in the shower washing the dust out of my hair when Clay arrived home. While I toweled my hair, I could hear him in the kitchen. Glasses clinked, and the bottle made its gurgling noise.

I put on my jeans, a flannel shirt over my sweater, and thick socks, and went to join him.

"I see Dad came through with the Crown Royal."

Clay had a happy smile as he handed me a glass of whiskey.

"I note the unusually generous level. Are we celebrating or is it bad news?"

"Come see," he said, opening the back door wide.

I looked out and whooped when I saw the white Ford F-250 supercab with TEXANA on the vanity plates.

"Merry Christmas," Clay said. "Why don't we try out the captain's seats in creamy fawn leather while we drink our Crown Royal."

"How did you manage this?" I said, getting in and taking a deep whiff of leather and polish. "We haven't gotten the insurance check yet, and this is nicer—"

"We have, and it is. I talked to the insurance man in

person, plus your father went in with me to get you all the extras.''

"Queen of the road, that's me.''

The telephone rang, and we hopped out to answer it. Out here the standard is nine or ten rings before you give up because the person you're calling may be in the barn or halfway across the pasture, or in my case, waiting on a customer.

"You were right," Andalon said. Clay and I held the receiver between us. "More than right."

I said, "What does that mean?"

"We found two skeletons in the grave. One on top of the other. From what we can tell, they appear to be in the same condition. We're assuming they died at the same time. We're sifting the grave now for small remains and any other identifying items that may be there. One skull shows a gunshot wound in the back of the head, the other has a compression fracture at the back of the skull. It gives validity to the assumption Haro might have killed the evangelista and Elisio Silva. His methods seem consistent. Have you got any ideas you'd care to share about the identity of the either body, Texana?"

"I have no idea whatsoever."

Andalon stared. "Well. That opens up an interesting line of thinking."

After Andalon left, Clay and I went to see my father to bring him up-to-date on events, but mostly for me to thank him for the contribution to my pickup. I also took him his present, a box of cigars. We each smoked one, and agreed that as good as these were, they didn't measure up to the private label that Ghee had sent me once.

When we got home, Carlos Haro waited in his red Jeep in the parking lot.

"Stay here," Clay said, cutting the motor. "I'll see what he wants."

"Be careful," I told Clay. I sat tight. If Federico's youngest son knew the full truth of what happened, he had no reason to feel friendly toward me.

Carlos got out, the two talked briefly, then he reached into his pocket. I jumped out of the pickup and got halfway to them before I realized what he had in his hand.

He gave the blue box to Clay, then turned to me. He'd aged overnight, his face exhausted, his eyes red-rimmed, his shoulders hunched.

"Carlos," I said, "I'm so sorry this is happening to you." I meant his pain, his father's death, his family's humiliation, his suffering.

"I nearly got you killed," he said.

"What?"

"Open the box."

Clay lifted the hinged lid of the Haro Silverworks box and lifted out the bookmark I'd commissioned, the gift I thought was gone forever, sold by the thief who'd run me off the road in the *comando*.

Carlos spoke, his voice a monotone of shock, indicative of a mind that has been faced with too much to assimilate. "That day you brought the medal in, I recognized it. Or at least I'd seen one identical to it. In my childhood the medal had always been in my father's room, dangling over the praying hands of a statue of Our Lady. I think it was that medal that interested me in silver and led me to the work I do now. When I first started to study silverwork in Taxco, I went through book after book trying to find a replica or anything similar. In all these years I've never seen anything like that medal. I used to ask my father about it, but all he would say was that it was a gift from the old priest in Guadalupita where he grew up. When you brought it in, I was so fascinated that after you left, I called my father to tell him about it. He was upset and rang off. I thought he was still angry with me because I'd told him earlier that I intended to consult a lawyer and fight his will if he left everything to Henry as he intended to do. I found this in his desk this morning. It means he set up the accident and the robbery. I'm sorry."

Clay said, "Come inside, Carlos. You need some food, a stiff drink, and some rest."

Carlos rubbed a hand across his weary face. "Gracias, but I have arrangements to make, questions still to answer for the authorities." He got back into the Jeep, made a tight turn, and was gone.

Clay looked at the bookmark. "You put a lot of thought into this. It's perfect."

"My father tanned the deerskin."

"That makes it even more special. Come on. Let's go in, put on an old movie, and forget our troubles and everybody else's for a couple of hours. We'll eat hot dogs and stuff ourselves on shoestring potatoes."

"That's a great plan. You cook."

TWENTY-EIGHT

ANDALON CAME TO SEE Clay and me on December 30, bringing the final answer to the puzzle, or at least all we were likely to get.

"This was in Haro's desk. It's not addressed to anyone. From the looks of it he wrote it years ago because he wanted his secret protected by his heirs. The secret of the grave, I mean."

"What does it say?" I asked.

"Read it for yourself. This is a copy. I'll help myself to coffee and a package of doughnuts out front."

We opened the large envelope and I took out a number of pages of lined paper filled with neat, firm handwriting, rather small and very masculine in form. Don Federico had not expected failure when he wrote this.

Clay said, "You start, and hand me the pages as you finish them."

As I read, I realized it was the conclusion to the tale of Guadalupita.

"I first thought of killing my brother when he lifted out of his saddlebag the reliquary with the saint's hand that he had taken from the church of our village. If the relic had remained, the bandits would not have come, destroyed the town, and slaughtered our family and friends. My brother the priest, my brother the traitor, the thief, the betrayer of his faith and family, had killed our mother, our sisters, our nieces and nephews as surely as if he had held the gun and fired the shots with his own hand.

"They had died by his most grievous fault. I watched

the pride in his face as he spoke of the government supporters his cristeros had killed. The ecstasy he once felt for God, he now felt for killing. I knew at that moment I wanted him to suffer, to discover for himself what he had become. And I knew how to make it happen. He would fail at what had become his obsession. I had the means to assure his failure. Meanwhile, I forced myself to applaud and smile as he boasted of his glorious achievements in battle, and he clasped me to his breast and called me brother once more. That night, I ate with him and his men, watched while they grew drunk on pulque and self-glorification.

"I ate little, poured my drink onto the ground, and waited. When they fell into a pulque-induced sleep, I crept out and removed the reliquary from my brother's saddlebag. I opened the gate of the corral for the horses to walk out and thus slow the pursuit of me, which surely would come. Now that I had the saint's hand, I knew that luck was with me and I was unafraid. In a matter of hours I came upon an old man with a mule and wagon stuck in the mud. I helped him free the wagon, and he gave me a ride into the next town. He and his wife fed me and gave me a bed. Because the town was large and friendly to the government cause, I told the couple I was hunted by the cristeros. I rested with them in safety for three days. My journeys after that were arduous, but not so hard as they might have been had not the saint's hand protected me. After more than a year I heard about a man of wealth who needed men to smuggle drink over the border. I went to work for him. Everything that came after led me here, to La Noria.

"Success followed success. Always the saint's hand protected me and then my family when I married and my wife bore me three sons and later a daughter. When the Second World War came, I was too old to go, and my sons were too young. It was then my brother found me. He came to the house and announced himself. He told me he had renewed his priestly vows, helped to rebuild Guadalupita and the church there. He asked my forgiveness for his past mistakes. He was happy, not sorrowful. He had come to reclaim the relic for the town. He talked as if it were a simple request. He had brought with him a silver *milagro* to show me his heart had been healed of its sins. He intended to place it in the reliquary with the saint's hand because he had prayed to José Zuño to heal him. My brother arrived on a Tuesday. My wife and sons were in Marfa. We had bought a small house, and she and the boys stayed there during the week so the boys could attend school. For the first day, I treated Bernardo as the prodigal he thought he was, welcoming him with food and wine while I made my plans. On the second day I invited him for a drive over the ranch. I stopped to show him the overlook from the rimrock. He was standing at the edge looking out and talking about his plans for Guadalupita when I swung the shovel against the back of his head. He toppled over the edge. I put the shovel into the truck and drove back to the building site of my new house.

"I had workers on the place, German POWs who stayed all week because it was too far to drive in to the camp. At night, I locked them in the old bunkhouse. The other workers, a few Mexicans, camped out and slept on the ground. I'd taken care to keep my brother away from contact with any of them. In that, too, the saint's hand had given me success. I went to the one POW who spoke a little English. He bossed the others. I took him aside and told him there had been an accident and I needed help. I don't know how much he understood, but he did as he was told and got in the truck. I told the Mexicans they could take a break while the man and I repaired some fence. I made it plain I would be gone for some hours. When we got to the rimrock and the German saw the situation he wanted to get others to help so we could hoist the body up by rope, but I shook my head. It took us most of the afternoon to get the body back up the mountainside. When we had it in the bed of the truck, I drew my pistol and shot the German in the back of the head. He fell forward. All I had to do was hoist his legs and shove him in beside my brother. I put a tarp over the bodies, and I drove back to headquarters, locked the truck in the barn, and checked the workers. The Mexicans were there. The other two POWs had run just as I had counted on them doing. That night I drove to the cemetery, carefully cut away the top sod in squares, and dug a grave. I took one thing from my brother's body, the medal that Father Juan, the old priest who taught us in Guadalupita, had given him, a medal struck in Guadalupita in the old days and handed down from priest to priest. I took it because it would have been a sacrilege to bury it with the body of a corrupt man. I buried both bodies together. After I smoothed the grave over and replaced the sod, only someone expecting to see something could have noticed the slight disturbance.

"The next morning I reported that all three POWs had run off during the night. The military authorities never questioned my word or came to the ranch. I counted on the Germans having enough time to get down the canyon road—the only way to get out, and get to the border. Or die trying. When they were picked up a couple of weeks later and denied the third man escaped with them, the military authorities assumed they were lying to give him more time to get away.

"One of the Mexicans working on the house was a stonemason. In the course of one day, at my instructions he made the gravemarker OSSA HUMILIATA. Like my brother, I had attended Father Juan's lessons in Latin. I sealed the reliquary inside another box, lifted a square of sod, put it just under the ground, and had the man place the marker—a marker for a saint, a sinner, and a stranger.

"As my sons came of age, I told each of them about the relic, saying only that I had taken it from my brother's saddlebag and brought it with me, and that when I died it would be in Eduardo's care, as the eldest. Every few years we removed the marker and replaced the outer container with a new one to protect the saint's hand.

"I have built up a dynasty. Henry will be a statesman. With the wealth I leave him, he will groom his sons for the highest political office. Someday, the nation will hail a Haro as president.

"In all my actions, I did what any man, any father would do. I destroyed that which endangered my family's future. I have explained. I do not apologize."

I handed the last page to Clay. After a few minutes, Clay put his hand on mine. "I know what you hoped for out of this whole plan, our making Haro think we knew he'd murdered the POW. You hoped he'd admit to arranging the death of Herbert Heinkel as well, and that it might help Claudia's cousin."

"Can't expect all the answers," Andalon said, coming in with a half-eaten doughnut in one hand, a coffee in the other. "It's pretty obvious, though, that he also killed the evangelista. Bashed her head in like he did his brother's."

I said, "Why cut her throat?"

"To make it look more like a vengeance killing by her former partners in the smuggling racket when her real identity came out from her fingerprints. My guess is—I'm catching up to you here—that he knew his son Alberto was involved in the smuggling of the illegal immigrants, and knew exactly who the evangelista was. Father Jack told me he thought she was arranging for church art in Mexico to be stolen and then selling it to collectors in this country and Europe. Her mistake was roping in Federico's granddaughter for her latest scheme, not only using the girl, but putting her in danger of getting killed by sending Alicia to do the preaching on the other side and to collect the art."

Clay said, "And the German? Johann's son?"

"A loose end tied up. Tina said the man came to the house and spent the day with Haro. We'll never know if the colonel knew anything or Haro only thought he might. He made arrangements, I imagine, to be safe. What's a little extra murder, after all he'd done?"

When Andalon had left, Clay looked at me. "You didn't tell him about Carlos and the medal."

"No. Carlos is only guessing that his father hired the comando, just as Andalon is guessing Federico hired whoever killed Herbert Heinkel. Someone in that family has to overcome this and try and make up for the past."

TWENTY-NINE

I CARRIED THE silver bowl into the church and set it on the table to the right of the door in front of the gold-framed painting of the Virgin of Guadalupe, then went back to the pickup for the artificial roses. I punched each wire stem in place.

"That's a fine offering to Our Lady," Father Jack said, emerging from the white curtains that divide the sacristy from the nave.

I didn't tell the priest I'd driven all the way to Marfa to try and give the bowl back after Carlos returned Clay's gift. I told him part of the truth, that Carlos and I had agreed it would make a fine gift for the church.

"And so it does. Thank you. I'll write to Carlos, also. I have something I think you should see that Carlos brought to me, also."

He led the way down the aisle and into the sacristy. On top of the built-in cabinet holding the altar linens was a wooden box, the reliquary from the grave. Someone had cleaned and polished the ancient wood. I could see the carvings lovingly done by the craftsman of Guadalupita whose name had been lost in time.

Father Jack said, "Carlos asked if I would give the saint's hand a home in the altar of our church."

"I thought you didn't believe in relics. Things Chaucer made fun of, you called them."

"I spoke in haste. Chaucer—and I—meant chicken bones sold by the unscrupulous as relics to the devout but ignorant. Genuine relics have a long history in the Church.

The early Christians risked their lives to recover the bodies of martyrs, and enshrining them in a portion of the altar became custom. It's just that some people innocently confuse worship at the altar with worship of the relic. That's the mistake Federico Haro and the villagers of Guadalupita made. I lack proof that this young man José Zuño died a saint, meaning among other things murdered in hatred of the faith, but if the priest in Guadalupita thought enough to enshrine him, who am I to doubt? José Zuño experienced a vision and his wounds healed miraculously. He took no advantage of his situation. He went back to his goats. These things are in his favor. Visions are tricky, serious business. They can wreak havoc. Just read Saint John of the Cross if you don't think so. I think José had a personal vision, possibly divine in origin. I'm trying to locate someone in the Church in Mexico who will research the existing archives for a letter from the village priest about the event. Even in those days the man would have written to his bishop, though the early local priests were too often ignorant, unlettered men. I must accept on faith that the village priest knew enough to accept him as a saint honored by popular opinion, if not officially by the Church. In the meantime, we'll keep the reliquary here, on hold, so to speak. By the way, I have something to tell you that I think you'll find comforting. Andalon passed on some information to me concerning Federico's death because he thought I should speak to Carlos and his brother Eduardo. I think it might help you to know, also. The men who cut Federico Haro from the wreckage say one thing is without doubt. He died with a rosary in his hand.''

"I remember what you told him that day. Between the saddle and the ground—"

"Salvation he found. Facing death, he fell back on the

teachings he learned as a child at the feet of his godparents.''

On the way out of the church, I met Claudia Reyes. She ducked her head, her round face flushed. She took three steps past me, then turned and called my name. I faced her, hoping for the best.

"I'm so sorry," she said. "I knew after what Father said that day at Mass I was wrong, but I was so ashamed..."

"I never did anything to hurt your cousin," I told her.

"I know that. Without your telling me I know that. I'm ashamed of the way I acted. Ruben says I was crazy."

"No. You were hurt and confused. As often as we doubt ourselves, it's much easier to doubt each other."

She moved down a step and hugged me. "I'll see you at the King's Day party?"

"Of course."

THIRTY

Toward sunset on a mild day in late January we met, Andalon, Carlos and Eduardo Haro, Clay, and I, at the private cemetery at La Noria to reinter the bones of Father Bernardo Haro beside the grave of his brother Federico.

His remains had been placed in a plain wooden casket, the kind religious orders traditionally use to bury their dead. The medal given to him by Padre Juan of Guadalupita all those years ago had been placed inside the casket by Carlos to honor the uncle he had never known.

Father Jack had said Mass at the church for the long-dead priest. He kept his words at the graveside simple and brief. "I read from Second Maccabees, chapter twelve, verse forty-six: 'Thus he made atonement for the dead that they might be freed from this sin.'" He closed the Bible, and said, "The community of the Church is not destroyed by death, for we have a foot in both the temporal and the eternal across a bridge of prayer. We offer our fervent petition that Father Bernardo be admitted into the company of the blessed, and that in turn his prayers may assist us through the years of our lives yet to come."

We stood for that awkward anticlimactic moment after any burial when no one seems to know what to do, and then Father Jack took a shovel and started to fill in the grave, but Carlos touched his arm. Father Jack held out the shovel, and Carlos set to work. Eduardo removed his jacket and waited his turn.

We left them to the burial of their dead, and walked in a straggling line to our vehicles. Andalon said, "I'd like to be buried like this. No fake grass carpet, the real sky instead of a tent, and the closure for the family of filling in the grave. You guys remember this if some drug dealer or drunk shoots me dead.''

I said, ''But not if you die in bed?''

''Smart mouth. Say, before we leave, I want to show you something we found that belonged to Johann Heinkel.'' He reached into his uniform pocket and brought out a coin that in size resembled the old American silver dollars. A single small hole had been punched through it near the rim, and a thin long chain ran through it. He handed it to Father Jack.

''It's a German mark,'' the priest said.

''We found it when we sifted the dirt of the grave, along with a few buttons and such.''

The priest held the silver coin up between his thumb and forefinger so that Clay and I could see the facing side. ''Look at that.''

We looked close. Clay said, ''Isn't that...?''

''Kaiser Wilhelm the Second.''

''What year is the coin?'' I asked. Father Jack obligingly turned it over and read the date. ''Nineteen oh seven.''

Clay said, ''Eleven years before his abdication and the dissolution of the German monarchy. I wouldn't think this would be a coin that a fanatical Nazi would be carrying. Seems to me at heart Johann must have been a monarchist.''

Andalon said, ''We'll never know but I like thinking this Johann Heinkel was on the right side of the coin himself.''

''That pun is so bad I might have phrased it, but I heartily agree with the sentiment,'' Father Jack said, handing the coin back to Andalon.

He dropped it back into his pocket. ''It goes back with the remains to Germany.''

Father Jack and Andalon had parked closer to the cemetery and reached their vehicles first, and left.

Clay said, "Good thing Andalon is following him. Look at that smoke coming out of Father Jack's pickup. With the amount of oil he's burning, I'll bet you he doesn't make it three miles."

"No bet. I already lost one to you this week."

"You should have trusted Dennis when he said he'd catch the person who spray-painted the trading post."

"Irene told him who to watch."

"Yes, but he already had his eye on Tommy Lopez for scratching up Charlie's Caddy. Be glad the kid didn't get caught until he spray-painted the Saint Francis Plaza. Now he'll be El Paso's problem again."

We reached the pickup. I turned to look back at Carlos and Eduardo still hard at work, but it was the sky that drew my eye. The waning crimson sunset shone along the faraway line of the horizon, giving the illusion that the earth was melting into the boundlessness of the universe.

THIRTY-ONE

THE WIND MOANED and whistled where the doorframe needed weather stripping. The propane heaters at either end of the trading post were stinking up the room with their fumes without warming it, and the dry air sucked the moisture from the pores of my skin faster than lotion could soothe it. It was March in the desert.

My visitor graciously ignored the discomforts and pulled a chair up to the counter. "When I asked you if there was anything my country could do to repay you for your part in solving the murders of two German citizens," Colonel Graf said, "I doubted my ability to honor your request."

"It looks as if you underestimated yourself," I said, referring to the red tied-flap folder in his hand.

"It was not I who knew whom to ask, nor had I the influence to obtain permission to copy the original." Using both hands, he presented the folder to me. "Though I'm not permitted to name names, I may tell you that the original document was in the extensive private collection of historical papers of an individual in Mexico City, and cataloged as being among items removed from the residence of the bishop of Zamora during the cristero revolution. This is only a copy, of course. The original was in Spanish. The owner agreed to allow a copy to be made. A linguist at our embassy did this English translation for you. I was permitted to read it. You'll find the saint's tale enlightening, and not only about the relic."

I said, "Father Jack wrote to both Spain and Rome to try to find more about this, but we had to estimate the time of the actual event, since it was an oral legend even to Federico Haro. Father Jack said it might take years for some archivist to take the time on such a small matter. I'm astonished at your success. And grateful.''

Graf made a little self-deprecating gesture. "I did nothing but forward the request to those who might fulfill it, but I was happy to help.'' He wished me good day.

I waited until the doors closed before opening the folder and reading what Graf had called the saint's tale.

My name is José Zuño. I am a herder of goats. I cannot read or write. Fray Francisco Albacete is putting down my words.

I am the oldest of five children. I was born in the year of the great eruption of the volcano that blackened the skies. I live in my own hut, built by my labor, on the mountain between the lands of the hacienda and the village the Spanish renamed Guadalupita.

My eyes were put out by the Spaniard who rode down an old woman named Simona as she crossed the street. After I helped her up and to get away, he turned the horse and rode after me. He kicked at my face and slashed my eyes with his spurs. The pain was great and I fell down as if dead. Later I heard the old woman whisper to me, 'Get up, get up before he comes back to kill us both.' She guided my steps. I could not see for the blood.

I remember little of the remainder of that day. The old woman washed my face and wrapped my wounds with cloth tied around my eyes. I tried to feel my eyes, but she pulled my hand down and I did not have the strength to resist. I lay in the darkness that was my eyes and listened to the old woman shuffling around the hut, making herself ready for the darkness of the night. I thought, How can a blind man herd goats? How will I live? I drank goat's milk the old woman gave me. She held the bowl for me to drink because my hands shook so. She put pulque in it to help me sleep and ease the pain. I must have slept because I remember nothing until the lady came in the night.

The rustle of cloth woke me. A voice said, "Wake." I raised up on my elbows. The hut glowed with white light. I touched my eyes. The bandages were wet and sticky with my blood. Yet with my torn eyes and through the blood-soaked cloth I saw her. A lady in a cloak. Around her head were rays of golden light and her hands were fixed in prayer. I heard her words, "My life is devoted," though her lips smiled without moving. She bent over me. I smelled a fragrance like the flowers of the fields after rain. She told me to rise and go forth to tend my goats.

I tore the bandages from my eyes and left the old woman's hut and went back to my own. Old Simona told the villagers I was gone. They came looking for me. When they saw I could see, they questioned me. They grew angry when I told them nothing. I could not. I did not understand what had happened or why. I was afraid. That afternoon the priest came to see me. To him, I told the story. He said I need not fear. He told me to come here to the church today. He promised to let me return to my goats if I would tell the story and let my words be taken down, and this I have done.

At the end of the document was a phrase no one had bothered to translate: *verificado el 24 de octubre de 1620*. Beneath the date, Fray Francisco Albacete had signed his name, and the translator had faithfully written it in also.

I sat lost in the world of José Zuño, who had, by his

own words, had a vision. Of the Madonna? Of a saint? I took the pages with me and went to the old rolltop desk where I keep the business accounts and trade bills. I found the slip of paper where I'd written down the Latin from the medal I'd returned to Carlos Haro. *Vota vita mea.* The same words. My life is devoted. And the image I recalled from the medal was very similar to the vision of the woman José Zuño described.

There was more. Another page.

I, Brother Francisco Albacete, write this in witness to what has happened. Sent here by the bishop to copy down the statement of the goat header José Zuño and to investigate whether the vision he experienced came from God or the devil, my mission is ended. The boy is dead, and I believe I know at whose hand the death occurred.

The local priest, Padre Agustín, is a weak man, moving in the darkness of sin. He drinks. He has seduced more than one of the village women. He lives in squalor and indulges himself in gluttony and sloth. On the day the boy was murdered, during the afternoon hours when most of the village retires inside, Padre Augustin passed the hut where I had gone to rest. He walked in the direction of the mountain where the goat herder lived. This behavior was so odd for such a slothful man, that I watched for his return. Padre Agustin did not return for three hours. When he did, he rushed into his hut, closed the door, and remained there until late that day, when several men of the village came to report that they had found the goat herder dead, murdered, and one of his hands cut off.

Later, after the body had been carried into the village to be washed and prepared for burial, I questioned

Padre Agustín about where he had gone that afternoon. He claimed to have spent the morning praying for a sign from Heaven. The priest has told the villagers that the Spaniard who blinded Zuño must have killed him. I know better. Padre Agustín, not satisfied with a living visionary blessed by God, wanted a martyrdom so that the village would gain a saint. He thinks to make the village important and raise himself up in the eyes of the bishop.

I would have nothing to do with Padre Agustín's taking the hand of José Zuño for enshrinement in the altar. The priest may believe he has his saint, but I will stop this here. The boy did not die in defense of the faith and therefore is not a candidate for sainthood. José Zuño, poor child, died for nothing. I fear Padre Agustín has obtained his relic for the church at the loss of his immortal soul.

EPILOGUE

"UP IT GOES. No, a little to the left. There, that's perfect."

The whole of Polvo cheered, toasting my new sign with soft drinks.

El Polvo

Population	125
Dogs	52
Elevation	2,594
Zip Code	79,845
Area Code	915
Total	83,531

TEXANA'S TRADING POST
WELCOMES YOU

Charlie had finished the sign in December, but I had waited until the weather warmed and invited the whole community to the sign-raising party. From the porch, where the buffet had been set up, the smell of Claudia and Ruben's enchiladas *placeras* made stomachs rumble in anticipation of the meal about to be served. Father Jack had loaned me the small church hall tables, now spread around the front parking lot, and each family had brought chairs, plates, and glasses for the icy cold beer.

Claudia called, "Come and get it," and everyone moved toward the porch in a bunch.

I waited, Clay with me, admiring the sign.

Nearby, at the edge of the parking lot, Charlie leaned

against his car, Max the dog panting proudly by his side. Charlie had had the paintwork on Bess refinished, and she gleamed in the sunlight.

"He's gained weight," Clay said.

"Charlie or Max?"

"I meant Max, but now that you mention it..."

The *evangelista's* dog had wandered into Polvo a few weeks ago, so thin you could hardly see him, but alive and in a fighting mood over a bowl of food set out for a town dog. The owner had called Clay to stitch up her pet, and he brought Max home. Clay and I both took turns hand-feeding him slowly and nursing him back to health, but for affection the fickle animal preferred Charlie, and it was mutual. Charlie had adopted Max as his pet.

"A real miracle, that," Father Jack said, coming along to wait out the line to the food and sipping mineral water. No beer. He was still on his diet.

"Yeah," Clay said. "I thought we might lose old Max at first."

"Not that. Your skills saved Max. No, I meant Charlie actually allowing a dog to ride in his Caddy. That's the miracle."

"He has three blankets protecting the seat where the dog sits," I said.

A child's voice squealed. "There a skunk in the pipe," a little boy yelled. Half the kids ran to look while the other half scattered to get away.

I sell a few drainage pipes to ranchers and I keep them stacked to one side of the parking lot.

"Leave it alone," Clay shouted, moving in that direction. Max growled, and Charlie quickly tugged on his leash and led the dog away from any temptation to roust the smelly varmint.

"The skunk is stuck in there," someone said.

I heard Pete's voice saying, "Stand back. I know exactly what to do. This will get him out."

I turned to see him pumping an acetylene and oxygen mixture from a welding rig mounted on a nearby pickup. Clay shouted, "No!" Pete ignited the explosive mixture and ducked for cover, arms over his head. The acetylene flamed with a whoosh and an echoing boom like a bomb going off in a sewer. The skunk shot out of the opposite end of the pipe, flew through the air and straight into the open front window of Charlie's Cadillac. Everybody scattered hands clamped over noses as the skunk let 'er rip and the stench spread in our direction.

A cry of pure anguish came from the porch. Pete took one look at Charlie's face and ran for the river. Charlie leaped over the porch rail and pounded after him. Max dashed after Charlie, baying like a bloodhound. All three disappeared in the line of salt cedars along the riverbank.

The skunk, nursing a little scorched fur on his tail but otherwise okay, was later found curled up asleep in the backseat of Charlie's car. Clay opened the door, and the skunk woke up and obligingly jumped out and headed for the river.

WILLIAM RELLING JR.

SWEET POISON

A JACK DONNE MYSTERY

Augustus Poole, the single most influential food and wine critic in the country, is also the most intensely loathed. He insists someone wants him dead. Still, he's been selected to receive a special award at an elite epicurean banquet.

Ex-ATF agent turned vintner Jack Donne has been persuaded to be Poole's bodyguard. As a job, it's murder. Unfortunately the dead man isn't Poole, but rather the banquet's chef, who drank the rare bottle of wine that had been a gift to Poole.

Donne soon finds himself uncorking a mystery as full-bodied as a fine burgundy—aged to murderous perfection by greed, desperation, jealousy…and sour grapes.

Available January 2000 at your favorite retail outlet.

 **WORLDWIDE LIBRARY** ®

Visit us at www.worldwidemystery.com   WWR336

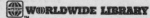

CHRISTIANE HEGGAN

"A master at creating taut, romantic suspense."
—*Literary Times*

ENEMY WITHIN

When Rachel Spaulding inherits her family's Napa Valley vineyard, it's a dream come true for the adopted daughter of loving parents. But her bitter sister, Annie, vows to do whatever it takes to discredit Rachel and claim the Spaulding vineyards for herself. Including digging into Rachel's past.

What she digs up uncovers three decades of deceit. And exposes Rachel to a killer who wants to keep the past buried.

On sale mid-February 2000 wherever paperbacks are sold!

MIRA®

Visit us at www.mirabooks.com

MCH577

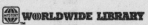